the LIVE-IN temptation

BRIGHTON WALSH

Edited by Lisa Hollett of Silently Correcting Your Grammar, LLC
Cover Design © Brighton Walsh
Illustration by Newton Henrique

The Live-In Temptation is a work of fiction. Names, characters, places, and incidents are either products of the author's imagination or are used fictitiously, and any resemblance to actual persons, living or dead, business establishments, events, or locales is coincidental.

Digital ISBN: 978-1-68518-054-6
Paperback ISBN: 978-1-68518-049-2
Special Edition ISBN: 978-1-68518-050-8

CONTENT NOTES

Please be advised that this book contains content that may be upsetting for some readers. Should you prefer detailed information in order to have the best reading experience, please visit the author's website or scan the QR code below to view a full list of content notes.

*For everyone who wants to be bossed
around and used by a Stern Brunch Daddy.
Not carelessly. Not cruelly.
But with purpose. With possession.*

Chief Growly Pants is ready for you.

CHAPTER ONE

XANDER

IN MY PROFESSIONAL OPINION, fighting a house fire was a hell of a lot easier than getting a four-year-old ready and out the door on time.

I liked to think I was a smart guy who not only faced challenges head on but conquered them. I'd been doing that my entire life. And yet, when faced with the challenge of my daughter's hair every single morning, I failed. Spectacularly.

"Ow, Daddy! That hurts," Emma said, her voice thin and watery, which meant she was on the verge of tears.

Something I was, unfortunately, all too familiar with, thanks to my previously mentioned failing.

"Sorry, peanut," I murmured, my brow furrowed as I stared at the absolute clusterfuck that was her hair. "I don't understand how you can go to bed with smooth hair and wake up with *this*."

It was just yet another unexplained mystery in my new life. The life I'd been blindsided by eleven weeks ago when a social worker had contacted me and told me I had a daughter.

That had knocked me on my ass. The bigger blow? I'd missed the first four years of her life. Which meant the first memory my daughter would always have of me was that I wasn't there.

As the grown-up version of a kid who had too many of those memories to count, I felt sick thinking Emma would have the same of me.

But I was here now. I was trying. That had to account for something.

Kids had never been part of my plan. After the childhood I'd had with the father I'd been saddled with, I figured it was best for everybody if I stayed out of the gene pool.

Fate, apparently, had had other ideas.

Emma's mom had been a single weekend of fun—something I rarely allowed myself. But I'd just been promoted to captain and wanted to celebrate. It hadn't been love by any stretch of the imagination. It had been sex. Pure and simple.

I'd thought Corinne was beautiful and kind and self-deprecatingly funny. But never in the weekend we'd spent together had I thought, *yeah, she'd definitely keep my kid from me for four years.*

It was a question I desperately wanted an answer to—what was it about me that made her not want to tell me she was having our child? That made her think it would be better to raise Emma alone rather than bothering to give me the most basic courtesy of a goddamn text telling me I was going to be a dad.

Unfortunately, now that Corinne was gone, that question was one that would forever remain a mystery.

The reality was, it didn't matter *why* I hadn't been there. Only that I hadn't been. And the guilt I felt over abandoning my little girl—unknowingly or not—would sit heavy on my chest for the rest of my life.

I looked down at the catastrophe that was my daughter's hair and sighed. This was going to have to be good enough. I grabbed the purple hair tie with unicorns on it—her current favorite—in hopes it could save this disaster. Though after this many days and weeks of the same mess, I knew that was futile.

Stepping back, I looked down at her. My beautiful little angel with her big green eyes that matched mine and her round cheeks and her cute little rosebud lips. And then topping it all off was a devil's disaster of a hairstyle.

Her ponytail was crooked, her hair nowhere near as smooth as it had been last night after her bath. But she still needed breakfast, and I wasn't even dressed yet, which meant we were out of time. As usual.

"All right, peanut." I lifted her off the vanity and carried her as I jogged downstairs. "What do you want for breakfast?"

She shrugged while clutching Pinkie, her tattered but still sparkly unicorn, to her chest. I blew out a frustrated sigh because I had a feeling this was going to go like yesterday had. And the day before that. And the week before that. And the month before that.

"Cereal?" I asked. When I got no reaction, I listed off the other items I'd stocked the house with. "Toast, oatmeal, banana, pancakes, yogurt?"

She just shrugged again, as if it didn't matter. As if I

could give her anything at all and she'd eat it. Except I'd already been tricked by that. Several times.

She didn't like *anything* I'd offered her for breakfast.

Lunches? No problem. Dinner? I had it down. Okay, I didn't *exactly* have it down, but we managed. Cooking boxed pasta and heating up a jar of spaghetti sauce still counted. But breakfast was kicking my ass.

Still, I tried. Every morning, I tried.

I set her down in her chair and pulled out the various breakfast items I'd listed, setting them in front of her like a smorgasbord. When she just sat, shoulders slumped, her tiny little fingers picking at the frayed seams of Pinkie, my heart broke a little.

Every morning when I offered her a variety of food, she looked at me like I'd told her I kicked puppies in my spare time. And I didn't know what the hell to do about it.

Hanging my head, I blew out a weary sigh, accepted defeat, and strode to the pantry. I bypassed the protein bars—those had been a hard fucking pass from her—oatmeal, and half a dozen other more nutritious options I'd picked up in the vain hope of her finally eating something. Then I plucked the chocolate chip granola bar out of the box and brought it over to her.

She still wasn't excited about it, but it was the one thing I'd managed to find that she would eat at least half of.

"How about I make you a deal?" I squatted down to her level, holding up the granola bar between us like a peace offering.

She glanced at me with a spark of interest in her gaze. It

wasn't much, but after the forlorn, my-daddy-kicks-puppies-in-his-spare-time sad eyes, I'd take it.

"If you eat the whole thing, we can have pizza for dinner and watch *Frozen* again. Sound good?"

She perked up. "Can Pinkie have a piece too?"

"Of course. You know Pinkie gets grumpy when she's not fed."

"Okay." Emma took a tentative bite of the granola bar—which was really just a candy bar, let's be honest—chewing as if it were as flavorful as sawdust.

But still, she ate.

When I was satisfied she'd continue when I was out of sight, I stood to my full height and headed for the stairs. "I'm going to change while you eat, peanut. We have to hurry to get to Mimi's because we're late." Muttering under my breath, I added, "Again."

I fucking hated being late. I had *always* been a punctual guy. But since Emma had come into my life, I hadn't been on time once. Not even once. It didn't matter how much I prepared for our departure, something always popped up. Spilled juice that required an outfit change, a last-minute potty emergency, the morning she'd insisted on counting every step from her bedroom to the front door—twice.

This morning, it had been missing shoes that held us up. Except it wasn't a single pair that had vanished. No, it was one of each.

Fortunately, the remaining shoes I could find were opposites, so she had one for each foot. Unfortunately, one of those was a winter boot and the other was a sneaker.

I glanced at my watch and muttered a curse as I bundled

her in her winter coat, hat, and mittens. Then I scooped Emma into my arms, grabbed my keys off the counter, and dashed out the front door.

Late January in Maine meant it was still mostly dark outside, just a hint of the sun beginning to peek over the horizon. The neighborhood was still quiet, thankfully, not even—

"Well, good morning, neighbor!" Mabel—my mom's book club buddy, Starlight Cove's sex toy dealer, and my too-nosy-for-her-own-damn-good neighbor—called from across the street. She wore her husband's winter boots and a housecoat, her gray hair done up in rollers. "You're looking a little worn down there, Chief."

"Thanks," I muttered.

I'd felt lucky when this house had come on the market at just the right time, but that had been before I'd realized who would be living across the street. I swore that woman set an alarm every morning just so she could witness my failures.

"And Emma, you're looking very *adventurous* today. Love the style choices!" Mabel's words rang with sincerity, but I couldn't help but feel them as a reminder of just how far out of my depth I was.

Adventurous wasn't exactly what I would call it. More like disastrous. Catastrophic. A complete fucking mess.

And it wasn't even seven a.m.

I WASN'T AN ARROGANT GUY. I was confident in my abilities, yes, but I wasn't ever cocky about it.

Or I hadn't thought so.

But when I'd transferred from the Chicago Fire Department to Starlight Cove's, I had to admit I thought it was going to be an easy change.

Statistically speaking, Starlight Cove had a minuscule number of calls compared to what I was used to on any given shift in Chicago. True, I hadn't been the fire chief while tackling those calls, but I thought I'd been prepared for that shift, considering the much smaller activity level here.

But now, after weeks in my new position back in my hometown, I could admit I was a complete fucking idiot.

This morning alone, I'd had to break up a heated discussion about which shift got to decorate the station's float for the St. Paddy's Day parade, discovered someone had "borrowed" one of the trucks to hang a *Welcome to Retirement* sign for Buster Thompson's party, and spent forty-five minutes trying to figure out why the hell there was a goat tied to our flagpole.

I wasn't used to dealing with all this...*shit*.

A knock sounded, and I glanced up from the paperwork spread across my desk to find Ford McKenzie leaning against the doorjamb. He was several years younger than me, having graduated with my youngest brother, Lincoln, so we hadn't been close. But I couldn't lie and say it hadn't been nice to see a friendly face my first day on the job.

"Ford, what can I do for you?" I asked.

He pushed off from the frame and strode toward me. "I got volunteered to tell you we're not usually this incompetent." Grinning, he took a seat in the chair across from me and leaned back without a care in the world. As if he hadn't just walked through a glitter explosion in the firehouse. "Who would have thought Stage Two meant something completely different in Chicago?"

Blowing out a heavy sigh, I tossed my pen onto the desk. "This is a fire station. It makes a hell of a lot more sense for that phrase to mean a two-story structure fire simulation than 'untangle string lights and find every bottle of glitter within a three-mile radius,' don't you think?"

Ford chuckled. "You would think. But this crew gets a little eager when we prep for festivals. Chief Brambert always bought a case of beer to whoever managed to untangle last year's lights the fastest without swearing, so they're invested."

"Would you say you're all very familiar with these festivals, then?"

"Definitely. Probably more familiar than we should be."

I braced my elbows on the desk and leaned forward. "And yet, not a single one of the grown-ass adults in this station wondered why the hell I'd order festival prep eight weeks early."

He cringed. "Not our best move. But to be fair, Mabel did just send an email with that exact phrase—capital S, capital T."

"Jesus Christ," I muttered, scrubbing a hand down my face. Of fucking course my menace of a neighbor was behind this clusterfuck.

"Other than this little shitstorm, you settling in okay?" he asked.

No, I absolutely wasn't. Because it wasn't just the Stage Two miscommunication. It had also been the inspection paperwork I'd forgotten to sign and the training schedule I thought I'd posted but never actually did and the rookie I'd snapped at for something that was probably my fault in the first place.

It was the fact that I couldn't remember the goddamn radio codes without double-checking the binder, and apparently the dispatch ladies thought I was mad at them every time I opened my mouth.

That wasn't even delving into the personal side of things, where there was an entire truck's worth of more bullshit I hadn't yet figured out, no matter how hard I tried.

Somehow, I thought I'd be able to make it work with a group of adults looking to me—the guy who'd had to send his daughter to preschool in mismatched shoes—for guidance. I'd figured coming back home was the smart move. The safe move. But it was turning out to be just more proof I was fucking this up.

I hadn't committed a lot of fuckups in my life, and I could officially say I wasn't a fan.

"I'm not sure *settling* is the word I'd use," I muttered. "Or okay, for that matter."

"You'll get it. Just gotta give it some time. Chief Brambert was here for decades, and everyone's used to how he did things. Plus, I think everybody assumed the promotion would come from in-house—someone we already had a relationship with. So there's gonna be an adjustment period."

I snapped my gaze to his, trying to get a read on his expression, but it was the same laid-back, never-bothered look he always had about him. "Shit, man, did I step on toes around here? Were *you* hoping—"

"God, no." Ford lifted a hand and shook his head. "No, not yet anyway. If Brambert had stuck around for another five or ten years, maybe. But now's not a good time for Quinn and me—with kids and everything."

I blinked at him, searching my memory for any mention of Ford and his wife having kids and coming up empty. "You have kids?"

"Not yet." He grinned widely. "But we're trying. Just want to make sure all my focus is on that, you know?"

"Right," I said, while internally I was second—third... fourth...*fifth*—guessing my move here and the change in position that had come along with it.

Because Ford's only thing he needed to be focused on was fucking his wife. And even then, he didn't want the distraction of being chief to interfere with that.

Meanwhile, I was the sole responsible party for a little girl I'd helped create but hadn't known three months ago. A little girl who'd just lost her mother and was thrust into a brand-new world with strangers. A little girl who was going to weekly therapy sessions in hopes of helping her work through the trauma she'd experienced in her short life.

But yeah, sure, pile chief duties on top of that.

What a fucking idiot.

When diving into single fatherhood, I'd known I wouldn't always make the right choice, but I'd hoped I'd make the sensible one. The trouble was, I thought this was it. Moving back home so I could be close to family—so *Emma* could be close to family—had seemed like a no-brainer. Especially when my mom had told me the chief position had opened up.

But right now, sitting here with a tally of fuckups under my belt for the day—split equally between work and home—I didn't feel like a chief. And I sure as hell didn't feel like much of a father.

All I felt like was a man barely holding his life together with duct tape and string, hoping no one noticed exactly how frayed the edges were.

———

AFTER A LONG-ASS DAY—AND three hours later than planned—I unlocked my front door and slipped into the dim, nearly silent house, my mom's subtle perfume hanging in the air. While that should have comforted me, all it seemed to do was remind me I was failing.

One of the other main reasons I'd taken the chief job was that the schedule was far more reasonable than I'd had as a firefighter. But I'd come to realize that Chief Brambert had worked long, unsustainable hours—no doubt one of the reasons his wife had forced him into an early retirement.

Stepping into his shoes meant a lot of adjustments, as well as shifting and moving pieces that couldn't always be planned for. Which also meant there were many days when I didn't get off work on time. Or even *close* to on time.

I toed off my boots and strode into the living room, finding Emma and my mom on the couch. Mom was running a gentle hand over Emma's hair as my daughter slept, her head resting in my mom's lap, her tattered unicorn plushie clutched to her chest.

"She was waiting up for you," Mom said, her voice barely

more than a whisper. "Said she wanted to make sure Daddy got home safe."

A knot lodged itself in my throat, and I cleared it, trying to force it down. Of course she'd been worried—her mom had been there one day and gone the next. And here I was, walking through the door hours late, probably confirming her worst fears. Christ, I was screwing this up in so many ways, I was starting to lose count.

"I'll take her up," I said, my voice gruff.

I scooped Emma into my arms before heading toward the stairs and up to her bedroom. It was hard to believe someone who weighed next to nothing had settled something so heavy on my shoulders. Something that felt like the weight of the entire fucking world.

I laid her down on her pink sheets and covered her with the unicorn blanket she'd picked out. When Emma had first come to stay with me, the social worker had suggested it might help my daughter with the adjustment if she picked out something herself for her new room.

But it turned out it didn't matter which bedroom set I purchased or the color of her bedding or how many stuffed animals filled the space to make it less lonely.

We were both still floundering.

The difference, though, was that I was supposed to have my shit together. I was the adult in this situation, and she was just a scared little girl who was looking to *me* to make everything better.

I stared down at her—at this tiny little peanut I was somehow in charge of. And though I'd been at it for months, I was still in over my head, screwing it up day after day. Every night, I promised myself tomorrow would be the day I finally got it right, knowing deep down I was nowhere near the father she needed.

I swept the hair back from her face, tucked the covers under her chin, and leaned down to brush a kiss across her forehead before slipping out of her room.

Mom was sitting in the same place I'd left her, an understanding smile on her face. "Rough day?"

Breathing out a sigh, I dropped down onto the couch, resting my head back on the cushions. "More like rough week. Sorry you had to stick around so late."

She made a dismissive sound and patted my knee. "You know I never mind staying. I missed the first four years of that little angel's life, so I'm going to soak up as much as I can now."

"I know. But I also know you have your own life."

She hummed. "Speaking of... I know this isn't an ideal time, considering the day you've had, but I'm afraid it can't wait any longer."

"What?" I asked, wariness heavy in my tone.

She tipped her head toward the open laptop sitting on the coffee table. The headline *Hiring a Live-In Nanny* was bold and prominent on the page.

"No," I said without hesitation. "Absolutely the fuck not."

My mom blew out a breath and hit me with her *I wish you would just listen to me for once in your life* stare. "And here I thought Declan was my dramatic one."

"He is. And I'm not being dramatic. I'm being *firm*."

"Well, you're going to have to unfirm yourself, honey. I'm sure I don't have to remind you since I've told you repeatedly, but I go back to full-time hours at work next week."

"Fuck," I said on an exhale and closed my eyes.

"Yeah, fuck. And my schedule at the library is as unpredictable as yours is at the firehouse. Some days, I'll be able to drop off or pick up Emma from preschool, or stay here with her until you get home, but not every day. In fact, not most days."

My chest tightened, the pressure of having to figure it out bearing down. "I'll handle it."

She hummed and stood from the couch. After shrugging into her coat, she pinned me with a stare that looked an awful lot like pity. "You are so much like your older brother."

Atlas had his shit together more than most people and always took care of what needed taking care of, so that was a win in my book.

"Thanks."

"That wasn't a compliment," she said dryly. "You and Atlas are both hardheaded and stubborn and think you need to take care of everything on your own. But isn't that the entire reason you moved home in the first place? So you wouldn't have to?"

Yeah. It was. But there was something very different from my family helping with Emma and having a literal stranger move in to my house.

"Just take a look at it." Shooting another glance at the open laptop, she hooked her purse over her shoulder and unlocked the door. "And, Xander? Don't wait."

The door shut softly behind her, leaving the house in silence. But there was nothing calm about the bomb she just dropped. For weeks, my mom had been dancing around my hiring some help, but she'd never come right out and told me I needed a nanny. And not just any nanny, but a *live-in* nanny? Someone here in our space when Emma and I were still trying to find our rhythm?

My gut told me it wasn't a good idea, and a quick glance at the website confirmed as much. I closed out of the tab without a moment's hesitation before shutting the laptop.

I'd figure this out. I didn't know how I was going to do that or what it would look like when I did. What I *did* know was I was that little girl's sole remaining parent. I didn't take that responsibility lightly.

And I sure as hell wasn't going to pawn it off on somebody else.

CHAPTER TWO

CHLOE

NORMALLY, when I'd already been in a place for six weeks, I started to get the itch. That ever-present hum under my skin that encouraged me to move—to flee, if I was being honest. I'd lived a lot of places in my twenty-eight years, and I'd never, without exception, been drawn to actually *stay*.

Which was why the lack of that buzz under my skin was...odd.

Though, I had to admit, Starlight Cove, Maine, was one of the cutest places I'd lived in recent or even distant memory. It could have been the picturesque downtown that looked straight out of a Hallmark movie, or the fact that I could step outside my front door and hear the ocean waves crashing against the shore, or that this town was also the home to my longest-lasting friend.

Regardless, I wasn't dying to leave. Not yet anyway. And that was a hard feat, especially in the winter. This was when I stayed in a place for the longest stretch of time. It was also when I tended to feel that buzz to leave the hardest.

But I was settling in here in my space. Finding short-term housing was always my biggest hurdle when moving to a new town, and this had been no different. Fortunately, said longest-lasting friend had come through for me.

Luna had somehow managed to sweet-talk Brady, her grumpy sheriff of a husband, into allowing me to shack up in their backyard cottage. Well, it was less of a cottage and more of a she-shed.

Okay, it was actually just a shed.

But it was cute, and the rent was a big fat zero, so it couldn't get much better than that.

And sure, it didn't have walls per se, but it did have fairy lights. And the tapestry I'd hung above the futon really warmed up the place. Well, that and the space heater.

Yeah, I only had a hot plate to cook on, and yeah, I had to run into the main house anytime I needed to use the bathroom—thank God I had a bladder of steel. But in a town this small, the number of people clamoring for a massage therapist wasn't exactly sizable, which meant my rent budget was firmly in ramen-and-vibes territory.

Since Luna had already established herself as the massage therapist/yoga instructor in town, my clients were few and far between. So that big fat zero I paid to rent this place looked pretty damn good.

But even besides rent, this girl had bills. And I needed to figure out how to pay them.

I sat on a floor pillow in front of the shed's single window. The sheer scarves I used as curtains were pulled back, giving me an unobstructed view of the full moon—aka the perfect time for my tried-and-true abundance spell.

After smoke-cleansing the space, I placed my smoldering mugwort and lavender bundle in a glass dish on the window ledge. Then I grabbed my green aventurine and citrine crystals, placing one in each palm, and rested my upturned hands on my knees.

Sitting up straight, I closed my eyes and breathed in deeply, imagining the life I wanted—full of love and laughter and abundance. Where money was never an issue because it constantly flowed to me. Opportunities came to me around every corner. So many, I was able to pick and choose my favorites—only the ones I was most drawn to. The ones that would be the best fit.

And hell...since this was an abundance spell, I could also do with an abundance of orgasms. Preferably given not by my trusty silicone friend but by an actual man who knew what he was doing.

A man who had muscles for days and eyes that could see into your soul and a filthy mouth that could make even Mabel blush. A man who loved going down, who wasn't intimidated by a battery-operated enhancement tool and wanted to tag team me with one. And last but not least, a man with an abundance of coc—

A burst of heat swept over me, and my lips twitched. Damn right it was getting hot in here. It had been far too long since a man had had the pleasure of my company. Maybe a little too long, if the increasing waves of heat rolling through my body were anything to go by.

Good lord, I didn't think I was that hard up.

My nose twitched as the scent of something smoky hit my nostrils. As if someone was having a bonfire. Not unusual, since the shed didn't have insulation. Or walls. But jeez, this was *really* strong. And since my thoughts had been derailed from the faceless hottie who was going to rock my world, my body shouldn't be this heated.

I loosened my grip on the crystals and fluttered open my eyes. Only to come face-to-face with a fucking *inferno*.

"Oh shit!" I jumped up from the floor, spinning in a circle and looking for something—anything—to smother the fire currently licking up the sheer scarf I'd bought in Marrakesh. "Oh god, oh my fuck, oh sweet sparkling Moses!"

The shrill blare of the smoke detector cut through the otherwise quiet night, and I swore under my breath. Brady was *definitely* not going to be happy if I burned down his shed.

I grabbed a blanket—thankfully not from Marrakesh—and swatted at the flames. In a perfect situation, I would have doused the fabric with water to help smother the fire. But also, in a perfect situation, I wouldn't have been dwelling in a garden shed that didn't have running water.

That was when I remembered it *did* have a fire extinguisher!

Brady hadn't been happy when Luna had asked if I could move in, but she'd worked some kind of magic—I was putting my money on something having to do with sex—that got him to agree. His two sticking points had been that the shed needed a smoke detector and a fire extinguisher.

Honestly, I could kiss that man! I wouldn't—because, you know, boundaries—but I was definitely going to do a spell for him so he got everything his heart desired.

Just as soon as I put out this fire.

I fumbled with the fire extinguisher as the alarm blared—which absolutely was not helping my focus. Finally figuring out how to work the damn thing, I directed the nozzle at my once-beautiful sheer scarves, now completely overcome by flames, and sprayed.

While it probably took all of 3.7 seconds for the fire to be extinguished, it felt more like 3.7 years. My heartbeat thudded wildly in my ears, and a haze of smoke filled the shed, which triggered a coughing fit. Now that the adrenaline wasn't thrumming through my veins as aggressively as it had been, my eyes and lungs began to sting.

I threw open the door and stumbled outside into the snow, breathing in deep lungfuls of clean air. Jesus*fuck*, that was a close call.

Thank god Brady had insisted on the extinguisher. And thank god I'd been able to figure out how to use the thing. More than that, thank god nobody had called the fire depart—

The wail of a siren pierced the cold January night, and I groaned toward the sky. Apparently, I could escape the fire but not the fallout. I was just grateful Luna had taken the grumpy sheriff to a full moon sound bath, so at least they weren't here to witness this.

Flashing lights from the fire truck swept over me, illuminating the smoke pouring out the shed's door. The engine rolled to a stop, the siren cutting off mid-wail before both doors flew open and out stepped firefighters coming to my rescue.

And honest to god, if I'd had a gun held to my head, I wouldn't have been able to tell you a single thing about who had stepped down from the passenger side. Not when all of my attention was focused on Gruff Mr. Hottie Pants, who came stalking toward me like I'd parked in a fire lane.

Damn, the Universe was working *fast* on this one. When I asked for more abundance in the dick department, I figured that was all I'd get. Instead, saucy Ms. Universe delivered this guy to me, who appeared to be abundant in *every* department—from his dark, shampoo-commercial hair that was tousled and yet somehow perfectly coiffed, to his piercing green eyes, those full lips, and that beard that was just enough to tickle me in all the right places.

And then there was his body.

Good *god*. Even beneath all his gear, I could see he was built. I didn't know what sort of fitness regimen firefighters were engaging in, but apparently they'd started lifting cars in their downtime.

"You did real good this time, Universe," I murmured. "I forgive you for ruining my Marrakesh scarves."

"Miss, I'm going to need you to step away from the shed," he said, his tone low and gruff and *commanding*.

So fucking commanding.

And, hell yeah, I'd let him boss me around in the bedroom if he did so in that voice. *Put me on my knees and tell me to open up, Daddy.*

"Don't worry, I already put out the fire," I said, swatting a hand through the smoke still pouring out of the shed. "It was really more of just a sparky misunderstanding anyway. I'm afraid my scarves from Marrakesh couldn't be saved, though. Which is a real shame because it definitely livened up the space. Made it a little more homey, you know?"

My Favorite Mistake in Uniform narrowed his gaze on me, eyeing me from head to toe. And it was only then that I realized I was out here in my fox slippers, indecently tiny pajama shorts, and a sweatshirt two sizes too big that read, *Manifest this, bitch.*

"What do you mean 'more homey'?" he asked. Or barked, really. "Are you *living* here?"

"Define 'living'... I prefer to call it thriving."

A muscle ticked in his jaw, and it sent a shiver straight down my spine. "Are you sleeping here?"

"Definitely. Well, I'm trying to anyway. Luna and the sheriff can get a little loud, if you know what I mean. And these walls aren't exactly soundproof. Or insulated."

His expression hardened even more, and I'd never been more grateful for my thick sweatshirt than I was right now. He didn't seem like he was in the mood to be assaulted by my nipples that were currently trying to cut their way through the fabric just to get closer to him.

Stepping around me, he poked his head into the shed, his scowl somehow deepening when he looked back at me. And just why in the ever-loving *fuck* did that make my pussy tingle? "You don't even *have* walls. You have studs covered in plywood."

I waved a hand through the air. "Semantics."

He stood to his full height and crossed his arms over his chest, providing a *very* delectable image. Good *god*, this was how all quality porn should start. And I volunteered as tribute for the Starlight Cove rendition of *Stop, Drop, and Rail Me.*

"I'm not sure who told you this was suitable for a living

space, but a garden shed is not zoned for a dwelling." He glanced toward the main house, his eyes narrowed. "I'm surprised the sheriff let you do it."

"'Let' is a bit misleading. He may have been persuaded by his wife." I held up my hands and shook my head. "I didn't ask for details, but I'm pretty sure it had something to do with the sudden lack of honey in the house."

His lips didn't so much as twitch as he glowered down at me, and *hooooo boy*, I wanted that mean mug focused on me while he ordered me to come again. "Fortunately, one of us who's in charge doesn't have a wife."

A fact I was *definitely* noting for future reference.

"And as the fire chief, I say you living here is illegal. If you don't find another place to reside by the end of the week, I'll evict you myself."

Well, that was a bucket of ice water on my libido.

"Wow. Okay. So, we're not doing the whole small-town welcome wagon thing." I crossed my arms over my chest and tipped my head to the side as I studied him. "Are you always this charming, or do I have my abundance spell to thank for it oozing out of you?"

He pressed his mouth into a firm line, his nostrils flaring as he gave me a slow once-over. And, yes, that look absolutely made me shiver, but I was no longer entertaining any kind of funny business with this man. Not when he was fully committed to being the villain of my cottagecore origin story.

"By the end of the week, chaos." He stepped close until he towered over me, his voice pitching low and scattering a rush of goose bumps across my skin. "I mean it."

And then he walked away, all dominance and

disapproval, and it was a sight to behold. Even with all the layers covering him, I knew I'd love what he had underneath it all. Too bad the stick up his ass wouldn't allow any fun to happen between us.

"Cool, cool, cool," I called after him. "Love this journey for me."

With one last scowl in my direction, he climbed back into the truck, his gaze locked on me through the windshield. He might've been an ass, but being on the receiving end of that glower and his *I'm going to ruin you and you're going to like it* vibe? Ten out of ten, would recommend.

CHAPTER THREE

XANDER

MY WEEK DIDN'T GET any better. In fact, it had somehow gotten *worse*.

Emma still wouldn't eat any of the options I provided for breakfast, I still couldn't find her damn missing shoes, and I still didn't know how the hell to do her hair. Not to mention, I wasn't on solid ground at the station yet either.

I felt like a lost cause. But I refused to give up, and I refused to give in. Neither was in my wheelhouse.

In Chicago, fire chief duties had meant coordinating multi-alarm fire responses, handling arson investigations, and fielding press conferences at a moment's notice. Here in Starlight Cove? It meant chasing down a raccoon that broke in to the station's snack stash, approving marshmallow-roasting proximity limits at the annual Let It Burn Bash, and making sure the undeniably hot—and also undeniably unhinged—tourist didn't burn down the shed she'd made a temporary home.

But that was a problem I'd tackle once I got to the station. First, I needed to drop Emma at my mom's.

I opened the back door, guiding Emma in ahead of me, and glanced around. Mom stood at the stove flipping pancakes, while my younger brothers, Declan and Lincoln, sat at the breakfast nook. Even though they'd probably both slept less than five hours last night, they looked a hell of a lot more well rested than I did. And I had no doubt they were going to remind me of as much. I couldn't fucking wait until they hit their late thirties.

"Good morning," my mom said over her shoulder, smiling at Emma and me.

Emma scrambled out of her mismatched shoes before running over to my mom and crashing into her legs with a tight hug. "Hi, Mimi!"

"Hi, angel. Did you eat for Daddy this morning?" Mom glanced up at me, and I gave one firm shake of my head and ran a tired hand down my face. "Well, let's see what we can do about that, should we?"

Mom pulled up a stool to the counter and guided Emma up, instructing her on how to help with the pancakes. And my brothers didn't waste any time digging into me.

"Jesus." Lincoln gave me a quick once-over, his brows pitching higher as he went. "You look like a walking cautionary tale, man."

"He's not lying," Declan muttered from where he scribbled what looked like an open book with flowers growing out of it on a napkin. "When's the last time your hair saw a goddamn brush?"

"Today, dickhead," I snapped. Though, I did run a hand

through my hair, because I couldn't remember if I'd actually done that this morning or not. I was just lucky I hadn't shown up in what I'd worn to bed. Again.

Lincoln raised a brow and lifted his coffee mug to his lips. "You finally gonna stop playing martyr and hire someone like Mom's been telling you to? Or are you just hoping caffeine and shame will carry you through to graduation?"

I stared at my pain-in-the-ass youngest brother, my jaw ticking as I bit back the slew of curses I wanted to lob his way. In the end, I just said, "Emma's four. I think we'll be fine by the time we get to graduation."

"It's not graduation we're worried about," Lincoln said. "It's *now*."

"I'm handling it," I snapped, ending the discussion.

Or so I'd hoped.

Unfortunately for me, my brothers didn't give a fuck about my cues. Gave even less about leaving me the hell alone.

Declan snorted but didn't bother lifting his eyes from his sketch. "You're not handling shit. I've seen you adjust to a propane tank explosion faster than you are to this."

Yeah, well, that was because I had actual training in dealing with a propane tank explosion. And I'd had exactly zero in the way of training for a child before my daughter was dropped on my doorstep.

So, yeah. It was taking me a little fucking time to adjust.

"I said I was figuring it out." I glanced at Emma, who sat at the eat-in island, enthralled in a book Mom had brought home from the library and—thank fucking god—eating a pancake. "I'm not going to pass her off on to somebody else just because it's difficult."

Mom cleared her throat, set an empty mug down in front of me, and filled it with coffee. "No one's telling you to pass her off on to someone. We're just trying to look out for you. Between this and the new job and me going back to work full time, you're on a one-way track to bleeding yourself dry. And you can't pour from an empty cup, honey."

"Listen to her, for fuck's sake," Declan grumbled.

Lincoln lifted his glass in a salute. "Can't argue with a wise woman."

"I didn't come over to get ganged up on by my entire family."

"That's not what's happening," Lincoln said. "Atlas isn't even here."

As if Linc had summoned our eldest brother, the back door swung open. Atlas stepped inside, all six-foot-six of him brimming with irritation, his signature game-day scowl already firmly in place.

I didn't have time to hide the dried applesauce on my hoodie or the disastrous state of Emma's hair or the fact that there were two different tiny shoes by the back door because he clocked it all in a nanosecond.

After sweeping the space, he glanced at each of us in turn, his brow raised. "This is what morning looks like now?"

"Yeah," Declan said dryly. "It's been a real treat."

Atlas didn't crack a smile, though that was nothing new. In fact, the only time I'd seen his lips so much as twitch usually involved one of three people—his new girlfriend, Sutton, her daughter, Laurel, or *my* daughter. Who knew

Brick Wall had a soft spot? One thing I did know was that I sure as hell wasn't included in that group.

He poured himself a cup of coffee then leaned back against the counter and crossed his arms as he took a sip from his mug. Finally, he said, "Still trying to prove something nobody has asked you to, huh?"

I stiffened at the same time Lincoln whistled lowly under his breath.

"Direct hit," he muttered.

As if I needed the reminder when I'd *felt* that hit in my chest.

Before I could tell Atlas where to shove his nonexistent expertise, he continued, "And while you're doing that, the only time you're spending with your daughter is full of tension."

I darted my gaze to Emma, who was still engrossed in her new book. Completely oblivious to the impromptu intervention my entire family had decided to spring on me. I didn't need a goddamn lecture, and I sure as hell didn't need a guilt trip.

What I needed was five fucking minutes when it didn't feel like I was drowning.

But if there was one thing I'd come to know in my thirty-eight years, it was that my older brother didn't speak unless it was important. He didn't sugarcoat things, but he also rarely missed.

Blowing out a deep sigh, I scrubbed a hand over my face. Then, quietly, I admitted, "I feel like I'm failing her if I bring in someone else to help."

"Yeah? And have you felt like you've been winning these past few weeks when you haven't?"

I didn't answer. I couldn't. Not when the truth hit harder than I wanted to admit.

No, I absolutely wasn't winning. Not by any stretch of the imagination. I was white-knuckling my way through every day, just fucking hoping I didn't drop a ball I couldn't afford to. Pushing through the exhaustion and defeat. Failing more than I wanted her to see.

"Daddy!" Emma called, the name still a shock to my system. "I read this whole page! Right, Mimi?" She grinned up at my mom, and my heart broke a little more.

Because Atlas was right.

That was how I wanted to spend my time with my daughter—reading with her and coloring with her and playing with her, instead of being swamped with laundry and cooking and cleaning and the long list of other things I'd had no idea even needed to be taken care of but now fell solely on my shoulders.

They were right. I did need help.

Now I just had to figure out where to find it.

Group text with Mom, Atlas, Xander, Declan, and Lincoln

1:47 p.m.

XANDER:

Fine.

LINCOLN:

Thanks, I put a lot of effort into my hair this
morning. Glad you noticed.

XANDER:

I mean, fine, I'll hire someone. You dipshit.

LINCOLN:

Idk man. One of us went to work with some
mysterious dried food on his shirt. Seems
like the clear dipshit in this situation
ain't me.

XANDER:

Whatever. I get it. Emma and I need help.

DECLAN:

You do for sure

XANDER:

Jesus, I should've just texted Mom instead
of all of you asshats. Or Sutton. They
would've helped.

ATLAS:

My girlfriend doesn't need to help you with
your problems.

Lincoln added Sutton and Laurel to this text group

LINCOLN:

Too late. And I figured this situation called
for Little L's sass too.

ATLAS:

Goddammit, you asshole. Her daughter doesn't need to worry about your shit either.

LAUREL:

This better be important

I'm in class

LINCOLN:

It is. Xander said he needs help.

LAUREL:

So he wants like therapist recs orrrrr???????

XANDER:

Thanks a lot for this, Linc.

LINCOLN:

You can always count on me.

SUTTON:

Is there an actual emergency or are you guys just fucking around? The clinic is slammed today.

ATLAS:

Ignore my idiot brothers, trouble. You too, kid. Focus on work and school, and I'll deal with this bullshit.

DECLAN:

Someone deal with the bullshit so I can stop getting these notifications.

MOM:

Oh, honey! I'm so glad you finally came around!!! Tell us what you're looking for in a nanny so we can help!

DECLAN:

Yeah, Xan. Definitely tell us what you've always looked for in a nanny.

XANDER:

Quit being a fucking pervert. Laurel's on this thread.

LAUREL:

I'm sixteen not six. And I read plenty of spicy books that your mom actually keeps me stocked in. I'm fully aware of the single dad nanny trope.

XANDER:

This isn't a fucking single dad and nanny trope romance book.

LINCOLN:

DUDE. You should read one! I'm not even joking. Mom hooked me up. I can't believe we've been sleeping on romances this whole time. Wtf was I even doing with my life??

ATLAS:

I haven't been sleeping on shit. Been reading and learning from those books for years.

SUTTON:

Can confirm.

LAUREL:

Don't be gross

But also read the books guys

Because you all seem pretty dumb when it comes to women

Daddy Grump included

ATLAS:

Thought I was getting better?

LAUREL:

Just because you're not drowning doesn't mean you're Michael Phelps

LINCOLN:

Brutal.

LAUREL:

You're no better

Should I roast you next?

LINCOLN:

Don't you have school right now?

LAUREL:

Yep so I'm muting this

MOM:

So we're looking for someone who will play and be silly with Emma, right? And they should be fun and love little kids, obviously!! Someone laid-back who can take things as they come would also be a perk!

DECLAN:

Definitely. Especially if they're going to be dealing with Xander and the two by four lodged up his ass.

XANDER:

Thanks, everyone. Appreciate the help.

SUTTON:

Ignore your brothers. I'll put out some feelers at the clinic.

MOM:

I'll do the same at the library, honey! We'll find someone perfect. Don't you worry!!!!

CHAPTER FOUR

CHLOE

IT TOOK a lot to make me panic.

Actually, I wasn't sure I'd ever tipped over into that territory. Life was too short to let all that bullshit weigh on me. Normally, stuff just rolled right off my back. But I could admit a tight, fluttery sensation under my ribs was beginning to seep in.

Chief Growly Pants, Destroyer of Ovaries, had done exactly what he'd warned. Not only had he kept an eye on me to make sure I got out of my sparkle sanctum, but he'd also tattled on me to *Dad*. Brady Luna's Husband was scary, but Brady The Sheriff was something else entirely.

I was trying my hardest to stay out of his way while he and Luna were letting me shack up in the guest room until I found a more permanent residence, but glitter was really hard to contain.

Thankfully, he was working a late shift tonight, which meant I could sit in the living room, eat my Lucky Charms, and read my tarot cards in peace.

I ate a spoonful of cereal, then shuffled my deck, one brow lifting as two rogue cards flew out and landed on the coffee table. Judgment and the Three of Cups. Awakening. Transformation. Friendship and community. Well, that was loud and—

Before I could even finish the thought, the front door opened and in strolled Luna, my moon-worshipping landlord and part-time life guru, and the reason I'd landed in Starlight Cove in the first place. Her sister-in-law Quinn, the town's resident doctor who made competence look like a superpower, walked in after. And last came Sutton—new to town like me, allergic to bullshit, and somehow already living out her small-town HEA with a former pro-football player built like a tank and half as talkative.

My new girl gang, all assembled.

I glanced down at the cards before lifting a brow in their direction. "If this is an exorcism, you should know I just ate my weight in Lucky Charms. I wouldn't be surprised if there was a little Linda Blair action happening."

"Not an exorcism." Sutton sat down next to me on the couch and set a charcuterie tray on the coffee table.

It should absolutely not look as good as it did, considering how much cereal I'd inhaled, but I was a slut for cheese.

"An intervention, then." I lifted my chin toward Quinn and Luna as they strode into the living room, one carrying two bottles of wine, the other four glasses. "In that case, I demand at least two glasses of wine and one scandal first."

"I can get you started on the wine." Quinn poured a therapeutically generous portion into my glass.

Luna sat in the chair across from me and leaned toward us, a smirk on her face. "And I can take the scandal."

I shimmied in my seat and rubbed my hands together, ready for the nitty-gritty. "Lay it on me."

"Well, let's just say Brady's dashboard cam caught a little more than traffic last week."

I raised a brow. "What does that mean?"

Quinn didn't bother to glance up from where she was filling the rest of the glasses with wine. "It means sex. Between them. While he was on duty. And his deputy saw the evidence."

I gasped. "*No!*"

"Unfortunately, yes." Luna nodded and grabbed her glass of wine. "Traeger's practically tripped over himself to avoid me the couple times I've gone into the station."

"Thank god Atlas didn't accidentally send our not-so-accidental video to his assistant coach," Sutton said. "I'm definitely not interested in traversing that kind of awkward."

"Ohhh...a not-so-accidental video, huh?" I waggled my brows at her. "Sounds like new coupledom is treating you well. Has he cracked a smile yet, or does he communicate solely through shoulder tension and grunts?"

She flipped me off with a black olive perched on the tip of her middle finger, but the corners of her mouth twitched as she ate it.

"No, seriously." I leaned forward and grabbed a cube of cheese before popping it in my mouth. "I need to figure out where he gets a paycheck for all the full-time glowering he does."

"If he got a paycheck for it, he'd be a billionaire," she said with an eye roll.

"At this point, I'd settle for being a hundredaire." I swallowed the last of my wine and held my glass toward Quinn for a refill because one was *definitely* not enough tonight.

Luna cleared her throat. "Speaking of..."

I held up a hand to stop her. "Don't worry, friends. I'm going to intervention myself."

Quinn raised a brow. "I don't think that's how it works."

"Well, I'm doing it anyway." I crossed my legs under me, straightened my back, and blew out a heavy sigh. "I need a new place, and I need it really damn quick. If I crash here much longer, I think Brady will literally have an aneurysm."

"Normally, I'd say Chloe is prone to exaggeration, but this time, it's true." Luna shrugged. "Turns out he can tolerate a lot from the woman who gives him blow jobs. Not so much from someone who leaves a path of glitter wherever she goes, like some kind of a hungover trash panda."

"Not the worst thing I've been called." I shot her a wink as I grabbed another wedge of cheese. "The trouble with GTFOing is that I need a job before I can get a place. Like, a reliable, full-time job. I've done one massage this month—two, if you count the one I was paid for in goat cheese. Which, while delicious, is not exactly sustainable."

"Are you still helping Mabel?" Sutton asked.

"Yeah. Only once a week, but it's something. Unfortunately, I haven't been able to find a landlord who accepts payment in vibrators."

"I'm not sure you'd want that landlord anyway," Quinn said dryly.

Sutton gasped and bolted upright with wide eyes. "Oh my god!"

"What?" I said, glancing around for whatever had caused that reaction. "*What?*"

She leaned toward me, eyes bright. "You like kids, right? You said you were an au pair once."

I nodded. "Sure. Love 'em. They're just drunk adults in smaller packaging with more whimsy and tiny socks."

Sutton glanced at Luna and Quinn before returning her attention to me. "And how do you feel about firemen? You don't mind them?"

"Oh, I mind them *very* much." I shot her a sly grin, memories of the dreams I'd been blessed with the past several days coming to mind. My subconscious had made Chief Grumble Buns a growler. And an absolute *maniac* at eating pussy. Bonus? He couldn't talk when his mouth was already occupied, which meant he couldn't harsh my vibe. "In the fun, sexy way, if at all possible."

"Believe me, after your little smoke-filled flirt-a-thon, the entire town knows firemen are your kink," Quinn said dryly.

I scoffed, my mouth dropping open. "That..." Was absolutely true.

"It's perfect!" Sutton said, eyes bright. "He's looking for a live-in nanny—housing *and* pay included. And the best part? You could start immediately."

I blinked twice, shook my head, then glanced into my still mostly full glass of wine. Shit, was this stronger than I thought? "Wait, *who's* looking?"

"I believe Sutton's talking about the same man you referred to as Mount Grumpus, God of Scowls and Silent Brooding," Quinn said.

My brows flew up toward my hairline. "The guy who evicted me from my spa sanctuary—"

"It was a *shed*, Chloe," Quinn interrupted with an eye roll.

"—and threatened my cleansing bundle?"

Sutton cleared her throat and nodded. "Yes."

I didn't bother to hold in my bark of laughter. "We'd kill each other. Maybe literally. I definitely wouldn't last more than a single day before he tossed my Himalayan salt lamp into the ocean and then me out the front door."

"I think you're being slightly dramatic," Luna said. "If Brady survived my moon water in the coffeepot, Xander Steele can survive a little glitter in his grout."

I snapped my head toward Sutton. "Wait, Xander *Steele?* As in grumpy Atlas's equally grumpy *brother?*"

"Yes," she said hesitantly. "But it's not about him. It's about Emma. That sweet little girl needs someone who's soft and fun and magical. Someone suspiciously like you."

I tipped my nose up and sniffed. "Your compliments won't work on me."

Quinn snorted. "Don't think all of us didn't see how you preened under her words."

"It doesn't matter." I shook my head. "That man is one pulsing forehead vein away from a breakdown. I am *positive* I'm not the vibe he's looking for."

"Maybe not." Sutton tipped her wineglass in my direction. "But maybe you're exactly what he needs."

"Or *maybe* he'd have a coronary the first time he came home to me teaching his daughter how to manifest snow days and burn down the patriarchy."

Sutton nudged me with her elbow. "Cut him some slack. He'd never admit to it, but he's drowning."

"Can confirm." Quinn nodded. "And that's coming from my always-looks-on-the-bright-side husband. But Ford said Xander's really been fumbling. This whole sudden single fatherhood has thrown him for a loop."

I didn't know much about Xander and Emma's situation —only the snippets I'd heard from Sutton in passing—but I felt for both of them. While Xander was definitely in need of some loosening up, he'd stepped up when the daughter he hadn't even known existed landed on his doorstep. And that poor little girl... Losing her mom and everything she'd known, plus being thrust into a life with strangers, couldn't have been easy.

But I was still almost definitely sure this wasn't the right direction for me.

I blew out a heavy sigh. "I'll think about it."

Luna cleared her throat, setting her phone down on the coffee table before picking up her wineglass and leaning back into her chair. "No need. Your interview's tomorrow at four."

I stared at her in silence for a beat. Two. Then, "I beg your finest pardon?"

"I love you, Chlo. You know I do. But I also love my husband's dick, and right now, it's holding a grudge. It's time to GTFO."

I huffed out an incredulous laugh. "Are you seriously kicking me out for some D?"

She didn't even have the decency to look repentant. "You're damn right I am. And any one of you bitches would do the exact same thing."

Quinn lifted a single shoulder. "She's not wrong. The McKenzie men are seriously blessed below the belt."

"The Steele men are too." Sutton grinned and shot me a look. "Though I definitely shouldn't tell you that, considering one of them is about to be your new boss."

I dropped my head back on my shoulders and groaned toward the ceiling. This was my fault, really. I'd asked the Universe for abundance, and that bitch delivered. "You are all emotionally manipulative witches. I hope you know that."

"But you love us," Luna said. "Now, finish your wine so we can help you pick out an outfit that says 'reliable mayhem' and not 'mayhem demon.'"

Well, the joke was on her, because I didn't own any clothes like that. And I also had no intention of changing who I was for Grumpzilla.

He'd take me as I was or not at all.

CHAPTER FIVE

XANDER

*Group text with Mom, Atlas, Xander, Declan, Lincoln,
Sutton, and Laurel*

8:42 p.m.

SUTTON:

I found you a nanny! She's perfect. And she
set up an interview tomorrow.

XANDER:

What's her name? I have several interviews
lined up.

SUTTON:

Chloe Bradshaw

LAUREL:

lmao no but what's really her name?

SUTTON:

Shut it, Lolo.

LAUREL:

Ummmmmmmmmmm

LINCOLN:

I've learned the more letters added to a word, the harder the emphasis. So what Lolo really means is, what the actual fuck?

LAUREL:

He said it not me

DECLAN:

I feel like this could've been done not in the group chat

MOM:

But then I would've missed out on hearing because you boys never tell me anything!! So glad to hear you found someone, Sutton!! I bet she's just perfect!!!

LAUREL:

Perfectly chaotic

XANDER:

Not feeling great about this suggestion.

SUTTON:

Don't listen to anyone else. Chloe is amazing! She was an au pair. And she'd have a ton of fun with Emma. Plus she's new to town and is looking for something immediately.

LAUREL:

Yeah cause she almost burned down her last place

SUTTON:

LOLO. Don't you have some studying
to do?

XANDER:

Wait. What does she mean by that?

SUTTON:

Nothing. Just a little mishap that could
happen to anyone. She's currently staying
with Luna and the sheriff, but she's looking
for her own place.

XANDER:

Excuse me?

SUTTON:

Oh, don't worry! She's ready to start
anytime.

XANDER:

I meant excuse the fuck out of me, you
think the tourist who nearly burned down
the sheriff's backyard shed should be my
new live-in nanny?

SUTTON:

Without question.

XANDER:

No. Absolutely the fuck not.

ATLAS:

Watch how you're texting my girlfriend. I
could kick your ass twenty years ago, and I
can kick your ass now.

XANDER:

Then tell your girlfriend she's out of her mind. That woman…Chloe, apparently…is UNHINGED. I'm not letting her anywhere near my daughter.

SUTTON:

We'll see.

MOM:

Keep an open mind, honey!! You never know what kind of magic she'll bring!

XANDER:

Fortunately, there are three other people bringing their magic before her. I'm sure I'll have someone hired before she even arrives.

LINCOLN:

Well, if you do, send her my way. I'd be happy to console the hot blonde with sunshine during a hurricane energy.

XANDER:

Don't you have a bar to run?

LINCOLN:

Don't you have a nanny to hire?

CHAPTER SIX

CHLOE

I WASN'T *mad* at Luna per se. More frustrated. And maybe not frustrated as much as clam jammed. Because when I got this job—and to be clear, I was absolutely going to get this job because I was a fucking magician with kids—that meant banging Sir-Broods-a-Lot was *officially* off the table.

And. Well. I deserved to mourn that a little bit. Because that ass? Good *god*. And that Stern Brunch Daddy thing he had going on? *Lord*. The Destroyer of Ovaries moniker wasn't just a pithy remark—I was pretty sure it was actually true.

But I guess her setting this whole thing up meant she was a good friend. Yeah, *technically*, I probably did need a job and money and, you know, a place to live or whatever more than I needed a dicking down that would rearrange my chakras *and* my guts.

Thank god one of us was an adult and could see past the sex haze.

At 4:07, I strode up the steps of the quaint Cape Cod.

Navy blue with white shutters, empty flower boxes clinging to the windows, and a porch dusted with snow. Yeah, technically, I was late. It was for a good reason, though. I'd had to turn around to grab my unicorn lunch box—aka the Kid Dazzler—because it never missed.

Was it overkill? Maybe. Probably.

But I hadn't yet met a child who wasn't enamored with at least one thing inside my magical kit, and I wasn't about to break that streak today when my homed status hung in the balance.

I rang the bell and plastered on my brightest smile, ready to charm. Xander Steele swung open the door wearing an expression that perfectly mirrored his name. Fortunately, my smile didn't waver, even while faced with his glower—a glower that only deepened as he swept his gaze over me from head to toe.

"You're late," he said, his voice sharp and commanding. "And you're wearing pajamas."

I glanced down at my leggings and oversized hoodie with an owl on the front proclaiming, *Owl always be reading.* "This is my power suit but make it cozy. Believe me, it's way too cold to wear my pajamas outside. You remember...you've seen them."

A spark of heat lit in his eyes, but it was there and gone so fast I wasn't sure I hadn't imagined it. Except the way my nipples responded made me think I definitely hadn't.

"And sorry about being late. I had to grab my briefcase." I held up the vintage metal box and tapped my fingernails against it. "We ready to get this party started?"

He studied me for long moments, those obscenely

muscled arms crossed over his obscenely muscled chest and that glower telling me without words to be a good girl. "*That* is your briefcase? Doesn't look like any briefcase I've ever seen."

"And exactly how many professional kid wranglers have you been in the company of, Chief? Boring leather briefcases aren't gonna cut it when you're dealing with preschoolers."

He clenched his jaw, his nostrils flaring as he blew out what was very clearly an aggravated sigh. "Let's get this over with," he muttered and held the door open wide for me.

Right. He'd clearly already decided he wasn't going to hire me, so I definitely had my work cut out for me with this one. Challenge accepted, Glower Ranger.

I stepped into the incredibly tidy, incredibly structured, incredibly boring home, and spotted a little girl. Her dark-brown hair was pulled back in a disaster of a ponytail, and she peeked out at me from behind a throw pillow, her green eyes wide.

Two seconds in Emma's presence, and I knew Sutton's assessment of her had been spot-on. Though I didn't blame the girl. Losing her mom and moving across the country with a father she'd never met before would have been scary for anybody, let alone a four-year-old.

Fortunately, this wasn't my first run-in with a shy kid. The key was not to overwhelm them. And to be intriguing enough to entice them to come to you.

So, instead of approaching her, I sank down onto the floor. Sitting cross-legged, I flipped open the latch of my kid dazzler kit and began rummaging around inside until I found what I needed. I pulled out the small notepad and a handful of crayons, scattering them on the floor next to me.

Then, without a word, I started drawing while humming and minding my own damn business.

"What the hell are you doing?" Xander asked.

I glanced up to find him looming over me, arms crossed, that scowl firmly in place. Shrugging a single shoulder, I turned my attention back to the paper and continued drawing. "Waiting for the interview to start. This is my pregame ritual. Helps me focus—really get in the zone, you know?"

Now it wasn't just his face I had to contend with—I could actually *feel* the waves of irritation rolling off him. Didn't matter, though. I knew it wasn't my job to impress *Xander* in this interview.

My job was to win over Emma.

And I'd never met a four-year-old who was won over by prim professionalism—regardless of the fact that I couldn't be primly professional if my collection of tarot decks depended on it.

"What's that, Mr. Dragon?" I leaned closer to my drawing and tipped my head to the side, as if I was listening. "Oh, okay. You want glitter wings and a...butt tattoo? Well, those are bold choices, but we love a brave queen."

Emma giggled softly from behind the pillow. And hearing that, knowing I'd earned it, was what I imagined winning gold at the Olympics felt like.

I smiled at her. "Are you laughing at my dragon's tattoo? I think it's ridiculous too, but who am I to argue with a mystical being?"

Emma lowered the pillow so I could see her entire face now—round cheeks, a little button nose, and green eyes that couldn't quite hide her sadness.

I raised a brow at her and tipped my head toward the picture. "You wanna help?"

Rather than answer, she pushed aside the pillow and scooted off the couch. She took a few tentative steps toward me before sitting on the floor just out of reach. After only a moment's hesitation, she grabbed a sparkly purple crayon and held it out toward me.

"Ohh, *glitter*. A girl after my own heart. You have amazing dragon instincts. I think that'll be the perfect color for his wings."

"He needs sparkles."

"Finally, someone with some vision! He *absolutely* needs sparkles. Everyone needs sparkles, am I right?"

Emma's grin widened, and she offered a small nod before scooting forward on her knees. "Can I draw the wings?"

"Only if you promise to help me name him. He needs something magical and majestic. Like Sir Waddlesnoot."

That earned me another giggle.

"That's a dignified name for a dignified dragon, don't you think?" I pointed to where she drew what I assumed was a crown on his head. "Have you done this before? You're very good at it."

Emma smiled and leaned over the paper, all of her attention focused on our make-believe creature.

"I can tell Sir Waddlesnoot approves too. He's *very* confident in your artistic ability."

Xander cleared his throat, and I glanced up to find him

watching us from the doorway, arms still crossed, an unreadable expression on his face. He split his gaze between me and his daughter before straightening and tipping his head toward the other room. "We should talk."

I couldn't tell a damn thing from his tone. But I had a fifty-fifty chance of snagging this job. I just had to pull out all the stops.

CHAPTER SEVEN

XANDER

I'D DEALT with a lot of emergencies in my life—had run into collapsing buildings, cut toddlers out of crushed cars, and dragged unconscious men out of infernos. But nothing had prepared me for the hurricane who showed up at my front door carrying a unicorn lunch box and shooting me a grin that screamed liability. The same one I'd had to all but haul out of a flaming shed a week ago.

I'd been hoping I'd find a Mary Poppins type with a clipboard and a firm handshake. What I'd gotten instead were three failed interviews and the woman with wild blond hair, a diamond stud in her nose, and tattoos I had absolutely no business noticing who'd managed to infiltrate my fucking dreams without my permission.

She looked like the kind of woman who made bad decisions on purpose just to see how much trouble they'd cause.

And I was supposed to *hire* her? To take care of my *daughter?*

Jesus Christ.

I didn't trust her. Not even a little. And yet, watching her with Emma—hearing that unrestrained, carefree laugh mixing with my daughter's—I couldn't deny it. Something about her tugged at me deep in my chest and low in my gut. It was constant and unwelcome. But it was relentless.

Which didn't make any sense. I didn't even *like* her.

She irritated the hell out of me, and I'd spent a grand total of twenty minutes in her presence. It was definitely just the proximity that had me feeling off. And the fact that she'd gotten Emma to giggle within the first five minutes of being here when it usually took my daughter hours or even days to warm up to someone new.

I should've been happy watching my little girl come out of her shell, even if it was with a stranger—a completely unhinged, utterly unprofessional, ridiculous-down-to-her-bones stranger.

But I couldn't lie and say it didn't sting.

Getting Emma to feel comfortable was *my* job. I was her father. I was the one who was supposed to protect her, keep her safe, make her feel secure enough to be the real her. But so far, I'd only seen Emma this relaxed with my mom. And now Chloe—a woman who was proving to be a thorn in my side and she'd only just set foot into my life.

After she told Emma to keep up the good work and that she'd be right back, she grabbed something out of her ridiculous lunch box—I refused to call it a briefcase—and followed me into the kitchen.

I stood on one side of the island, and she stepped up to the other, unfolding the piece of paper she'd brought in before sliding it across the counter toward me. It was a résumé—if you could call this hodgepodge mix of jobs listed on a single sheet of paper a résumé.

"Figured you might want to see my qualifications."

I eyed the "résumé" filled with more jobs than I'd had in my lifetime by double. "How old are you?"

"Twenty-eight. How old are you?"

A hell of a lot older than that.

Rather than answer, I said, "You think being a dog walker for a poodle with separation anxiety, a chaos coordinator—"

"That's an unofficial title."

"—at a mountain goat yoga retreat, and a massage therapist for a parrot rescue in Key West are all pertinent to *this* job?"

She shrugged. "That last one was deeply educational. Birds are hornier than you'd think."

I didn't even know how to respond to that, so I just stared at her, wondering how the hell I'd gotten here.

I'd completed three other interviews today, each one worse than the last. First, there'd been the guy who'd thought this would be perfect to pair with his delivery job because Emma could just *tag along*. Then, there'd been the recent divorcée who admitted she wasn't great with kids but *needed a reason to get out of the house*. And finally, the retiree who'd asked if she could day drink while watching Emma, as long as she stuck to white wine.

And now, pure mayhem.

"Don't forget the au pair in Monaco," she said, pointing to the paper. "You'd think that was the most directly related, but I actually think all the skills I've gained from the other jobs will come in handy too."

"How do you figure that?"

"I could handle a poodle with separation anxiety, so I know I can help your daughter feel comfortable in whatever environment she's in. The goat yoga retreat? If I can corral twenty goats, I can corral a four-year-old."

"And the massage therapist for an overly sexualized parrot?" I asked dryly.

"Easy—boundaries. I'm very good at setting them, Chief," she said.

Something in my chest tightened at her words—some weird flicker I refused to name. And for a second, I felt... disappointed? Which made no goddamn sense.

Why the hell should I care if she set boundaries? I had my own already locked and loaded.

Yeah, she was gorgeous. Objectively speaking, of course. Mischievous eyes, untamed hair, and a mouth that was made by the devil himself.

But that wasn't the point.

The point was, she was sunshine chaos, a decade younger than me, and absolutely the wrong choice in every measurable way.

And, if I actually said yes to this absolutely insane plan, she'd be the one person besides me tasked with looking after my daughter.

"Uh-huh, and how about the professional mermaid?"

"That's just a bonus. Think of me like a Swiss Army Knife—lots of tools, no clear owner's manual."

"That's actually not comforting at all."

She shrugged. "Sutton said you needed help. I can multitask, I can improvise, and I can clearly entertain your daughter. Besides that, I don't burn down houses anymore."

I snapped my gaze to hers. "I thought you said the shed was an accident?"

"I wasn't talking about that one." She waved away my concern like she was swatting a fly. "Never mind. That's more of a third-date sort of discussion. Or something reserved for therapy. Not so much a job interview."

When I was three seconds away from telling her this was over and I was obviously going to have to go with the divorcée because she was the best worst choice, Chloe blew out a long sigh.

Bracing her hands on the island, she looked up at me with the first serious expression I'd ever seen from her. "I know I look like nothing but a mess, but I'm dependable where it counts. Ask the count in Monaco. Or Mabel."

"Mabel isn't helping your case. She wouldn't be my first choice as a character witness."

"Well, that's rude—she's a pillar of this community thanks to the *pillars* she offers the community, if you know what I mean."

Jesus fucking Christ.

I had no choice but to know about Mabel's *pillars*, since the Pleasure Palace where she housed all her stock was directly across the street.

Before I could tell Chloe this just wasn't going to work, Emma came running into the kitchen with a smile. She held up a picture showing a tall stick figure with brown hair and what I hoped was a beard, a small one with pigtails, and a person-shaped blob made up entirely of sparkly crayons that might have been Chloe. All three of them were standing in front of a blue house with white shutters.

"Do you like the picture of us, Daddy?"

My throat tightened as I took the paper from my daughter and stared down at it. It wasn't the first drawing she'd made since she'd come to live with me, but it *was* the first one depicting us. I cleared my throat, attempting to swallow down the swell of emotion that had overcome me, but it wasn't helping.

Chloe, clearly sensing I needed a minute, squatted down to Emma's level. "You're a very good artist, doodlebug."

Emma's smile widened until she was beaming at Chloe. "Can we use paints next time?"

And fuck me—*next time*. As if she was certain there'd be one.

Chloe noticed it too, if the way she slid her gaze to mine was any indication. Then she returned her attention to my daughter. "That's up to your dad. I'm not sure if he's ready to welcome paint into his house."

From the way she said it, it was obvious she didn't mean *paint* so much as *her*.

"Please, Daddy?" Emma said. "You could help us!"

As soon as she turned those eyes on me, I no longer had a leg to stand on. I'd been a dad for less than three months, but I already loved this little girl more than I'd loved anything. Ever. And I knew I'd give her whatever she wanted.

Chaos goblin included.

Blowing out a heavy sigh, I pinched the bridge of my nose, knowing I was going to deeply regret this. But I was backed into a corner without much of a choice. "You'd need to be available full time beginning as soon as possible. My schedule is unreliable at the moment."

Chloe shot me a beaming smile, one that lit up her entire face, and I ignored the pang in my gut at the sight. I knew I shouldn't have had nachos for lunch. "Totally fine. I just need Thursday nights off."

"Why?"

"I help Mabel with her...community outreach."

"Right." I nodded. "Book club."

Something my mom was also a part of. And based on the books Atlas had mentioned Sutton reading for the club, I didn't need to know any more details.

"Um...sure."

I clenched my jaw, studying her for a long moment before sighing. "Fine."

"Yay!" Emma wrapped her arms around my leg and squeezed tight. "Can it be sparkle paint?"

Chloe stood and booped Emma's nose. "You got it."

With a grin, my daughter ran off into the living room, muttering about another picture she wanted to draw, and Chloe turned toward me.

"So, I'm hired, huh?"

I cleared my throat and crossed my arms over my chest, ready to set those boundaries right along with her. "Just until I get my feet under me."

She nodded. "Of course. Totally temporary. I never stay long anyway. I'll be headed to Sedona the end of March, so that's perfect."

There was no reason her words should have made my

stomach sink. I was probably just worried about my daughter growing attached to someone, only for them to leave. Again. I'd have to be cautious around Chloe and protect my daughter to ensure that didn't happen.

I grabbed the house key I'd had made and slid it across the island toward her. "You can move in anytime, but I'll need you to start Monday morning at 6."

"You got it, Chief." She saluted me, and her little sass shouldn't have made my jeans tight. Jesus, I was really hard up. "Do I need to bring my own fire extinguisher, or is that part of the starter kit?"

I couldn't tell if she was joking, and the mischievous grin she aimed my way didn't help the matter. But as I watched her interact with my daughter before she headed out, promising Emma she'd be back this weekend to *have all the fun*, I couldn't help but wonder what the hell I'd done.

Inviting this tornado of mayhem into my life—the life I'd worked hard to keep structured and controlled and utterly predictable—was surely a mistake.

But it was too late to stop it now.

CHAPTER EIGHT

CHLOE

NORMALLY, I didn't get first-day jitters. Starting a new job was totally routine for me. Just another Monday in Chloeland.

What was *not* routine, however, was running into my boss. Literally.

And doing so before I'd even brushed my teeth, all while said boss was wearing nothing but a very small, very thin towel. And while droplets of water cascaded down his very broad, very defined, very drool-worthy chest before coasting over those basically photoshopped abs.

And Jesus Christ, he had a *tattoo?*

I knew it probably wouldn't be professional of me to lean over to get a closer look. But I wanted to. Desperately.

Wanted to know what those lines peeking out from the top of that low-hung towel led to. Never mind getting a closer peek at the appendage down a bit and just to the left. And dear god in heaven, did it *twitch?* Or did he somehow have a third leg under there? That *had* to be it, right? It couldn't possibly be his di—

"Chloe," he said, his voice low and rough in a way that shot straight to my pussy. "Of course you're an early riser."

He was *also* an early riser, apparently. Or a shower, not a grower. Or—sweet fuck—*both*.

I snapped my gaze up to his, feeling like a kid who'd been caught with their hand in the cookie jar. And though my hand hadn't been anywhere near his cookie jar, the thought had definitely crossed my mind. Was crossing it right now, in fact.

Shaking the thoughts from my head, I straightened and plastered on a smile that was entirely fake.

Nothing to see here, boss man! Definitely not your brand-new nanny picturing her hand wrapped around your third leg.

"Sorry! Wanted to get a jump on the day, you know?"

He raised a brow. "I didn't take you for much of a planner."

"Oh, I'm not. Just want to make sure I have all the tools ready for our first day."

"What kinds of tools?" he asked, skepticism heavy in his tone.

"Nothing for you to worry about, Chief." I nearly patted his bare chest as I stepped around him, but I somehow managed to keep my hands to myself. "A girl's gotta have some secrets."

Like the fact that I was definitely picturing him losing the towel, hauling me up, pressing me to the wall, and having his gruff, stern, wicked way with me.

Ahem.

While Xander was getting ready for his day—and I was trying very hard not to recall every delicious inch of him I'd seen—I focused on a far less scandalous but far more important mission.

Cracking the case of Emma's elusive appetite.

She sat at the table, her little legs swinging, her eyes weary but hopeful. Xander had already filled me in on the daily breakfast battles, and I was making it my mission to win today's round. It would go a long way in proving my worth to him, and I didn't know why that was so important to me. Just that it was.

"There are so many yummy breakfast foods, don't you think?" I smiled brightly at Emma and gathered up the supplies I'd whipped up late last night. "I was thinking we could play a game."

That piqued her interest, and she sat up a little straighter, her eyes intent on me.

I grabbed the page that read *Doodlebug Diner: serving anything your belly desires.* Smoothing it out, I taped it to the wall above the table as if it were a gold-plated plaque and not a piece of notebook paper I'd scribbled on in pink marker at midnight when I'd hatched this little plan.

"Welcome to Doodlebug Diner, Miss Emma," I said, adopting a horrendous French accent.

She giggled at my funny voice and perked up as I set a hand-drawn menu in front of her. I'd drawn everything I could think of for breakfast—even throwing in some unconventional choices like spaghetti and pizza. Though, to be fair, pizza wasn't unconventional for *me.* But I had a sneaking suspicion buttoned-up, Type-A Xander would probably report me to the breakfast police for that one.

"Today's specials include a chef with absolutely zero professional training that she makes up for with a lot of enthusiasm *and* an exclusive VIP guest." I leaned over and dropped my voice to a conspiratorial whisper. "That's *you.*"

She grinned up at me before turning her attention back to the menu, her gaze darting over the page. From the toast wearing a top hat and monocle to the waffle wearing sunglasses. Then she straightened and pointed to the muffin with the ponytail coming out of the top.

Check. Mate.

"An excellent choice, Miss Emma." I bowed dramatically before taking her menu. "Our famous blueberry muffins, coming right up."

As I was whipping up a batch, nobody could tell me anything. Day one, and I was *nailing* this. Boss bitch level, achieved.

I was riding my high as we said goodbye to Xander, as I French braided Emma's hair while the muffins were baking, as I pulled the baked deliciousness from the oven and plated two for the VIP. I was riding it all the way until I set the dish in front of her and...watched her face immediately fall.

It would've been comical if it weren't so heartbreaking. The excitement in her eyes dimmed, her smile vanished, and her shoulders slumped.

Dammit all to hell.

I'd gotten cocky, and look where that had gotten me. It *had* been easy—because I hadn't solved shit.

She picked at the muffin, eating only half of it, her former excitement nowhere to be found.

I squatted down next to her and gave her a smile. "Looks like the chef got something wrong, huh? No biggie. Trying and failing is my favorite thing to do. Do you know why?"

She shook her head, but there was a bit of interest in those sad eyes.

"Because failing just means I get to try again. And I'm going to try again until I get it right."

Emma looked up at me with reluctant hope. "Pinkie promise?"

I held out my pinkie toward her without hesitation. "Pinkie promise."

After she'd linked her finger with mine, I flipped over the menu, grabbed a crayon, and drew a big rectangle with bubble letters above it proclaiming: *Doodlebug's Wish Box.* "That would be a great place to drop some clues on what tomorrow's breakfast could be. Why don't you draw me something delicious while I clean up?"

She slid the piece of paper toward herself and dipped her chin in a small nod. "Okay."

"I knew I could count on you!" I set down several crayons for her then picked up her plate, smiling to myself when she started to draw. "After you're done, what do you say we go on a scavenger hunt for some missing shoes before we head off for our first adventure to school?"

This time, the smile she aimed my way was a little broader, a little brighter. And my tension eased a bit.

I might not have gotten the breakfast situation solved, but

as someone who was frequently on the losing end of shoes, I knew this was something I could tackle and win.

＜CHAPTER NINE

XANDER

IT WAS late by the time I got home the following evening. I hadn't planned it that way—we'd been one person short today, so the shift had run long and paperwork had stacked up—but maybe minimizing my time at home wasn't a bad thing. Not when Chloe and Emma were still finding their footing. And definitely not when I couldn't take a full breath without catching a trace of Chloe in it.

Eventually, things would level out. She'd settle into the job, I'd get used to her being here, and my body would stop reacting like a hormone-addled teenager every time I caught a whiff of her shampoo.

Or so I fucking hoped.

I unlocked the door and strode inside, immediately tripping over something as I went.

"Daddy!" Emma yelled, running straight for me. "Chloe found all the missing shoes!"

I picked her up before she could crash into me, holding her as I glanced down and spotted the culprits. All six of them. "I see that. Did they need to go right in front of the door?"

"All the matching pairs deserve prime placement, Chief," Chloe said. She was leaning over the kitchen island, wearing an oversized hoodie and a pair of skintight leggings, her hair piled in a ridiculous mess on top of her head, and goddammit.

Goddammit.

All I could think about was bending her over that island while I stuffed her full of my cock. Or laying her out on top of it while I feasted on her cunt until the evidence of just how much she loved my tongue dripped down my chin.

And after the way she'd hungrily drunk me in when I'd run into her after my shower yesterday morning, I wasn't sure she'd stop me.

"Yeah, Daddy!" Emma said, pulling me out of my misplaced thoughts of fucking the hell out of my pain-in-the-ass nanny. "Prime pracement!"

I cleared my throat and looked to my daughter. "Uh-huh, and the pairless shoes?"

"They're in the shoe orpha-midge," she said very seriously, wrapping an arm around my neck.

"Do you mean orphanage?"

"That's what I said."

"That seems very official."

For some unknown reason, I glanced again at Chloe, who only smiled back, the picture of serenity. As if she hadn't made my cock twitch with one look in her direction...with one hint of her scent. As if she weren't a chaos demon sent straight from hell with the sole purpose of driving me out of my goddamn mind.

"Come see!" Emma pushed against my chest until I set her down. Then she grabbed my hand and tugged me toward the corner of the living room, her body practically humming with excitement.

What had once been a lovely, beautiful, *empty* space now held a house made from a decorated cardboard box, complete with ribbons down the front, tied back like curtains. And, of fucking course, glitter.

Everywhere.

"This is where they stay, Daddy." Emma dropped to her knees and arranged the shoes like they were dolls in a dollhouse. "So we can take very good care of them until they find their pairs. Kind of like Dottie did for me after Mommy went away. Right, Daddy?"

The way she said it—so matter-of-fact—nearly broke my heart as much as the words themselves. Thank god for the older neighbor who'd looked after Emma until CPS had located me. Thank fucking god. I hated the thought of my little girl, alone, grief weighing her down, and not knowing what was happening.

My throat tightened, that familiar heaviness of guilt and regret sitting squarely on my shoulders. It was so goddamn heavy some days, it was hard to breathe. But better I carry it than her. After all, it was mine to bear.

I tugged Emma toward me and hugged her tight, pressing a kiss to her temple. "Yeah, peanut. Just like that."

IF I THOUGHT RUNNING into Chloe in the hallway while wearing only a towel or picturing her bent over the kitchen island was bad, neither of those instances had anything on the sight of her when I got home Wednesday night.

I walked in—careful not to trip over any more shoes—shut the door behind me, and turned around to find Chloe bent over in front of me wearing only skintight leggings and a sports bra. A yoga mat was stretched out beneath her, and her ass was at the perfect height for me to grab. To step right up behind, grip those lush hips, and fuck this infatuation straight out of me.

"You're doing great, doodlebug! Excellent Downward Dragon," Chloe said, reminding me that my daughter was, in fact, in the room.

Emma stood next to her in an inverted V, her hands braced on her very own yoga mat, and gave a loud roar. Cosplaying the dragon, I assumed. But even my daughter being adorable as hell couldn't distract me from the temptation that was Chloe.

Not to mention the X-rated fantasies of her that had been playing on a constant loop through my mind.

I scrubbed a hand over my face, closed my eyes, and muttered a soft, "Fuck."

And then I did the only thing I could. I turned on my heel and stalked off to my bedroom to hide my very prominent, very inconvenient, very persistent hard-on and get my shit together before diving into Daddy Mode.

THOUGH WE'D MANAGED to avoid any other post-shower run-ins, I wasn't sure Chloe standing in the kitchen in her pajamas was any better. Especially when those "pajamas" consisted of shorts so tiny they might as well have been panties, and a sweatshirt so big it might as well have been a dress.

Logically, I knew she had bottoms on under it. But I couldn't *see* them. And because I couldn't see them, it was easy to imagine she was walking around with a bare pussy beneath all that material.

Every day that passed, it was getting harder and harder to tamp down my body's reaction to the infuriating woman.

We stood side by side in the kitchen, her humming something softly under her breath and me trying valiantly not to lose my shit before I'd even left for work.

This was usually *my* time—the early morning before Emma woke up, a dark kitchen, and nothing but silence.

Now, Chloe was here.

Humming.

Smiling.

Taking up space like she owned it.

Not just in the kitchen but in my goddamn head.

We reached for a mug at the same time, our fingers brushing, and a jolt of electricity I had absolutely no business feeling shot down my arm.

"That's mine," I said, sharper than necessary.

Just more proof this woman absolutely undid me without even trying. And I hated every goddamn second of it.

Chloe glanced at me and raised a brow. "Sorry, Chief. Didn't think you'd be territorial over mugs."

"Didn't think you'd be in my way every morning," I said before I could stop myself.

As if I needed the reminder of Monday morning—or every morning that had followed. Didn't matter if every other encounter between us had been innocent. That had only been on the surface. Because god knew I'd fucked her in seventeen different ways in my mind.

It was only the early hour that made my voice husky and definitely not anything to do with remembering the lust in her eyes when she'd run into me straight out of the shower.

Lust that was in her eyes even now.

It would be so goddamn easy to lean in. To crowd her against the cabinets, brace my hands on either side of her hips, and kiss her. I could lift her onto the counter, slip those tiny shorts to the side, and sink inside. Could bend her over it and fuck her from behind. Could sink to my knees and feast on her like she was my last meal. I could—

"Daddy! I can't find my sparkle sweater!" Emma called from upstairs.

Her voice was like a bucket of ice water poured over my head, effectively breaking the horny trance I was in.

And reminding me what a monumentally bad idea it would be to cross that line with the woman tasked with caring for my daughter.

I cleared my throat and stepped away from Chloe, unsure what to say to brush aside the want she'd no doubt seen in my eyes.

So, in the end, I didn't say anything at all. Just turned around and left. Walked away from the flame that was Chloe Bradshaw before it could burn me again.

CHAPTER TEN

CHLOE

AFTER MY FIRST week on the job, three things had become abundantly clear.

First, getting Emma out of the house and to school on time was basically like training for an Olympic sport.

Second, there were *rules* in this house, and the number one was not to touch Xander's sacred coffee mug.

And finally, if I wanted this job to last, there was no way I could spend the entire weekend in the house with him.

I'd barely held on during the grand total of ninety minutes we'd spent in each other's company this week. All day and all night in a confined space together with only a very independent four-year-old to serve as a buffer?

Absolutely not.

I'd either get fired or fucked—maybe both. And while one of those sounded pretty damn good, I couldn't afford the other. Which meant I couldn't afford *either*.

Since Xander wasn't on call and didn't have a shift this

weekend, he was available for full-time Emma wrangling, so I was taking the opportunity to get the hell out.

CHLOE:

SOS

I need a distraction

Preferably one that involves tequila, battery-powered friendship, and zero proximity to Chief DILF

Do you need help hawking flavored lube again?

MABEL:

Oh honey, I always need help hawking flavored lube.

CHLOE:

Thank god

My resolve is dangling by a thread

And that thread is wrapped around Xander's towel

(Which he was wearing when I LITERALLY ran into him on Monday)

I have to GTFO before I dry hump my boss with nothing but Emma's stuffed unicorn as witness

MABEL:

I'm not sure I see the problem…

CHLOE:

MABEL!!!!!!!!!!!!

MABEL:

Fine, fine. Distress call answered. You, me, and three pleasure parties this weekend.

Tonight, we've got a birthday girl who just turned 69. Tomorrow's a church basement full of horny PTA moms. And on Sunday, we're crashing Bev's divorce party. The woman is in need of a high-speed come-to-Jesus courtesy of our Pussy Destroyer.

CHLOE:

Sounds like an experience

MABEL:

The parties or the PD?

CHLOE:

Yes

MABEL:

Right on both counts. Meet me at my house in 20. I've got a trunk full of orgasms, a matching set of penis tiaras, and a fresh batch of pot brownies with your name on them.

CHAPTER ELEVEN

XANDER

CHLOE HAD BEEN in our life for a grand total of six days, and yet she'd already shifted *everything*. It was irritating as hell.

Between the glitter every-fucking-where, the shoe orphanage, and the motivational Post-it Notes stuck to the bathroom mirror, I barely recognized my space. She'd taken my ordered and tidy house and turned it into a den of mayhem. Not to mention how she'd infiltrated my goddamn dreams.

I couldn't take it anymore, and I had to get out.

My mom had the weekend off from the library, and she'd asked me to drop by. Since moving back to full-time hours, she was missing the afternoons she'd gotten used to spending with Emma. Visiting her gave me the perfect excuse to escape my once peaceful, now completely unhinged house, so I was all too willing.

"Can I do it, Daddy?" Emma asked as we walked up to my mom's back door.

"Go for it." I stepped aside and pulled off Emma's mitten, allowing her to press her thumb to the scanner.

When it flashed green, her eyes lit up with joy, and she beamed up at me. "I did it!"

"Great work, peanut. I heard Mimi say you're the best door unlocker she's ever met."

"Really?" Emma whispered, her eyes wide, tone threaded with awe.

I huffed out a laugh. I wasn't sure I'd ever get used to seeing the world through her eyes. A world filled with magic and wonder and possibility. I was thirty-eight years old, which meant those years were long gone for me. But even when I'd been Emma's age, I couldn't imagine I'd been as bright-eyed as she was. Not with the life my brothers and I'd had.

"Really," I confirmed. "You should ask her about it."

I pushed open the door, and we stepped inside, the scents of fresh-baked cookies and laundry detergent hitting me. Ever since I was a kid, I'd associated that combination with home. After living the first twelve years of my life in the back of a tour bus, a home that smelled like something other than stale beer and pot was a welcome change.

"Mom," I called as Emma shrugged out of her coat and tugged off her snow boots—the matching set, thanks to Chloe —as fast as humanly possible.

"Is that my little angel and her daddy here to visit me?" Mom called from the living room. She stepped into the kitchen, a bright smile on her face.

"Mimi!" Emma ran full speed toward my mom and

crashed into her legs for a hug. "Did you really tell Daddy I'm the best unblocker in the world?"

Mom glanced up at me with a raised brow, and I quickly flipped the dead bolt to clue her in. She smiled down at my daughter. "I *did* say that. The very best, and your uncles are all very good at unlocking doors, so you had a lot of competition."

Emma straightened, beaming at my mom and regarding her with nothing but love. I didn't know if it was because Mom had been the first person other than me Emma had met, or that she'd done so right here in this kitchen, but the two of them had forged a bond I was grateful for. Especially since Corinne hadn't had any family.

That meant we were it for Emma.

"We have so much to catch up on," Mom said, clutching Emma's hand and guiding her into the family room. "I want to hear everything you did at school this week. And you have to tell me all about your new nanny."

While Emma was soft-spoken, quiet, and incredibly shy with those she didn't know or hadn't developed a relationship with, once she was comfortable around someone, all bets were off. She spoke a mile a minute, filling my mom in on everything she'd done in school, as well as her week with Chloe—the torture yoga that had starred in too damn many of my dreams included.

"And how does Daddy think things are going?" my mom asked.

"What do you think, Daddy?"

I grunted out a non-answer because no way in hell was I

getting into that with Emma in earshot. "Why don't you go grab the stack of library books Mimi brought home for you and pick out your favorite one to read?"

"Okay!" She scrambled off the couch and ran down the hall toward the bedroom my mom had taken great pleasure in redecorating for Emma.

As soon as my daughter was out of sight, Mom turned to me with a raised brow. "That good, huh?"

I scrubbed a hand down my face and released a groan. "She's a fucking disaster, Mom. There's no schedule, no routine. And the house is a mess."

"I was just there Thursday afternoon, and it didn't look like a mess to me."

"Did you see the shoe orphanage?"

My mom's lips twitched as if she was highly amused by the entire situation. "Yes, I saw. And I thought it was a great idea."

"It's ridiculous, is what it is."

"Those things aren't mutually exclusive, Xander."

In my life, they were and always had been. And I fully intended to keep it that way.

"Mimi!" Emma ran back into the living room at full speed before dive-bombing the couch. She scrambled up and sat next to my mom, holding up a book. "LoLee has this one!"

"LoLee?" my mom asked.

"It's what she started calling Chloe," I grumbled.

"Well, that's sweet," Mom said, apparently seeing no problem with the fact that my daughter and my nanny already had nicknames for each other after less than a week.

I did, though.

The last thing I needed was Emma getting attached to someone who wasn't going to stick around. She'd already had enough of that for a lifetime.

"Can we make the gooey glitter stuff like LoLee does?" Emma asked.

Mom tipped her head to the side and regarded Emma. "Gooey glitter stuff?"

Emma nodded rapidly. "It's sparkly and smells like bainbows. Daddy doesn't like it 'cause it feels like a jellyfish."

I didn't like it because it was messy and disgusting and, yes, because Chloe insisted on putting glitter in every-fucking-thing she possibly could. Yesterday, I found sparkles in my goddamn boxer briefs. How the fuck they'd gotten there, I had no idea. Because no one—glitter-laden or not—had been around my dick in a very, very long time.

"Do you mean homemade slime?" Mom asked with a smile.

"Yeah!"

"Well, I'm not sure it'll be exactly the same, but we'll try our best. And next time I see Chloe, I'll ask her what magic she uses to make it smell like rainbows."

"And also, what kind of glitter. LoLee has the *best* sparkles."

"Is that right?" my mom asked, sliding a glance to me.

"Oh, I'm very familiar with her glitter," I said dryly.

My mom shot me a look, and I immediately shut down whatever well-meaning delusions she'd concocted in her fantasy land.

"Don't even think it."

Instead of answering me, she turned to Emma and gave her a list of ingredients to hunt down so they could make the slime. And then my daughter was off like a rocket, and there were just three of us in the room—me, my mom, and the unmistakable glint in her eye.

"No." I pointed a finger at her. "I mean it, Mom. Get that thought out of your head."

"What?" She shrugged, but her innocent act wasn't working on me. "The only thing I'm thinking is that Chloe seems to have made herself part of the family already."

"It's been a week. And she's not staying," I said firmly, ignoring the unease churning in my gut at that thought. Unease stemming solely from how that would affect my daughter.

Obviously.

"Neither was Bert Johnson. He was *just passing through* in '99, and now he coordinates the annual chili cook-off."

"Chloe isn't Bert. She's just..." I trailed off, unsure how to finish the sentence. She was just...what? A pain in my ass? A perpetual wet dream? A glitter gremlin I couldn't seem to get out of my mind?

Luckily, the back door swung open, and Lincoln came strolling in, saving me from myself.

"Morning, my lovely family. I came to see if the rumor about Xander's scowl deepening a full centimeter since he hired the hot nanny was true." He gave me a quick glance and nodded. "Two seconds in, and I can confirm."

"Get out," I said without hesitation.

Mom laughed, swatted my shoulder, and greeted my brother with a hug. "It's a little early for goading, Lincoln."

"No such thing, Mom." He turned toward Emma, his hand outstretched for their special handshake. "How's my little bean today?"

"Good! Me and Mimi are making slime!"

"Is that right?" he asked, and I didn't have to be looking at him to know his attention was on me. "That sounds like something your nanny introduced you to."

"How did you *know*?" Emma asked, awe in her voice.

"Lucky guess."

Emma and my mom dove into making the slime, their attention focused completely on that. Which meant mine was, unfortunately, on Lincoln.

He sat down on the chair next to me. "If you want my opinion—"

"I don't."

"Bean obviously loves her." Lincoln shrugged, as if that was all that mattered. That *should* have been all that mattered, and instead, I was allowing my dick to rule my life. "And while you're definitely homicidal with her in the picture, I don't really see how that's any different from usual."

"You'd be homicidal too if she turned your home into a glitter-fueled circus."

Lincoln leaned back in his chair, propped his feet on the coffee table, and aimed a lazy grin in my direction. "I don't know, man. If I had her for scenery, I'm pretty sure I'd take whatever she dished out and ask for seconds."

There was absolutely no good reason why my brother's

interest in Chloe should have ignited something inside me. Regardless, it did, and my retort was automatic. "Shut your damn mouth, Linc."

"That's a quarter in the swear jar, Daddy," Emma said without looking up from the mess of goop in front of her.

"See?" I gestured to the crap all over the table. "This is what I mean."

Mom huffed out a laugh and looked up, still helping Emma mix the slime. "I think you need to have more of an open mind about her, Xander. Because, frankly, she sounds very fun."

"Who said any of us needs more fun?" I grumbled.

Lincoln snorted, and my mom shook her head.

"Do you even hear yourself? Besides..." She pointedly glanced over at Emma, who was having the time of her life. "I feel like *this one* could use a little more of it, don't you think?"

My mom was right. I *knew* she was right. And so did she from the look she leveled me with.

"As always, Mom nailed it," Lincoln said.

"Nobody asked you."

"Oh, I thought we were here to give advice to the single dad who's woefully in over his head. Are we not? That's what my invitation said."

"You're not qualified to give a gopher advice, much less a single dad. How's the bar anyway?"

"Less dramatic than your life, which you should be absolutely horrified about." Lincoln stood, twirling his keys around his finger. "But speaking of, I've gotta run. Willa is meeting me there at eleven, and she's grumpier than usual if I'm late."

"How is Willa?" Mom asked as she helped Emma.

"Yeah, Linc, how *is* your best friend's baby sister?" I goaded because the asshole deserved it.

He flipped me off before turning his attention to Mom. "Fed up with my shit."

"She's not the only one," I said dryly.

"Careful, Xan. Or you might find yourself on the other end of a double shift at the bar next weekend. Hell, maybe I'll swing by your house while you're working to see how the hot nanny is handling things."

"The hell you will. The last thing Chloe needs is a distraction." Never mind that *I* would be the one most distracted thinking about him there, charming her. Pulling her focus away from my daughter, which was why I paid her. "And don't call her hot."

SUNDAY NIGHT, I was knee-deep in tangles and in desperate need of a miracle.

I didn't know how or when I'd pissed off the God of Hair, but I had no doubt I had. That was the only explanation I had for the torment I faced every time I brushed this clusterfuck. Or attempted to anyway.

"Ow, Daddy!"

"Sorry, peanut," I said, cringing along with her. "I don't understand how there're already so many tangles. I just brushed it before your bath."

"You're pulling too hard."

"I'm trying to be careful. Just sit still."

"I wish LoLee was here to do it," she whispered, her bottom lip quivering.

And I didn't know if it was the tremor in her voice or my little girl asking for a practical stranger over me that had my gut twisting. Probably both.

"When's she coming home?" Though Emma didn't say the words, I could hear the underlying "*is* she coming home?" fear threaded into the sentence.

"Soon." Both too soon and not soon enough, in my book.

As if she'd heard Emma's plea, Chloe unlocked the front door and strode in, a bright smile on her face. And Jesus, I'd thought getting some distance from her would help tamp down this uncontrollable draw I couldn't seem to stop feeling around her.

But fuck me, it had actually gotten *worse*.

Because seeing her now, after two days without, was like jumper cables to my chest. Let alone my cock.

She wore jeans and a V-neck sweater that dipped too fucking low for my sanity. Her hair was pulled back from her face, leaving the long column of her neck and her collarbone on full display—as if I needed the reminder of how goddamn soft her skin looked—not to mention the tattoo in sloping script below it that I shouldn't be dissecting as closely as I was.

"LoLee!" Emma escaped mid-brush, running straight to Chloe. "I missed you."

"I missed you too, doodlebug. Tell me all the things!" Chloe ran a hand down Emma's tangled hair. "What's happening here?"

"Daddy's trying to brush my hair." Emma glanced at me

over her shoulder, then leaned toward Chloe to whisper, "It's not going so good."

Chloe snorted and looked at me, her amusement at the situation only making my scowl deepen. "Want some help, Chief?"

"I got it," I said sharply.

Emma grabbed Chloe's hand and dragged her over to the couch before pushing her onto the cushion next to me. "Daddy's fibbing. He doesn't got it."

Chloe glanced at me and shrugged. "You heard the boss. You don't got it."

"I'm handling it fine."

"Please, Daddy. Can LoLee do it?" Emma tugged on my hand, those puppy-dog eyes demolishing my resolve in an instant.

I blew out a heavy sigh. "Fine."

"*Yes!*" Emma fist-pumped the air.

"First, we need our supplies," Chloe said. "Will you grab the magic bag from my room?"

Before Chloe had even finished the question, Emma took off up the stairs, leaving the two of us alone. I wanted Chloe to sit in silence. Just not say a damn word. But of course that was too much to ask for the human version of the Energizer Bunny.

"Rough weekend, Chief?" she asked, glancing over at me.

"It was fine," I snapped, irritated at myself that I was this far in and still hadn't figured out Emma's hair—or anything, really. And even more irritated that that very fact was so obvious to Chloe.

I hated the idea of failing my daughter. And for some

reason, I equally hated the idea of failing her in front of my new nanny.

"Got it!" Emma cried, running into the room and skidding to a stop between Chloe's legs.

Chloe accepted the bag with a smile before unzipping the pouch. She pulled out a spray bottle of detangler, a glittery hairbrush, and a scrunchie with—what else—unicorns on it.

She rested her hands on Emma's shoulders. "Are you ready for the most gentle hair magic this side of the fairy realm?"

Emma grinned broadly and nodded. "Yes!"

Right. As if a glitter brush, some placebo spray that probably amounted to water, and a decorative scrunchie were going to be the answer to my daughter's nightmare hair.

But once again, Chloe proved me wrong.

I sat in stunned silence as she patiently, expertly, untangled Emma's rat's nest before French braiding her hair. And doing it all in under five minutes. Not only had it taken her a third of the time I'd already been working on it, but Emma didn't whimper once—not even a grimace—as Chloe worked whatever demon magic she held in her body.

I wanted to be grateful. I *should* have been grateful. But instead, all I felt like was a failure. Something I seemed to be feeling more and more as the days went on.

"All done, doodlebug," Chloe said.

"Thank you, LoLee!" Emma spun around and threw her arms around Chloe's neck. "Can you teach Daddy how to do it so it doesn't hurt?"

"Sure." Chloe slid her gaze to mine, that ever-present

heat that just wouldn't go the fuck away arcing between us. "I'll give you a lesson anytime, Chief. Just say the word."

She was talking about fixing Emma's hair. Clearly. So then why did I hear an undercurrent of desire laced in her tone?

And why the hell was my cock half hard thanks to it?

CHAPTER TWELVE

XANDER

AFTER TWENTY YEARS of being on my own, it had been jarring that, suddenly, another person relied on me. Even though I'd been trained for years to wake up at the slightest sound, I'd been worried when Emma had first come to live with me that I'd sleep straight through her calling for me in the middle of the night. That, even if I was ten feet away, I wouldn't be there for her.

I'd never been more grateful to be wrong.

From the first night she'd spent with me, I'd become so attuned to her that I would wake up if she so much as coughed.

So it was no surprise that I jolted upright at 1 a.m., thanks to her crying out. What *was* a surprise was that in the mere seconds it had taken me to throw off my covers and tug on a pair of flannel pants, Chloe had beaten me to my daughter's room.

She sat on Emma's bed, whispering softly to her as she smoothed a hand down Emma's arm. I couldn't hear what

Chloe said, just the low cadence of her words, but it didn't matter. I hated how she looked, so soft and perfect...with her sleep-mussed hair and bare face and that goddamn sweatshirt that haunted my dreams.

Even more, I hated that she looked like that while she soothed my little girl after a nightmare. A nightmare caused by trauma I was all too familiar with.

True, our parents hadn't left for the same reason—I hadn't known Corinne well, but I was confident she would've done anything in her power to stay with Emma. Whereas my father bailed and traded us in for a new model without a second thought.

The bottom line was, I knew what it felt like to be left behind. That was something Emma and I shared, when some days, it felt like we didn't share anything else at all.

So, seeing Chloe—a woman who'd been in Emma's life for what amounted to a blink of time—step into that role and comfort my daughter instead of me pissed me the hell off.

Before I could walk in and take over, Chloe stood, said goodnight to Emma, and stepped out into the hall, stopping short at the sight of me. Her gaze darted over my bare chest before dipping down to the waistband of my flannel pants, and my body's answering response to her attention only pissed me off more.

"I didn't know you were awake," she whispered.

I clenched my jaw, making a concerted effort to keep my voice low. "My daughter had a nightmare. Of course I'm awake."

Chloe blinked up at me, obviously hearing the sharpness in my tone. "Right. Sorry, I just thought—"

"That you'd overstep? Clearly."

I knew I was laying into her harder than necessary. But goddamn it, this was the *one* thing I knew I was qualified to handle. The *one* thing I was somehow getting right. And when I was floundering in every other aspect, that meant something.

"Let me be very clear—when my daughter needs a tarot reading for her stuffed animals, you're the first one we'll call. But when it comes to nightmares stemming from her trauma? Let her father handle it."

Hurt flashed in Chloe's eyes, but I didn't apologize. And I didn't stick around to wait for a response. She was a fully grown woman who knew exactly what she'd been hired to do, and I had a scared little girl to reassure.

Without giving Chloe another thought, I stepped into Emma's room, the floor creaking under my feet.

Emma's eyes fluttered open as I stood next to her bed. "I had a bad dream, Daddy." Her voice was thin and watery, the sound breaking my heart.

"I'm here, peanut." I sank down to my usual spot on the floor next to her bed. "Everything's okay."

She shifted on her mattress to be closer, curling herself around me. One arm dangled over my shoulder, her tiny fingers running through the hair on my chest, the other clutching her stuffed unicorn. I reached up and grabbed her hand, bringing it to my lips for a quick kiss.

Then I settled in, resting my head back on the mattress, content to stay as long as she needed me.

CHLOE

IT TOOK a lot for me to wake up on the wrong side of the bed. Usually, I was one of those irritating assholes who was chipper even before that first cup of coffee—hell, I didn't even *need* coffee. But I should have known if anyone could piss me off before sunrise, it would be the infuriatingly hot, infuriatingly grumpy, infuriatingly rude single daddy who also happened to be my boss.

Honestly, the *nerve* of that man! To snap at me when all I'd been trying to do was help!

How the hell was I supposed to know he wouldn't sleep through Emma's whimpers? It wasn't like I'd dashed out of my room at the first soft cry. I'd been in the kitchen grabbing a glass of water before bed when I heard her.

What? Like I was just going to ignore her? What kind of asshole did he take me for?

He couldn't even find matching shoes, but I was supposed to believe that he was some kind of emotional guru at nightmares? Yeah, okay, sure, buddy.

I'd planned to make a double batch of muffins this morning so the grumpy asshole could eat. But fuck that. He was on his own.

If he wanted to treat me like that, he could—

My thoughts came to a skidding halt—right along with my feet—as I stood outside Emma's bedroom. The door was still cracked open like it had been last night, soft morning light just beginning to filter in through the curtains, illuminating a sight that had my ovaries damn near combusting.

"Goddammit," I muttered under my breath.

Xander sat on the hardwood floor, leaning against the side of Emma's bed, his head bent back and resting on the mattress. And Emma was curled around him like a comma, her head on his shoulder, her arms wrapped around his neck, both of them sound asleep.

All at once, every bit of ire seeped out of me. And somehow, that allowed my rational brain to come back online since the vacation it'd taken last night.

Given what Emma had been through, of *course* Xander would want to be there to reassure her after a nightmare—one where she told me she'd been in a strange house where no one knew her name. I didn't need a degree in psychology to figure that one out.

It was hard to remain annoyed when I could look at this now for what it was—a father trying to hold it all together for his little girl who'd been through hell.

With one last look at the sleeping pair—the gruff man who looked calm and peaceful but still ever the protector and the little girl who'd been through so much—I blew out a heavy sigh and closed her door.

And then I padded my way downstairs to the kitchen to make that double batch of muffins. Even assholes needed to eat.

CHAPTER THIRTEEN

CHLOE

LATER THAT NIGHT, when I'd finished folding my third pile of hobbit-sized leggings and unicorn-covered tops, I was beginning to second-guess my life choices.

Not what had gotten me here—to Starlight Cove, being a nanny to a super-awesome four-year-old. But *here*—in this house with her grumpy but obscenely hot dad. *Here*, sitting on the couch this late while a reality show I absolutely knew better than to watch flickered on the TV and I'd just downed my second glass of wine.

My inhibitions were already fairly low, and, as a rule, adding alcohol to the mix wasn't a great idea.

That went double when Xander was home.

God knew I didn't need to run my mouth—or my hands—while he was around. Apparently, it didn't matter if I was mad at him—I still wanted to jump his bones.

And true, I wasn't *really* mad at him. Not anymore. Not after the sight I'd walked in on this morning.

If there was one thing that could melt my indignation, it

was seeing a big, stoic, grumbly, shirtless man like Xander protecting his little girl like a knight in flannel-bottomed armor.

Welp, *that* was definitely not what I was supposed to be doing.

I wasn't supposed to be reminiscing about my boss or all the delectable ways he'd infiltrated my mind with his piercing eyes or his fuckhot body or that rough, growly voice. It was why I'd turned on this bingeable nightmare in the first place —to distract me from real life.

And there was nothing more distracting than watching a group of people with boobs for days and ten-packs—six-packs were for losers, and even eight-packs weren't enough—with no shame unloading their baggage while sitting in a hot tub and sobbing into a glass of wine.

Honestly, who hadn't been there?

Witnessing emotional trauma bonding between strangers was bound to make me feel better about my life choices.

I blew out a heavy sigh and glanced down at the disproportionately large pile of socks in front of me. I loved Emma, but that girl changed socks more than most people changed their minds.

"And how is it that none of you match?" I muttered as Brantley wailed on the television about how his childhood hamster never loved him back. "We're going to have to build a sock orphanage too. I'm sure the grumpy boss man is just going to *love* that."

I'd managed to match exactly five pairs when the floor creaked behind me. I didn't have to turn around to know who it was. Besides the fact that Emma moved about as stealthily as an elephant on crack, the air changed whenever Xander was close. It practically hummed with his presence, and my body always, always responded in kind.

After several long moments of silence, I couldn't take it anymore and finally glanced back.

He stood a few feet behind me, wearing a pair of gray sweatpants and a faded Fire Department T-shirt, hair mussed from his post-shower towel-dry. And Jesus tap-dancing Christ riding a unicycle, he should *not* look that good. Not at eleven o'clock at night. Not when my ovaries were still having a parade over the sight of him sleeping in Emma's room.

And certainly not when I was trying to beat back the horny beast that lived inside me.

That T-shirt fit him like a second skin, reminding me of every inch I'd come eye-to-chest with my first day on the job. And those joggers? They might as well have had huge letters across the waistband reading, *Here's Your Dick in a Box* for how well his substantial package was presented in them.

"You're still up?" His voice was low and rough, laced with something that could've been surprise or disappointment, but I didn't need two guesses to figure out which it probably was.

"The princess needed clean socks for tomorrow. And you're just in time." I motioned to the pile in front of me. "Tonight's meeting is about to start."

"What meeting is that?"

"The Sock Orphanage Support Group, obviously. We're welcoming new members who've been abandoned by their partners in the dryer."

"Sounds tragic," Xander deadpanned.

"You have no idea." I patted the cushion next to me. "Grab a seat. I found you can really repress your feelings through aggressive folding."

He stared at me for a beat. Two... And I worried he'd ask what kind of feelings I needed to repress. But instead, he shocked the hell out of me and took the seat next to me. Like, *voluntarily.*

With his brow furrowed, he reached out, riffling through the pile. "None of these match."

"I know. It's probably going to give you an aneurysm, but we're just going to roll with it. We'll call it the Sock Rebellion. Emma will be thrilled to start a new trend, and you won't have to buy a dozen new pairs of socks only for this to happen again in a week."

He stared at me for a long moment, and I could guess what was going through his mind. Namely—who the hell was this weird girl, and what had he been thinking to invite her into his home and be in charge of his impressionable daughter?

Finally, he grabbed two socks, his face twisted in disgust as he matched hot dogs with tutu-wearing dinosaurs, rolled them into a tight knot, and discarded them onto the table like they'd called him Chief Cuddles in front of his crew.

"Wow," I said, drawing out the word. "You really showed those socks who's boss."

He slid me a glance, and I could've sworn I saw the corner of his mouth twitch. But that couldn't be right. It was definitely the two glasses of wine I'd had going to my head and not Xander Steele actually *smiling.*

"They asked for it," he said. "They should be ashamed of themselves, making me pair them together."

"Don't think of it like that."

"How should I think of it, then?"

"Be happy you just reunited star-crossed lovers."

His brows hit his hairline. "I did what now?"

"A public service, if you ask me. Let's keep playing Cupid, shall we?" I grabbed two random socks—one with dancing lemons, the other solid pink. "Take these two, for instance. They met in a laundromat in Tennessee. This one comes with a trust fund and daddy issues. This one just got out of jail. They fell in love despite their differences. Now they run a record store in Vermont."

Xander just stared at me, blank-faced, then shook his head. "Exactly how much wine have you had, chaos?"

"Enough to assign fictional life paths to socks. Which, in my opinion, is just the right amount." I grinned at him, and though he didn't return it, I could make out something softer in his eyes as he regarded me.

And there was that goddamn charge again.

It arced between us, sending goose bumps scattering across my skin. Making me drop my gaze to his lips. Wondering what they'd feel like contrasting with the scrape of his beard.

Before I could do something really stupid—like inch forward and find out for myself—Xander cleared his throat and turned his attention to the TV.

On the screen, Brantley was mid-confession, sobbing into another glass of wine as the man he was on a date with shifted uncomfortably across the table.

Xander made a face like he'd smelled something rotten. "Is this what dating's like now? Exposing all your traumas over appetizers and wine?"

"Only on reality TV. I can't remember the last time a man sobbed during the first course. Is your dating experience different, Chief?"

"Don't have much in that area."

I snorted and let out a little laugh. One that died on my tongue when I realized he wasn't joking. "You're serious? But you're—" *Older, hot, well established. A complete fucking catch, if one could get past the surliness.* "—you."

He huffed out a breath. "Exactly why I don't do it."

"I get that." I darted my gaze over his face, trying to get a read on all the things he wasn't saying, but he was locked up tight. "That's why I usually live vicariously through these idiots on TV. Sometimes it's nice to pretend people don't leave."

The words were out of my mouth before I could stop them. I wanted so desperately to snatch them back. Or to laugh. Just play it off like it was a joke and not something that kept me company more often than I'd like to admit.

But before I could do any of that, Xander stared at me for a long beat. Then he glanced back to the laundry and said, "My dad left when I was twenty-one."

And that was it. Nothing more.

Just those handful of words, given without inflection or emotion. As if he were reporting on the weather.

He didn't look at me, just folded another mismatched pair of socks. All the while, I sat in silence, waiting—*hoping*—for more.

But I knew it wouldn't come.

I hadn't known him long, but it didn't take a genius to figure out he was normally a closed book. Hell, I was probably lucky he'd told me his name. So, this? *This* had been huge. And he wouldn't have done it for no reason.

The pieces started clicking together in my mind—not just how he'd snapped at me last night, but the quiet guilt I'd noticed underlying everything he did. The way he treated Emma like he was trying to earn back time. How he wanted everything just perfectly so.

I realized he didn't need to say more. Not about this. His reactions when it came to his daughter weren't about control.

They were about shame. And loss.

"Jesus," I muttered, my eyes still on him. "So, when Emma had a nightmare about—"

"It felt like I'd failed her when you got there first." He avoided my gaze, suddenly very interested in the socks he paired together—cartoon donuts and wiener dogs. "Like I was repeating history. After I'd unknowingly repeated it the first four years of her life."

My chest tightened like someone had cinched up a corset too tight, leaving me struggling for breath. "That's a hell of a lot of weight to carry on four-year-old shoulders."

"That's what I'm trying to stop. I don't *want* her to carry it. That's on me."

"It's not," I said too quickly and far too loud for the quiet space between us.

I didn't know this man, not really. I'd only been in his life for less than two weeks—just a handful of days. But still, I knew *this*.

I knew he was good. I knew he was trying. And I knew if he had known about Emma, he never, ever would've abandoned her.

I cleared my throat and tried again. "Someone else's choices aren't on you. All you can do going forward is try to make the right ones."

He didn't respond, but I caught the slightest dip of his chin. Like maybe my words had landed somewhere unexpected.

This whole night was turning out to be quite unexpected.

"Anyway." He cleared his throat. "I wanted to say I'm sorry for snapping at you."

I smiled and bumped my shoulder into his. "Was that painful for you?"

"Little bit."

We folded in silence for a while, matching up various designs. And for some reason, I had this itch under my skin to reassure him. Despite the fact that we were oil and water. Despite the fact that we couldn't seem to exist in the same space without nearing combustion. That didn't matter right now.

He thought he was failing, but he was succeeding more than he knew just by showing up. After all, I was an expert on being on the receiving end when people didn't bother.

"Emma says she loves when you read to her, because you do the best voices."

He snapped his head toward me, his eyes hopeful in a way I'd never seen from him before. In a way I was sure he didn't mean to show me. "She says that?"

"Yep. But she also says my dragon voices are unrealistic, so maybe take it with a grain of salt."

His lips twitched again—another trick of the light. "Well, you are kind of dramatic."

I flicked my hair behind my shoulder and grinned. "Thank you."

Snorting, he shook his head and glanced back at the pile of socks. And I couldn't do anything but stare at his profile—at those ridiculously long eyelashes and the short beard I wanted to feel on my thighs and those lips I so desperately wanted to lick and suck.

Okay, *wow*.

Simmer down, libido. This is not that kind of show.

I needed to get out of this room. Immediately. Or I was going to do something incredibly ill-advised—like shove him down on the couch, climb up, and ride that beard until I came all over those lips I was just admiring.

So, I gathered up an armful of paired socks and stood, heading toward the stairs. With one foot on the bottom step, I turned to him. "You're good at more than just not leaving, you know. And she sees that."

And then before he could reply, I raced up the stairs. Because if I stayed another second, I was either going to ride his beard or trauma dump, and neither seemed wise to do with my boss.

CHAPTER FOURTEEN

CHLOE

WHEN XANDER HAD ASKED if I'd come with him and Emma to the weekly family dinner at his mom's, I'd had a momentary blip of panic. I didn't do meeting the family, and I certainly didn't do family dinners.

And then he'd reminded me that I was panicking for a reason I'd entirely manufactured on my own. He was on call this weekend, and since I was the *nanny*, he needed me there with Emma in case he had to take off.

So, I wasn't going to be there *meeting the family*. Yes, his family would all be there, and I assumed they wouldn't just ignore me, but it wasn't going to be like *that*. I'd be there strictly professionally. Obviously.

Except now, walking up to the back door of his mom's house with Emma's hand in mine while she talked a mile a minute about all the things she wanted to show me at Mimi's house, it didn't feel professional.

It felt...cozy.

"And Mimi has this magic door unblocker! Only some

people can unblock the door, and *I'm* one of them! She says I'm the best unblocker in the *whole world.* Watch!" Emma ran ahead of Xander and me, tugging off her mitten as she pressed her thumb to the keypad. The lock disengaged, and she shot a bright-eyed smile over her shoulder. "*See?*"

"Wow!" I grinned at her infectious enthusiasm. "That's some magic thumb you have."

"Thanks!" With one more smile tossed our way, she turned the knob and pushed open the door, revealing the kind of home I'd never known.

The kitchen was big and bright, all warm woods and soft light, with a breakfast nook tucked under bay windows overflowing with potted plants and herbs. A wide, double archway led to a dining room and a family room just beyond that with a wall of filled-to-bursting bookshelves anchoring the space. The scent of garlic, meat, and something vaguely sweet hung in the air like a hug I didn't even know I needed.

Though I'd met everyone in Xander's family at one time or the other since I'd first come to Starlight Cove, seeing them here, in this environment, was something altogether new.

Declan—my single-time tattoo artist—sat at the dining table, glaring daggers at a half-folded napkin while Sutton stood beside him, patiently explaining the difference between a swan and whatever crumpled-up object he had in his hand. Laurel sat across from them, phone in hand, her mouth quirked in the kind of *I'm absolutely up to no good* grin I'd come to expect from Sutton's teenage daughter. Atlas stood at the head of the table, arms crossed and expression carved from stone as he watched over the whole production.

Lincoln's voice drifted toward us from the other room,

calling something about napkin travesties before he appeared in the doorway, eyebrows raised like he was the only sane one in a house full of lunatics. "Oh good, you're here. Just in time to witness Dec's humiliation at the hands of origami swans."

"Give it a rest, Lincoln," Xander's mom said, exasperation in her tone. "They haven't even taken off their shoes yet."

"I have, Mimi!" Emma called, kicking off her boots as fast as humanly possible. "Are you making psghetti for me?"

Holly turned around just in time for Emma to crash into her for a hug. "I *am*. A little birdie told me that's what you were hoping for."

Emma stared up at her with wide eyes, her mouth hanging open. "You talk to birds?"

"Big, grumpy ones," Lincoln said. "She's got three of them barking in her ear every day."

"Birds don't bark, Uncle Linc," Emma said, the duh heavy in her tone. "They *chirp*."

Lincoln crossed his arms and leaned back against the counter. "I'm afraid only one of her birdies chirps. And he's *definitely* her favorite."

Holly rolled her eyes, absently smoothing a hand down Emma's hair as she regarded Lincoln. "I don't have favorites—with little birdies or sons."

"Who said anything about sons?" he asked.

"Hello again, Chloe," Holly said with a smile, completely ignoring Lincoln. "I'm so glad you were able to join us!"

"Oh, sure." I nodded, shrugging out of my coat when Xander reached for it. "Thanks for having me. I'm happy to go where the tiny human goes."

"What's going on in there?" Xander asked, stepping up

behind me in a way that made every nerve ending in my body stand at attention.

Why? I had no idea.

He wasn't even close. Not really. About as far away as someone would be while standing in line at the grocery store. But when it came to Xander Steele, I was coming to realize it didn't matter. If I was anywhere in his vicinity, I felt it like static through my entire body.

Irritating and inconvenient.

Lincoln grinned. "Declan lost a bet, so he's folding napkins into swans. Sutton's instructing him. Laurel's recording the entire thing for future blackmail potential. And Atlas is supervising."

"Right." Xander nodded. "So just a normal Sunday, then."

"Pretty much."

"Since Declan is so busy with the fancy napkins you just had to have, that means *you're* on table-setting duty," Holly said, gesturing toward a stack of dinnerware on the counter.

"*Mom.*" Lincoln huffed in a way that I would've expected from a teenager, not a grown-ass man. "Dec was supposed to do it this week!"

"And yet you insisted on making a bet with him that you *knew* he was going to lose, all so he could make some stupid swans out of napkins." She patted his chest. "That means it falls on you, my lovely child."

"What about Xander?" Lincoln gestured toward where Xander still stood next to me—far too close and yet not nearly close enough. "He's not doing anything."

"I didn't ask Xander, now did I? I asked *you*, my sweet, chirpy little bird."

"Come on, Uncle Linc," Emma said, grabbing his hand and tugging him toward the dining room. "I'll help you!"

The petulant look melted off his face as he smiled at Emma. "You've got a deal, little bean. Just make sure to give Uncle Dec the cracked plate because it's his favorite…"

As they headed into the other room, Holly turned to me with a smile. "I hope you like spaghetti, Chloe. It tends to be a fan favorite around here."

"Oh, I—"

"Holly's specialty," Sutton said, strolling into the kitchen and shooting me a grin like she knew something I didn't. "She made it for Laurel and me, too. The first time we came to family dinner."

Before I could freak out about that little detail my wily friend slipped in *way* too casually, Holly asked Sutton to grab the garlic knots as she dished up the spaghetti in a large serving bowl.

"Well, it's a crowd-pleaser, so I figure I can't go wrong with it." She glanced at me, her brow furrowed. "As long as you're not a vegetarian…"

I shook my head. "Oh god, no. I like bacon too much for that. Although I did give it a go when I was in Thailand for a month, but it didn't stick. Once I got back to the States, I basically ate my weight in bacon every day for a month."

"Oh, I *love* Thailand!" Holly said. "What were you doing there?"

"I was a caretaker at an elephant sanctuary."

"Really?" Holly's brows lifted as she studied me with

curiosity. "That sounds so interesting! Sutton tells me you have a bit of an eclectic résumé."

I slid a glance to my friend, who only returned my stare with a smile. "Eclectic is a very nice word for what others might call a mess."

Holly laughed and glanced back at Xander before returning her gaze to me. "Well, I'm just glad those people—whoever they are—could see past the mess and realize what a great addition you'd be to any...job."

I didn't have much experience with family dinners—by the time I'd oopsie-babied my way into my family's lives, my older siblings were out of the house and my parents weren't all that interested in doing the whole raising-a-kid-thing again. But this? This was...something.

It was loud and funny and addictive. Not to mention delicious. There were too many conversations happening all at once, nonstop bickering between the brothers as Sutton attempted to play referee and Laurel egged them on, and my little sidekick passing me bits of her garlic knot under the table like we were part of some kind of secret mission.

It was pretty perfect.

So perfect, in fact, I had to keep reminding myself it wasn't mine.

I BUCKLED myself into the passenger's seat of Xander's SUV and peeked behind me toward Emma. She was already passed out with Pinkie clutched tight to her chest, her mouth hanging open, not a care in the world. "She's gonna sleep well tonight."

"She conked out mid-sentence," Xander said as he started the car. "Something about a dragon who runs a food truck."

I smiled, warmth bubbling in my chest at her reciting one of the bedtime stories I'd told her this week. "All that trash-talking she did while challenging everyone to Uno really wore her out."

Xander huffed out what might've passed for a laugh and shook his head. "It's hard to believe."

"What is?"

He glanced over at me as he drove us through the quiet of Starlight Cove, the glow of lampposts intermittently lighting up the dark interior as we passed. "Hard to believe she's the same kid I brought here to meet them only a couple months ago. Hell, she doesn't even seem like the same kid she was a couple *weeks* ago."

My heart hiccupped, and I looked out the window quickly, glad there was no visible sign that my throat suddenly felt too tight.

But he didn't mean it like *that*. He didn't mean because of *me*. I knew that.

Obviously.

It was just Emma's natural growth while becoming more comfortable around people—especially those in her inner circle—and the hard work she was doing with her therapist.

But still.

I couldn't help my stomach from doing a tiny little pirouette, my heart warming at the thought that I might've had a little something to do with coaxing that sweet little girl out of her shell.

"Thanks for coming tonight," Xander murmured. "Even though it turned out to be unnecessary."

I shrugged. "No big deal. I had fun. Your family's kind of..."

"Annoying? Irritating? Obnoxious as hell?"

I breathed out a laugh and glanced over at him, running my gaze over his profile. "I was going to say great. Your family's kind of great."

"Yeah. I guess they're that too."

Silence stretched for a beat as we drove through the quiet town toward his house. I picked at the hem of my sleeve, pretending like I wasn't reliving every second of tonight while also shoving down that incessant bitch inside me who was begging to join in that again.

"I didn't realize you'd met Declan before," Xander said, his voice cutting through the silence.

"What?"

"At dinner." He cleared his throat, very diligently staring straight out the windshield. "Dec asked how your tattoo was healing."

"Oh. Yeah." I nodded, tucking my hair behind my ear. "When I first got here. Wanted to add to my collection."

"Collection?" He snapped his head toward me, his gaze flicking down to my collarbone hidden beneath my sweater, and just why in the hell did that make my clit tingle?

"Well, maybe not a collection, but definitely tattoos, plural."

I didn't know if it was the heavy silence in the car, the

way Xander seemed to be white-knuckling the steering wheel, or the fact that I couldn't get my mind off the memory of him in his towel, the black lines of his tattoo poking out of the top, but something made me lose my mind and blurt out a question I had no business asking.

"How about you? Just the one?"

"I have a few."

God. The way he'd said it, in that low, smoky rumble, nearly did me in. Had me imagining all kinds of things I had no business imagining. Like where else on his body was permanently marked. And what they would taste like when I traced them with my tongue.

"Well." I cleared my throat and shifted in my seat, crossing my legs and hoping it wasn't obvious just exactly what I was doing. "That feels like dangerous information to have."

Xander glanced over at me for the briefest second before returning his attention to the road. It could've been that fleeting look, or how he tightened his grip on the steering wheel, or that not-so-subtle tic of his jaw, but I began to wonder if maybe that wasn't the only thing dangerous between us.

CHAPTER FIFTEEN

XANDER

Group text with Atlas, Xander, Declan, and Lincoln

11:07 p.m.

LINCOLN:

Someone just called the bar to ask if we host bachelorette brunches with bottomless mimosa jello shots.

I didn't even know it was a thing, but we should definitely do that. What do you think?

ATLAS:

I think it's almost midnight. Wtf is wrong with you?

LINCOLN:

It's 11:07, grandpa. Calm down.

ATLAS:

Some of us are trying to sleep. Xander's got a 4yo for fuck's sake

XANDER:

I'm up

LINCOLN:

See? He's up.

LINCOLN:

Wait. Why are you up? Isn't your bedtime 9?

XANDER:

Fuck off

DECLAN:

Also awake. Finishing up with my last client.

LINCOLN:

So it's only the grandpa of our group who takes personal offense to this hour of texting. And it's his fault in the first place.

ATLAS:

How the fuck do you figure that?

LINCOLN:

Normally when it's slow at the bar, I do a little swiping

ATLAS:

...sweeping?

DECLAN:

He means on the hookup apps

ATLAS:

Still not seeing how that's my fault

LINCOLN:

Your girlfriend is the one who held me to
that bullshit bet I made at Mom's.

ATLAS:

I have no idea wtf you're talking about

DECLAN:

He said he'd delete all his dating apps if
Xander brought more than a carry-on with
him. And since he brought a whole ass
daughter, Linc lost.

LINCOLN:

So actually it's Atlas AND Xander's fault

XANDER:

I'm going to pretend you didn't just
compare my daughter to excess baggage.

LINCOLN:

Don't be a shit about it. You know I love that
little bean.

But fuck.

The lack of co-ed company is getting to me.
I got hard today from someone yelling at me
in a certain tone.

That's probably fine, right?

DECLAN:

Pretty sure that's just one specific person.

XANDER:

He's not wrong. It sounds like a normal
Wednesday for you.

LINCOLN:

How did the hot librarian piss you off this
week, Dec? And how're things going with
the hot nanny, Xan?

XANDER:

This is why I usually have this thread muted.

DECLAN:

Same

ATLAS:

Can everyone just go the fuck to sleep?
Jesus Christ.

I WAS A GLUTTON FOR PUNISHMENT. There was no
other answer for why I continued to test fate with these late-
night, unnecessary trips downstairs. It was the same reason I
hadn't altered my morning shower or coffee routines since
running into Chloe during both of those.

After last week—when she and I'd had a civil
conversation with an audience of socks—I'd been craving
more. And even though I could barely admit it to myself, I
wanted it again.

Why? I had no fucking idea.

Apparently, I had a bit of sadism in me. That was the
only plausible answer. I liked to torture myself with things I
couldn't have. Namely, my daughter's too-beautiful-for-her-
own-good and too-chaotic-for-my-own-sanity nanny who was

ten years my junior and who made me feel like I was losing my mind at least four times a day.

Maybe I was still reeling from the fact that I'd told her about my dad. How little I'd actually shared about him was irrelevant. My relationship—or lack thereof—with Stan Steele wasn't something I talked about. Ever.

Hell, I tried to never even think about it.

But somehow, with her, it had just...slipped out. Somehow, with her, I'd let my guard down.

That seemed to be a common thread when I was in her presence.

I should've taken that group text with my brothers as the stoplight on the whole evening. It was late. I *should* have been sleeping. I definitely should not have been creeping around my own house in the dark of night in the hopes of running into a little bit of chaos.

And yet...

I rounded the corner into the kitchen and stopped short, my chest squeezing uncomfortably at the sight in front of me.

Chloe stood by the fridge. She wore those goddamn pajama shorts that haunted my dreams—or I assumed that was what she was wearing. I couldn't actually see them since that hoodie practically swallowed her whole. It was longer than some of the dresses I'd seen her wear, but it might as well have been lingerie for the way my body reacted to her in it. Her hair was messy and piled on top of her head in the sort of unrestrained bun she preferred—the kind that looked like it had barely survived the day.

That made two of us.

I felt like I was barely surviving most days since Chloe had barreled into my life.

She held a tub of cookie dough in one hand and a spoon in the other. Just as she took a bite, she lifted her eyes to meet mine, not an ounce of surprise in her expression. As if she'd been waiting for me...expecting me.

"Hey, Chief. You want some?"

I knew she was talking about the cookie dough. I *knew* that.

My cock, however, did not. Or chose to ignore it entirely. Instead, it focused on her saying those words in an alternate version of reality—one where she was sitting on the counter, wearing one of *my* hoodies and nothing else, legs spread, fingers playing between them.

I cleared my throat, but my voice still came out rough. "Is that safe to eat?"

"Honestly? Probably not." She scooped another spoonful and held it out toward me with a raised brow, the light from above the stove glowing behind her like some kind of seductive halo for troublemakers and temptations.

God knew she was both.

I hesitated. This was such a bad fucking idea. True, all she was offering me was cookie dough, and the most dangerous thing in that was a minuscule amount of raw egg. But that wasn't what had me hesitating.

It was the siren of a woman I couldn't seem to get out of my mind and literally couldn't get out of my house that made me want to turn around, lock myself in my bedroom, and get my shit under control.

I *had* to. Because I didn't have another choice.

I was sharing a roof with her. Sharing a *wall* with her. And that wasn't going to change anytime soon.

But even knowing all those things, I didn't turn around.

I didn't go upstairs.

I didn't lock myself in my bedroom.

Instead, I stepped closer to her. Too close, considering it was nearly midnight and she looked like this and I was her boss. Not to mention, I had no doubt I'd be dreaming about her coming on my fingers and my tongue and my cock as soon as my head hit the pillow. Just like I'd been doing every goddamn night since the day I'd seen her stumbling out of that fucking shed in the sheriff's backyard.

But I didn't stop myself.

I dipped my head toward the spoon she held out for me. Her gaze flicked down to my mouth, that slow, seductive brush of her tongue against her lower lip nearly enough to buckle my knees. Send me to the floor right here, grip her waist, and beg for what I *really* wanted to eat.

Settling for something I knew wouldn't be nearly half as sweet, I wrapped my lips around the spoon, our gazes still locked and my cock hard enough to pound nails.

This close to her, I could see the flecks of gold in her eyes, feel each of her exhales against me. It would take nothing to close the space between us. To capture that plump lower lip between my teeth and tug until she gasped. To see how fucking delicious her tongue tasted—how fucking delicious *she* tasted.

Blowing out a shaky breath, Chloe turned away from me and set the tub of cookie dough on the counter. "Okay. Well, that was—"

Her words cut off, but I could fill in a dozen different adjectives for her. Hot. Dangerous. Combustible. Unprofessional.

A bad fucking idea.

But instead of continuing her sentence, she turned around to face me, her brows raised. "This is new."

This constant pull I felt when I was around her? Yes, it was. And it was becoming a real pain in my ass.

But that wasn't what she meant.

She glanced at the coffee cup she held up between us. It was obnoxious and gaudy, featuring a pink dragon wearing a sparkly tutu and heart-shaped sunglasses while holding a latte in one claw and a glitter wand in the other. In bold letters arched above, it read, *I am the drama.*

Fucking ridiculous. Just like her.

I cleared my throat and glanced away, avoiding her gaze. "I saw it and figured it'd finally stop you from stealing my mug."

"You *bought* me this?"

I didn't like the surprise in her voice. Not even a little. Whether it was surprise over the fact that someone—period— had bought her something, or that I—specifically—had done so, neither sat right with me.

Fuck knew why.

Why should I care if my nanny got gifts? Worse—why the hell had I bought the damn thing for her in the first place?

"I bought you a warning label, chaos," I corrected. "Besides, it was on sale."

She breathed out a laugh, the sound like wind chimes,

and shook her head, cradling the mug in her hands like it meant something.

I valiantly ignored the satisfaction that grew in my chest at her response.

"That was sweet." She bit her bottom lip and glanced to the side as she set the mug back on the counter. "Now, we just need to work on your hair skills. Emma looked like a feral poodle when I picked her up from pre-K today."

I grunted and took a much-needed step back, grateful for the reminder of my daughter—the very reason Chloe and I were here in the first place. "Emma wouldn't let me near her with a brush. As usual."

"Well, if you'd finally let me give you those lessons, we could probably fix that, Chief."

"What lessons?"

Chloe hesitated for a second before reaching up and undoing the knot at the top of her head. And that simple act should not have been as hot as it was.

Her hair fell around her shoulders in a mass of unruly waves, the scent of her shampoo overwhelming me and going straight to my cock—as if the bastard needed any help.

She should've looked like a mess—a beautiful disaster with smudged eyeliner, her hair an absolute riot around her, and a tiny crumb of cookie dough at the corner of her mouth.

But, to me, all she looked like was something I wanted to devour.

I wanted to slide my fingers into that mass of hair, tip her head back, and capture those lips with mine. Slip my tongue inside her mouth. See if she tasted as sweet as I knew she would. See if she was a moaner or a whimperer when she had the hell kissed out of her.

"Emma asked me to teach you how to do her hair, remember?" Chloe said, reminding me what the hell we were doing here in the first place. "Are you ready to learn?"

My throat went dry at what she was suggesting we do. Here. *Now*.

"On you?" I croaked, my voice sounding like death warmed over.

She shot me a smirk that was pure trouble. "I might be younger than you, but I'm sure there are things I can teach you."

She was talking about hair, nothing more. But the tone of her voice and the way she was staring at me with those pouty lips and those fuck-me eyes said something else entirely.

Something I wanted to explore.

Something I absolutely should *not* explore.

I didn't say anything, but she must've seen the acquiescence in my expression. She turned her back to me and finger-combed through her hair, the unruly strands becoming controlled far easier than I would've thought.

I stepped in close—too fucking close, considering I was her boss—and inhaled deeply. I didn't know if it was her shampoo or her body wash or just *her*, but her scent nearly did me in. Something soft and fresh.

Sunshine, somehow, even in February.

Reaching up, I gathered her hair in my hands, my fingers brushing her nape. A shiver stole through her at the brief touch, and I shouldn't have liked that as much as I did.

And my dick definitely needed to settle the fuck down about it.

Her hair was thick and so fucking soft. I couldn't help but think of it gathered in my fist while I guided her mouth over my cock. While I fucked her from behind.

"Split the hair into three equal pieces," she said, interrupting my thoughts, and not a moment too soon. Her voice was rough, illustrating just how much this was affecting her too, and that wasn't helping matters.

She guided me through the braid—left over middle, right over middle, repeat. Her voice was soft and gentle and far more intimate than it should've been while discussing a hairstyle.

When I finished the braid—lopsided and pathetic-looking, but a million times better than I'd ever done before—and tied it off, Chloe turned to face me, leaning back against the counter.

I could have stepped back.

I *should* have.

But I didn't. I just stood there. Near enough that I could feel the heat pouring off her body. And if she stepped even an inch closer, she'd feel exactly what she did to me.

"You're turning out to be different than I expected," I said, breaking the silence.

She lifted a brow as she stared up at me. "Is that a good thing?"

No, it fucking wasn't a good thing.

Because it had been a hell of a lot easier to deny this pull I felt between us when I'd been able to put her squarely inside a neat little box labeled in bold, permanent marker: TRAINWRECK.

Instead of saying any of that, I braced my hands on the counter on either side of her hips and leaned toward her, the magnetic draw between us too much to ignore even a second longer.

She pressed a hand against my chest, and though I was sure she was going to use it to push me away or pause my descent, she didn't. Clutching my T-shirt in her fist, she tugged me down toward her mouth and lifted onto her tiptoes to meet me halfway.

And then, suddenly, we were kissing, her lips under mine and her little body tucked up right against me.

It started soft. Slow. Tentative. But the second her tongue swiped across my lower lip, all bets were off.

I groaned into her mouth and cupped her face as I deepened the kiss, licking my way inside. Her moans only spurred me on as she met my tongue stroke for stroke, her sounds making me even harder for her.

"Xander," she breathed, my name on her lips like a fucking prayer I was desperate to answer.

What the hell was this woman *doing* to me?

When she wrapped an arm around my neck and tugged me down, I couldn't stop myself from satisfying her unspoken plea.

Closer.

Without breaking the kiss, I reached down, gripped her waist, and lifted her onto the counter. Then I stepped between those thighs I couldn't stop thinking about and ground my cock against her.

Her pussy was so hot, I could feel the heat of it through her pajama shorts and my joggers. But I wanted to *feel* it. Wanted to reach between us and see if she was as wet as I was hard. Wanted to sink my cock inside her until she thought she couldn't take any more and then coax her to take the rest. I wanted to hear my name on her lips again, but this time while I was thrusting deep. Wanted to hear her scream it. Wanted to—

"*Daddy?*" Emma called from upstairs, and I jerked away from Chloe as if I'd been electrocuted.

We were both breathing hard, our chests heaving as we stared at each other in the near-dark, a thousand unspoken things hanging in the silence between us. But two main points flashed through my mind unrelentingly.

First—that was the hottest kiss of my life.

Second—and more importantly—that was a mistake. A colossal fuckup I couldn't afford.

When Emma called for me again, I gave Chloe one last look before turning on my heel and leaving without a word. All the while, the image of her standing there—utterly wrecked by my hands and utterly confused by my actions—was burned into my brain.

CHAPTER SIXTEEN

CHLOE

THE MOMENT LUNA walked through the back door of Wicked Little Things the following night, I knew I was screwed.

Starlight Cove's newly opened lingerie boutique—funded by none other than Mabel herself—was always closed to the public on Thursdays so it could be rented out for events or used for Mabel's infamous pleasure parties.

And since the party we were working tonight wasn't set to start until seven, that meant it was just me and my repressed feelings in the store. Honestly, it was pretty much all we had room for.

Luna didn't even offer a hello before she pinned me with a look, one brow raised. "So. You kissed him."

I froze, hand in midair as I restocked the *Twilight*-themed lube—*glittered for her pleasure*—and stared at her in shock. The only way she could possibly know that was if she'd had a live feed into Xander's house or if—

"*Mabel*," I spat her name like a curse.

Luna dipped her chin in a nod. "The one and only."

"She wasn't supposed to say anything! I don't exactly need the entire town to know I made out with my boss."

"Okay, first—" Luna held up a finger. "We are definitely coming back to the whole '*made out*' thing. And second, she didn't tell the whole town. Just us. She said you needed a vent session and a blocked exit to keep you from, and I quote, 'ghosting like a horny little Houdini.' So, we're here."

"We?"

As if on cue, in strolled the rest of my little girl gang.

Quinn glanced at me out of the corner of her eye. "Don't even think about running."

Sutton hummed in agreement as she picked up our special of the month—a tentacle vibrator, complete with textured ridges down the shaft and vibrating beads at the base. "You might be quick, but I'm quicker. If I can dodge projectile vomit in the ER, I can tackle you without breaking a sweat."

I rolled my eyes. "I think you're all being a little dramatic. I kissed him. Pretty sure I'm safe from having to flee into WITSEC."

"Normally, I'd agree with you," Luna said. "But we're talking about *you*. Chloe of the mid-date disappearing act."

"And even if we weren't, this is kind of a big deal," Quinn said, making that knot in my stomach tighten further.

"They're right," Sutton said, not helping matters. "You kissed your *boss*. In his *kitchen*."

"Brief interruption to mention she said *made out*, not just kissed," Luna—the traitor—said.

Quinn held up her hands. "I stand corrected. The only

way it could've been more scandalous is if you'd done it on the fire truck while parked on Main Street."

"Well, I didn't know the fire truck was an option," I deadpanned.

"Been there, done that." Quinn shrugged. "I'm just saying, maybe don't rule it out."

"I don't have to rule out anything. He already did that for me," I said and then snapped my mouth shut and studiously avoided each of their gazes.

Fuck. I hadn't meant to say that. And definitely not in the tone I'd used—all bitter and affected. Like I actually *cared*. I didn't care. I never cared. Repressed feelings over here, party of one!

"What did he do?" Sutton asked, her voice carrying an underlying threat of violence that made me feel a little bit sorry for her sixteen-year-old daughter. It was a tone you didn't mess with. And one you certainly didn't challenge.

"Nothing. He did nothing." I shrugged like it was no big deal and definitely hadn't been all I'd thought about today. "He greeted me with a grunt that passed as 'good morning' and went about his day. Obviously because the *kiss* meant nothing. To both of us."

All three of them huffed as one, an unholy trinity of disbelief.

"Your scoffs mean nothing to me," I said.

"Just like that kiss, huh?" Quinn said dryly.

I opened my mouth to confirm exactly that when Luna held up a hand to stop me.

"Before you lie again and say it was nothing, or it wasn't a big deal, or it was just a one-time lapse in judgment—"

"It *was* all of those things."

"—let me just ask one question." She paused, obviously for dramatic effect. "Why are you wearing his sweatshirt?"

I froze with a handful of sparkle condoms—to go with the lube, natch—and glanced down. Fuck me. That was indeed Xander's hoodie I was wearing. The one I'd basically been secretly living in for days. Like a complete *loser*.

Shit.

I straightened my spine and cleared my throat. "I ran out of clean ones. And I was cold. And it was there."

"Uh-huh," Quinn said flatly. "And I'm sure it has nothing to do with the fact that it smells like him."

"Of course not." I rolled my eyes. "That would be weird. And inappropriate. And crossing a boundary an employee definitely shouldn't cross with her boss."

"I don't know, babe," Sutton said. "Seems like less of a boundary to wear his hoodie than it does to stick your tongue down his throat, all while dry humping the shit out of him. But what do I know?"

I dropped my mouth open on a shocked gasp. "That meddling little narc. I'm never telling Mabel anything again!"

"Be mad at her all you want, but she's right," Luna said. "You need support. And we're here to provide it."

"Well, as much as I appreciate that, I have to finish getting ready for our party tonight. So we'll just have to table this little support session."

"Tomorrow, then," Sutton said, her tone daring me to argue.

But I'd spent a lifetime repressing my emotions and hiding from uncomfortable truths, so I took that dare head on.

"Can't. Xander's on shift, so I've got Emma duty."

Luna narrowed her eyes at me. "Is he *really* on shift, or is this your not-so-sly way of dodging the conversation?"

I gasped and pressed a hand to my chest in mock outrage. "You think so little of me?"

Sutton snorted. Luna rolled her eyes. And Quinn nailed the coffin shut with two little sentences.

"Did you forget my husband works with Xander? I can confirm that with one text."

"Motherfuck."

"Tomorrow night it is!" Sutton said with exaggerated cheer. "I'll bring the wine. Luna will bring a variety of weird cheeses. And Quinn will bring the passive-aggressive concern."

"I prefer to call it accountability," Quinn said.

"I hate you all. I hope you know that."

"We love you too," they said in unison as they strode out the way they came, leaving me just as they'd found me.

Well, *almost* as they'd found me. Except now, I was on the group calendar. To account for my sins, to have a complete breakdown, or possibly both.

CHAPTER SEVENTEEN

XANDER

THURSDAY NIGHTS at One Night Stan's were usually quiet, filled with a few regulars and maybe a couple of tourists. But we didn't get many of those in February in Maine. Still, it was enough to keep my mind occupied.

Since it was Chloe's night off, I'd planned to do just that with Emma. But Laurel had stopped by after school and stolen my daughter for an impromptu cousin hangout, and Emma had looked so excited I hadn't been able to say no.

Thankfully, our family's bar—and the one and only leftover from our bailing father—was good for something and that was a distraction. Namely, a distraction from the five-foot-four goblin of mayhem who'd infiltrated my home and my mind and even my fucking dreams.

"Not that I don't love the help," Lincoln said as he slid a row of clean glasses into place. "But maybe you could do me a solid and come on a night when I actually need you. Like, I don't know...the weekend?"

"Yeah, yeah, I get it. I have a lot of time to make up for

because I was a shit brother and bailed as soon as I could." I blew out a breath and rested my hands on the bar top. "But I'm still trying to find my footing with Emma, so it's going to take me a little while before I can step up."

When nothing but silence greeted me, I glanced over and found Lincoln staring at me with raised brows. "Shit, man. I just meant it'd be nice to have a night off so I could take a pretty girl out once in a while. I wasn't lying last night when I said I'm hard up. But I didn't know you'd buried all *that*."

"All what?"

"You tell me." He tossed a towel over his shoulder and leaned one elbow on the bar top, attention focused on me. "I deal with this shit every day, so lay it on me."

"Lay *what* on you?"

"Whatever's got the unemotional Xander feeling some kind of way."

"I'm not *feeling some kind of way*."

"*Right*," he said, drawing out the word. "Granted, I don't have a lot of experience with this sort of thing, but I do seem to recall Atlas having a similar reaction when a certain smoke show single mom showed up in town and moved in to his backyard."

"Good for him and Sutton," I said flatly. "But I don't see what that has to do with me."

"Oh, you don't see?" Lincoln snorted. "Well, I'm not sure if you're aware, but you've got your own smoke show living under your roof. A smoke show half the men in town—and at least a quarter of the women—are panting after."

I clenched my jaw and averted my gaze, ignoring the pit

in my stomach that opened up at his words. "I don't know why you think I'd care about that. She's just my—"

Before I could finish that thought, the front door opened, and Mabel and her little militia stormed the bar. And there, in the middle of all that mayhem, was who else but Chloe?

"Excellent work," Lincoln murmured. "Very subtle. Definitely believe the whole, 'she's just my' speech."

I ignored him, too busy focusing on the woman I hadn't been able to get out of my head. Thankfully, she hadn't seen me yet. Probably didn't expect me to be here since it was her night off and my designated night with Emma.

She was mid-speech, holding up a vibrator like it was a party favor, beaming as if she hadn't rearranged my entire fucking grip on reality last night with that kiss.

Her sweater was pale pink and hung off one shoulder, tempting me with the curve of her neck and the swooping script below her collarbone that read *wanderlust*. But it had nothing on the rest of her. Fishnets that were wide enough to slip my hand under climbed her legs and disappeared beneath a black skirt that wasn't technically indecent but definitely should have been classified as such. Especially when she'd paired it with those knee-high boots I wanted over my shoulders.

She was a sin-soaked fever dream in the flesh. And all I could think about—*all I could fucking think about*—was what she had on under that skirt.

If she had on anything at all.

An image slammed into me like a freight train. Bending her over the bar top, flipping up that little skirt, pulling her panties to the side—if there were any—and then fucking her through those goddamn fishnets. Fucking her until she came all over me. Until she begged for more. Until she said my name the way she had last night in the dark.

Only, this time? She'd scream it.

I gripped the edge of the bar top in an effort to hold myself up—or maybe to keep myself from going to her. Because god knew my self-control was damn near nonexistent when it came to Chloe and I needed all the help I could get.

I'd already had to fight myself this morning when we'd met in front of the coffee maker—her holding that ridiculous, obnoxious mug I'd bought her, all while shooting me a sly look out of the corner of her eye. As if she was remembering, in great detail, what had happened right there in that spot mere hours before.

I knew because I'd looked at her the same.

But I couldn't. *We* couldn't.

So I'd turned away from her. As if the kiss had meant nothing. As if it hadn't shaken my very foundation. As if it had been a mistake.

It *was* a mistake.

Now, Chloe glanced in my direction, freezing when she saw me behind the bar. And then she pasted on a fake smile that didn't reach her eyes, and I fucking hated it.

Hated even more that I deserved it.

I was the one playing hot and cold with her when I shouldn't have been playing anything at all.

"Hey, Chief," she called, holding up a sparkly pink vibrator like it was a microphone. "We were thinking about some impromptu karaoke. Any chance you'd be up for it?"

"He's up for something, all right," Lincoln muttered, and I threw a towel at his face without glancing his way.

Mabel grinned in our direction and clapped her hands. "Perfect timing, fellas! Lincoln, I don't think you need any help in this area, but I'm sure Xander could use a little. Chloe was just telling us about the adjustable settings on this baby." She turned toward my nanny, a brow raised. "What were you saying? If you set the speed to four and tweak your wrist just so, it can—"

"*Mabel*," Chloe hissed, her cheeks flushing as she darted her gaze toward me.

And I couldn't do anything but stare, slack-jawed, and imagine her performing that exact thing with the vibrator buried in her cunt, her tits pointed toward the ceiling, and her lips parted on a moan.

Jesus. Fucking. Christ.

"What?" Mabel asked, all feigned innocence. "You were all too willing to share over at Wicked Little Things."

"Well, my boss wasn't at Wicked Little Things, now was he?" Chloe bit out.

"Your boss." Mabel shot her an exaggerated wink. "*Right.*"

Chloe leaned forward and snapped, "I swear to god, Mabel, I'll tell George about your little addiction if you don't shut your meddling mouth."

I had no idea what little addiction Chloe was talking about, but it was clear Mabel did.

The older woman's eyes went wide before she turned her back on Lincoln and me and addressed her group. "What were we talking about, ladies? The best way to achieve simultaneous orga—"

I stopped listening because there were some things I didn't need to hear. And because I needed to focus on something other than the hot mess express my hot mess nanny happened to be a part of.

That worked for all of three minutes until the front door opened and in strolled Eli Schultz. Cocky smirk he absolutely couldn't back up and that peaked-in-high-school-and-didn't-know-it energy he wore like a cloak.

"Eli! What a surprise you're here," Bonnie Schultz, one of Mabel's misfits, said in a completely unconvincing voice, gesturing toward him while he stared at the table of women. One, in particular.

I knew this fucking guy. Had gone to school with him. Witnessed the DUIs and restraining orders he'd racked up like frequent flyer miles. And now this walking red flag had his eyes trained on Chloe like she was dessert and he hadn't eaten in days.

"Easy there, Xan," Lincoln said. "You wanna loosen your grip on the bar top so we don't have to replace it?"

"Fuck off," I muttered. Because I was pretty sure gripping the bar top was the only thing keeping me rooted in place. Keeping me from claiming Chloe in front of this shit stain and dragging her into the back room.

Even though she wasn't mine to claim.

"Ladies, you know my son, Eli," Bonnie said. "Eli, you remember the ladies. And this is *Chloe,* our pleasure consultant for the evening."

Eli aimed a slime-coated grin in her direction. "Pleasure consultant, huh? I'm suddenly rethinking my career path."

Chloe breathed out a laugh that sounded forced. "Well, you know what they say—if you love what you do..."

There was that creepy-ass smile again. "This definitely explains the line of customers waiting outside."

This time, her laugh was genuine, and I clenched my teeth hard enough to crack a molar. The group got distracted by the lube samples Mabel handed out, which left Chloe and Eli in a semi-private conversation. Semi-private because while I couldn't hear what they were saying, I could see every bit of their interaction.

And I hated every goddamn second of it.

Eli pressed a hand to the small of Chloe's back and brought his mouth close to her ear to tell her something. Something that made her toss her head back and laugh. And why the hell did it feel like a meat grinder was working its way through my insides?

"Denial doesn't look good on you, man." Lincoln clapped a hand on my shoulder and stepped out from behind the bar, heading off to do...something.

I had no fucking idea what it was, and I didn't care. I couldn't tear my gaze away from Chloe and Eli for even a second.

I didn't know how long I stood there, glaring at the two of them. Long enough for the patrons to get the hint that they'd have better luck getting a refill from my brother than from me.

When Chloe bent to grab something off the floor, Eli's gaze didn't leave her ass. And mine didn't leave him. My jaw was tight, my eyes narrowed, my fists clenched around a bar towel like I was seconds from ripping it to shreds.

Before I could even think about schooling my expression, Chloe broke away from the group and sauntered over to the bar, that smirk that nearly did me in curving up one side of her lips.

Lips I'd had on mine less than twenty-four hours ago.

"You keep scowling like that and people are gonna think you don't like them."

"Good. That's what I'm going for. If douchebags like that kept their eyes to themselves, it wouldn't be a fucking problem," I said before I could stop myself. Then internally cursed when Chloe just stared at me, her brows hitched the tiniest bit.

Sure, it could have been the words themselves that caused her reaction. But I worried she'd heard the underlying tension beneath them—heard what I didn't want her to.

That she was so deep in my head, I couldn't hope to get her out.

After several long moments where I felt her scrutiny like I was under a microscope, she rested her elbows on the bar top and leaned toward me, that fucking sunshine scent coming with her and my fucking dick perking up thanks to it.

She met my gaze, something challenging in hers, and dropped her voice low enough so it stayed between us. "Still want to pretend that kiss didn't mean anything, Chief?"

And just like that, the bottom dropped out from under me.

She didn't wait for a response. She didn't need to. I was sure my thoughts were written over every inch of my face.

She just smiled—a little knowing and a little daring—and walked back to the table of troublemakers.

All I could do was stand there and watch.

I didn't go after her. I couldn't. Not now. Not yet.

Because for the first time in years—maybe the first time in my entire life—I didn't know what the plan was. Didn't know my next step. Didn't know where to go from here.

All I knew was I couldn't pretend anymore, and I was damn tired of trying.

CHAPTER EIGHTEEN

CHLOE

IF I JUST FOCUSED ON the damn muffins, I wouldn't have to think about Xander. And if I didn't think about Xander, everything would be *fine*.

That was what I'd been telling myself all morning since I'd woken up from yet another dream featuring the dark-haired, green-eyed devil I couldn't seem to escape.

I'd needed something—*anything*—to distract me. Because thinking about Xander, about the kiss that had melted my brain, the complete radio silence afterward as if nothing had happened, and then the way he'd watched me at One Night Stan's...as if I were *his*—wasn't helping anything.

Certainly not my mental state.

Muffins were the infinitely safer choice. They made sense. I could handle muffins. As long as I followed the recipe, muffins did exactly what was expected of them.

They certainly didn't kiss you like they'd waited decades for the honor, blow you off like it was nothing, attempt to incinerate a guy flirting with you by using only their eyes, and then conveniently flee the next morning for a twenty-four-hour shift.

So yeah.

Muffins were my focus. And the reason I'd decided to go full breakfast scientist when I'd woken up this morning.

I'd been testing theories for almost three weeks—ever since that breakfast disaster on day one—trying to crack the case of Emma's elusive appetite.

It was so strange because she ate fine literally every other time of the day. It was just breakfast that held the hiccups. Which led me to believe Emma wasn't looking for a specific ingredient. She was aching for something else—a moment or a memory, maybe. And I desperately wanted to help her find it.

This morning, I'd pored over the suggestion box she'd been filling with various renditions of the same thing—a muffin with what I'd assumed was a ponytail sticking out the top, just like I'd made that first day. But yesterday, she'd colored it yellow and added sparks all around it, and suddenly, I knew.

It wasn't a damn ponytail. It was a *candle*.

And maybe that memory she'd been craving.

"Okay, bug," I called. "Time for breakfast!"

I heard her sigh all the way from the other room, followed by the tiny patter of her feet, until she stopped short at the entryway to the kitchen. Her eyes lit up as she darted her gaze around before focusing on where I stood.

"Thank you so much for choosing to dine at Doodlebug's Café," I said in my horrible French accent. "It is my absolute pleasure to introduce you to the Breakfast Cupcake Creation Station!"

She grinned as I grabbed her little apron and slipped it over her head before tying it at her back.

I gestured to the spread on the table. "Please proceed right this way for decorations, candle selection, and wish deployment."

She gasped and looked at me, eyes wide and hopeful. "Can we light the candle?"

"Definitely."

"Can I make a wish?"

"Of course. I don't know about you, but I think wishes should happen more than once a year."

A smile swept across her face—bold and bright and vibrant—and her pure happiness stitched up a part of my heart I didn't even know was broken. "That's what Mommy used to say!"

I felt the weight of her words settle deep inside. Warmth bloomed in my chest and only continued to grow as she decorated her muffin. She worked so hard to find the perfect balance of sprinkles and strawberry Greek yogurt disguised as frosting, her tongue poking out between her teeth as she decorated.

Once she was satisfied, she studied the assortment of candles I'd set out, picking the one I'd guessed she would.

It was a unicorn on its hind legs, posed like it was jumping over a rainbow, the wick poking out of its horn.

"Excellent choice, Miss Emma," I said, slipping into that awful French accent again. "If you please, take your seat."

I pulled out the chair for her, and she scrambled up, eyes

bright with excitement as I set her breakfast cupcake in front of her. After placing the unicorn candle in the top of the muffin, I grabbed the matchbook and lit the candle, grinning as her eyes sparkled in the flame.

"Time for your wish, bug."

She closed her eyes tight, her lips moving silently on her wish, and then she blew out the candle before turning her beaming smile on me. "I did it!"

"You sure did." I squatted down to her level. "That was a great wish. I can tell."

She bit her lip and nodded before glancing at the unicorn candle, the tip of the horn partially melted away. Worry crept into her eyes. "What happens when the horn's all gone? Does that mean no more wishes?"

"Absolutely not. Because your LoLee is prepared." I grabbed the bag from the party supply store and overturned it onto the table, two dozen unicorn candles scattering across the top. "This should keep us in business for a few years."

Emma clapped and squealed, her laughter contagious. And then she did the most amazing thing—she devoured the muffin, not leaving a single bite.

After she'd finished the entire thing and grinned proudly at me, I nearly cried. *Nearly.* But I didn't.

Because crying was something you did when you were attached, and I *definitely* wasn't attached.

I was just happy. Satisfied. Proud. Of her. Of me.

And *that* deserved a dance party, complete with karaoke.

"It's time to celebrate, bug!" I called as I spun into the kitchen, grabbed a whisk like a mic, and launched into an off-key rendition of "Walking on Sunshine."

Emma joined in—belting out gibberish lyrics and dancing next to me like we were headlining at Coachella. My cheeks hurt from smiling as we sang and danced, our socks slipping on the hardwood floor and her laughter filling the house.

And for once, my focus was blessedly not on Xander.

At least until the front door opened, and in he strolled, his presence hitting the air like gravity shifting.

Even after a twenty-four-hour shift, he looked like sex on a stick in his uniform pants and a department tee under the coat he shrugged off. And good *god*. The way that T-shirt clung to him, molding around those biceps and broad shoulders and that chest I just *knew* would be firm and solid, should have been illegal.

I froze, the whisk halfway to my mouth, the off-key note dying in my throat.

He blinked once, then looked from me to Emma before shifting his gaze to the mess of the kitchen. And then—God help me—he smiled. Or what passed for a smile in Xanderville anyway.

Just the corner of his lips tilted the tiniest bit.

Just enough to make my stomach drop-kick my ribs.

"Morning," he said, his voice low and rough in a way that shot straight through me.

"Morning," I said casually. As if he didn't affect me at all. As if he hadn't just caught me making a fool of myself.

"Looks like I missed quite the show."

"And you missed breakfast cupcakes, Daddy!" Emma raced toward him, and he scooped her up before she could crash into his legs.

He toed off his boots, then walked into the kitchen, brow raised. "Cupcakes? I thought those were muffins."

I lifted a shoulder in a shrug. "They're breakfast cupcakes when we're feeling fancy."

"And when they have a candle!" Emma said.

I dipped my chin in a nod. "The most important part. And the missing clue in the case of Emma's elusive appetite."

He raised his brows, looking from her to the demolished plate in front of her seat at the table, then to me, a silent question hanging in the air between us.

"She ate," I confirmed, my voice catching for some dumb reason. It wasn't like I'd discovered a Taylor Swift easter egg or anything. I'd just gotten a little girl to eat. "Every bit. Happily."

His whole face softened then, relief and gratitude and something else I couldn't quite name settling over him.

"That's my girl," he murmured before pressing a kiss to Emma's temple. "Did you help LoLee with this breakfast cupcake decorating station?"

"Yeah!" Emma pushed to get down from his arms, then grabbed his hand and tugged. "Come on! I'll make you one too!"

He didn't even hesitate as he allowed her to pull him to the table and guide him to sit down. She dashed around the space, grabbing a plate, then a cooled muffin, before scooping a heaping spoonful of pink yogurt on top and absolutely drowning it in edible glitter.

With a huge smile on her face, she set it down in front of Xander, then reached over and grabbed her fancy candle. She stuck it into the top and turned to me. "Can you light it for Daddy, LoLee?"

Obviously, I couldn't say no to that, even though my first instinct was to run. Get the hell away from him and whatever voodoo magic he worked on me anytime I was in his presence.

Instead, I did as she asked, leaning close to him to light the candle. "Make a wish, Chief."

He lifted his eyes to mine...and didn't look away. The weight of his stare was heavy. More meaningful than it should've been for eye contact over a muffin. But even so, everything in me went still. Just froze entirely.

Xander didn't say anything. Didn't even smile. He just darted his gaze across my face, as if I were a puzzle he hadn't been able to solve. As if he were desperate to.

And then he blinked and looked away, snapping the moment between us as if it'd been all in my mind. Without a word, he turned his attention to the candle and blew it out.

"Yay, Daddy! You did it!"

He smiled at Emma then—something soft and private between them—and gathered her on his lap, pressing another kiss to her temple. "Thanks, peanut." Then he turned his eyes on me. "And thank you, Chloe."

My breath caught in my throat at my name falling from his lips with something other than exasperation or derision. Without sarcasm or frustration.

It had been laced with something that sounded a hell of a lot like want.

I turned away before he could see how flushed my cheeks

were. And so I could try to focus on something other than the thudding pulse of my heart in my ears.

I shouldn't care this much about his reaction. Shouldn't care whether he was going to kiss me again. And I definitely shouldn't care that he'd acted like it had never happened.

But I did.

And based on his reaction the other night at the bar and the way he'd looked at me just now—like I was everything he wasn't supposed to want—it had been nothing more than a lie on his end.

What was happening between us *wasn't* nothing.

And I had no idea what to do with that.

CHAPTER NINETEEN

XANDER

A SOFT NOISE broke through my subconscious, and I was off the couch in a blink. Halfway up the stairs before I even registered what I was doing. I'd heard...something. Something loud enough to tug me out of a dream and into reality.

Emma.

I'd woken just like this so many times before, I moved on autopilot as I headed straight to her room. Once inside, I darted my gaze around the space until it landed on her. She was sprawled across her mattress, her arms and legs taking up every inch of her twin bed, and her mouth hung open in a way that would definitely lead to drool.

Completely, blissfully asleep.

I exhaled a relieved breath, my shoulders sagging even as my pulse still beat wildly in my ears. Reaching down, I brushed the hair back from her face and pressed a kiss to the top of her head, grateful she was dreaming peacefully tonight instead of having another nightmare.

After stepping out into the hallway, I closed her door behind me, the strong sense of déjà vu washing over me. I shook my head and scrubbed a hand down my face. I was tired. Fucking exhausted. Apparently, catching a total of four hours of sleep sprinkled throughout my twenty-four-hour shift wasn't enough to keep me going once back in my own house, despite my plan to stay awake for the evening.

The last thing I remembered was Emma snuggling up next to me after dinner, Chloe on the opposite end of the couch, as we started our 672nd viewing of *Frozen*.

Now, I made my way down the hallway toward my bedroom, desperate to crash and fall back into whatever dream I'd been woken from. I couldn't remember it exactly, just that I'd enjoyed it. I had that vague, hazy recollection of something I was dying to experience all over again.

Something involving Chloe, no doubt.

Before I could close myself off in my room, the soft noise that must've pulled me from my dream in the first place sounded again, closer this time.

Like I was repeating something I'd done a hundred times before, I crept down the hallway, stopping just outside Chloe's partially open door.

She sat on her bed, her back braced against the headboard, bare legs outstretched on top of her dark purple sheets. As usual, she wore a hoodie so large it could've fit three of her inside it. But this time, it wasn't one of her generic sweatshirts.

It was *mine*.

Starlight Cove Fire Department was stamped across the front, directly over her tits, and my name was etched above it.

I'd seen her in that same hoodie a dozen times before. But every single one of those times had been in my dreams. And every single one of those times, I'd woken up with a hard cock and the knowledge that it hadn't been real.

None of it had been real.

Her cheeks were flushed, that plump lower lip caught between her teeth as she whimpered soft and low. She held her phone in one hand as the other was tucked between her legs, her fingers moving against her pale pink pajama shorts just peeking out beneath my hoodie. And all the while, she stared, transfixed, at whatever was on the screen.

"Are you watching porn, chaos?"

Gasping, Chloe snatched her hand from between her legs, her wide-eyed gaze flying to me. "Xander! What are you doing?"

I raised a brow. "What are *you* doing?"

"Nothing!" She placed her phone down on the bed and shook her head. "It's just a book. I swear."

"Must be some book. What's it about?"

"It's—wait." She furrowed her brow as she looked at me. "You're not judging me?"

"No. I'm not judging you." I raked my gaze down her body in a slow, deliberate perusal, cataloging every inch of her I could see. Cataloging every inch of her I *couldn't*. "But I am interested in what you're doing."

She narrowed her eyes at me, confusion sweeping over her features. "What's happening here?"

I leaned against the doorframe—something I'd done a dozen times before—and crossed my arms over my chest.

"Looks to me like you were touching yourself while wearing my hoodie."

She cleared her throat and averted her gaze, her cheeks flushing scarlet. "I...thought you were asleep."

"Maybe I am. Maybe I'm still dreaming."

"Okay..." she said, drawing out the word. Sweeping her gaze over me from head to toe, she studied me as if seeing me for the first time. "I'm not really sure what to do here."

"Tell me what your book's about."

"And why would I do that?"

"Because I told you to," I said, the command in my voice low but unmistakable.

Her brows flew up, her body jolting as if she hadn't been expecting the words or the tone. Hadn't been expecting her response to them either. But then she parted her lips, her eyelids growing heavy as she stared at me with undisguised want.

Want I was all too willing to be on the receiving end of.

"This is...new."

Not new to me. If only she were aware of just how many times some variation of this fantasy had played out in my mind...

"Do you want me to stop?"

Her chest rose and fell with her breaths, and her eyes stayed locked on mine for so long I thought for sure she'd say yes. Yes, she absolutely wanted me to stop. Wanted me to get the hell out of her room. Leave her alone and let her read her book in peace.

Instead, she whispered, "No. I don't want you to stop."

Somehow, my cock grew even harder at her admission

until it was throbbing incessantly in my jeans, desperate for her. Just like fucking always.

"Good girl. Tell me what you're reading and why it made you slip your hand between your thighs and touch that sweet little pussy."

"Oh my god," she murmured, barely more than a breath. Definitely not something she'd intended for me to hear. Then, louder, she said, "Are you sure about this?"

"Are you?"

She hesitated for only a second before biting her lower lip and nodding.

"The words, chaos. I need the words."

"I'm sure."

Christ. If my cock got any harder, I was going to pass out from loss of blood to my brain.

"Good. Now tell me."

She shifted her gaze to the side before meeting my eyes again. "It's a romance."

"I figured as much. What about this romance made your pussy so needy you had to touch it over your shorts?"

She exhaled a shaky breath, her eyes locked on mine as she swallowed. "This scene...the couple. They're, um... They're not supposed to be together. He's her boss. But then, the guy finally snapped. Dragged her into a back room at their office..."

"Then what?"

"He told her he was tired of fighting it. That he didn't care if he lost his job. He just needed to be inside her."

"Did he fuck her? Is that what made you wet?"

"He hasn't yet. He...he was telling her what to do. Telling her to touch herself and watching while she got herself off."

Fuck. I desperately wanted to reach down and grip my shaft just to get a handle on myself. Precome was already leaking from my cock because of nothing more than a handful of words spoken by my wet dream.

"Which part got you hotter? How he bossed her around or that she fingered herself while he watched?"

She licked her lips, her gaze darting across my face as if she couldn't believe I was still here or that I was asking her this. That made two of us. "Both."

"Show me."

"What?"

"Show me," I said, firmer this time. "If I hadn't interrupted, show me what you would've done."

"I...I don't—"

"Do you need direction? You want me to tell you what to do?"

A pause before a stilted nod.

"The words, chaos."

"Yes," she whispered. "I want you to tell me what to do."

I hummed low in my throat. "There's my dirty girl. Slide your hand inside your panties. Tell me how wet you are."

"Fuck," she breathed. Hesitating only the briefest moment, she did as I asked, spreading her legs just wide enough to allow me a glimpse of her pale pink shorts and the shape of her fingers beneath the wet spot on the fabric.

I knew the second her fingers brushed over her clit because a shudder rolled through her as she whimpered, her legs falling open even more. "Well?"

"I'm...wet. So fucking wet."

"I know you are. You leaked through your bottoms, didn't you?"

"Yes," she admitted, her fingers moving faster now. "*God.* I need..."

"What? What do you need?"

"I don't know..."

"I don't believe that. I think you know exactly what you need."

She locked her gaze on me, desperate and needy and trusting as she worked herself over with her fingers. "I want you to tell me what to do. Please, Xander."

Jesus fucking Christ.

I didn't know why the hell my name on her lips was so hot, only that it was. Only that it made me all the more eager to fuck her until it was the only word she said. The only one she screamed.

"Tell me how many fingers you have buried in your needy cunt right now."

Her breath hitched, her legs closing and trapping her hand between them. As if she'd been caught doing something she shouldn't have been.

"Don't. Don't hide from me. I want to see it all. Wish you didn't have those fucking cocktease shorts on that you're always wearing. Wish I could see exactly how deep you've shoved your fingers inside your sweet little pussy. Now tell me how many you've stuffed inside."

"Two."

I made a rough sound in the back of my throat. "You'd need more than that, wouldn't you? If you were going to take my cock, you'd need all four. Slide another one nice and deep for me." I raked my gaze over her again, desperate to see beneath the fabric covering her. "As much as I fucking love seeing you in my sweatshirt, I wish it were gone so I could finally get an eyeful of those perfect tits I've been dreaming about every fucking night."

"Oh god," she breathed, her other hand slipping under my hoodie and going straight for the tits I wanted in my mouth. "Don't stop."

"Not until you come. You know that, don't you? There's no fucking way I could stop once I had a taste. Once I sank even a fucking millimeter inside that heaven between your thighs. It's why I'm all the way over here and you're going to come on your fingers instead of against my tongue."

"Xander."

My cock was throbbing in time with my heartbeat, the overwhelming urge I had to go to her unrelenting. To rip a hole in the crotch of her shorts, feast my eyes on what I knew would be the prettiest pussy I'd ever seen, and sink deep without wasting another second. Find out if she'd gotten herself wet enough to take every fucking inch or if I'd have to make her come on my tongue first.

But instead, I stood rooted in place, in the doorway of my daughter's nanny's bedroom. And I watched her fuck herself with her fingers. Watched those tits heave beneath my sweatshirt as she gasped in lungfuls of air. Watched her bite that plump lower lip as whimpers and moans escaped her mouth. Watched her hips roll as she moved her fingers faster and faster beneath the material of her shorts.

I was close—so fucking close—to coming undone with

nothing more than a zipper pressed tight against my dick. And I had no hope of stopping this runaway train now.

"Jesus Christ. Look at you. Even covered up so I can't see a damn thing, you're still a fucking wet dream, aren't you? Still the hottest goddamn thing I've ever laid eyes on."

Her breath hitched, her eyes growing even heavier, and goose bumps broke out over her skin at my words. I knew I shouldn't have said it. Shouldn't have said a damn fucking word because I'd shared too much.

But what did it matter in this quiet space in the dark of night? I'd already established I shouldn't even be here in the first place. So what was one more line I'd crossed?

I wanted to tell her to add another finger to get her ready to take my cock. Wanted to tell her to lick those fingers clean, taste herself, and tell me how sweet she was. Wanted to demand she admit she thought of me just as much as I thought of her—that she couldn't get me out of her head either.

But I didn't say any of those things. Instead, I gripped the doorframe until my knuckles turned white and watched in awe as the girl who'd starred in every single one of my fantasies since she'd stumbled into my life inched closer and closer to orgasm.

"You're close, aren't you? You gonna come?"

"*Yes.*"

"Good. Shove those fingers deep, dirty girl. Pretend it's my cock filling you up. Come all over me, Chloe."

"*Fuck.*" She snapped her legs together, her head dropping back as she softly cried out my name. Her hips rolled beneath her hand, her fingers buried in the pussy I'd give anything to feel as she came undone.

And, like I was a goddamn teenager all over again, I went right over the edge with her, shooting off in my jeans as if I had zero self-control.

Although I was quickly coming to realize that, when it came to Chloe Bradshaw? Zero was exactly how much self-control I had.

CHAPTER TWENTY

CHLOE

FIRST OF ALL, I wasn't spiraling. I wanted to get that out of the way just so everyone was on the same page. I absolutely, one hundred percent was *not* losing my shit.

Sure, I'd been reading a spicy book last night when I'd been interrupted. And yes, my boss—my *boss*—had directed me to touch myself as he stood in the doorway watching, his eyes devouring me like I was his favorite late-night fantasy while I came apart.

And okay, fine, the way he'd voiced his orders in that deep rasp had very nearly triggered a spontaneous religious experience on top of the best orgasm I'd had in years.

But I was absolutely *not* thinking about that.

I wasn't replaying the way his eyes had heated when they'd landed on me. Or the rough sound that had come from his throat. Or how his entire body was tensed as he stood there, his knuckles white on the doorframe as if holding himself back. Or how out of character it'd been for him to do, well, *any* of that.

And I sure as hell wasn't thinking about how just my name on his lips had sent me over the edge and wrecked me more than any orgasm should have the power to.

No, sir. I wasn't thinking about any of that.

Also not wondering if, when he'd turned to leave without a word and silently shut my door behind him, he'd gone into his own room, wrapped his hand around his cock, and came to the memory of me.

Nope. Nope. Nope.

I wasn't doing any of those things.

Instead, I was devoting my entire day to winter shenanigans. Core memories, edible glitter to make things sparkle, maybe some mild snow-induced hypothermia. The usual.

Avoidance? Never met her.

It was a sunny—if cold—day, and Emma and I had been outside for twenty minutes playing in the snow. She'd already declared herself Queen of the Backyard Kingdom and appointed our pitiful-looking snowman as her official royal guard.

Captain Sparklepants was shaping up...well, not quite beautifully, but he was shaping up, nonetheless.

"Arms," Emma called, reaching back as if the candy canes I placed in her hand were scalpels and she was performing surgery.

"Yes, Doctor. Right away, Doctor."

We'd already given Captain Sparklepants a yellow scarf I'd stolen from the coat closet, pinecones for his eyes, a mouth made of chocolate chips—half of which Emma had already eaten—and a stalk of asparagus for his nose because we were all out of carrots.

A snowman had never looked more unhinged.

But my absolute favorite part of him and the pièce de résistance? A glitter beard.

"He's not sparkly enough." Emma propped her hands on her hips as she stared at our ridiculous masterpiece.

"No? I think he's got just the right amount of sparkle. Really accentuates his green nose."

"He needs *more*." Without waiting for a response from me, she grabbed the container of iridescent edible glitter and upended the entire thing over Captain Sparklepants's head.

So much for subtlety.

"Well, he's certainly luminescent now. And perfect," I said, brushing snow off my mittens and admiring our creation.

"He needs a hat!" Emma yelled, as if I weren't standing five feet away from her.

"A hat, of course," I said, glancing around for the plastic tiara I'd brought out.

I snatched it from the pile of discarded accessories and placed it on top of Captain Sparklepants's head before bowing dramatically. "Your Majesty."

Emma fell into a fit of giggles at my terrible British accent. And, yeah, okay—apparently, I liked to do accents and I wasn't very good at them. But with the way she laughed, literally falling over in the snow, thanks to her amusement, I'd do every bad accent I could think of.

I fell onto the snow next to her, a bright smile on my face as I glanced over at her. She had changed and blossomed so much in the few short weeks I'd been here. It was hard to believe this girl next to me with rosy cheeks and vibrant eyes and a smile big enough and bright enough to light up the whole sky was the same girl who'd been hiding behind a pillow the first time we'd met.

The thought that maybe—just maybe—I had a little something to do with that made something warm and soft unfurl in my chest.

But I shook that off. Now wasn't the time to get bogged down by those pesky things called attachments. Safer for everyone that way.

"Time for snow angels?" I asked.

"Snow angels!" she yelled back and immediately began flapping her arms and kicking her feet, sending snow flying in every direction.

My own angel was slightly lopsided and a hot mess— much like my emotional state. But for the first time in days, I wasn't consumed with the ever-present question: *what did that mean?* Or trying to figure out how to function around my boss without spontaneously combusting. I was just here, basking in the giggles of a little girl I adored.

At least until the back door creaked open behind us.

I froze mid-flap, the cold seeping into my body through my coat. But that wasn't what made me shiver. It was him.

It was *always* him.

I didn't have to glance over to confirm what I already knew. I could feel it—the weight of his gaze on me, all quiet hunger and unmatched restraint, just like it'd been last night.

But I knew I couldn't avoid him forever. Couldn't avoid the giant pink elephant sure to be in the room with us either. Yeah, he'd watched me come. And yeah, he'd told me to shove three fingers into my pussy to get it ready to take his cock. But so what? That was probably just another Saturday night for most people.

So, I sat up, shielding my eyes against the sun, and glanced toward the house.

And sure enough, there he was, all six feet and a handful of inches of growly, off-duty fire chief. Xander's beanie was pulled low, his jaw shadowed with that tight-cropped beard that had starred in every single one of my dreams. The same one I'd wanted to feel on my thighs last night.

He wore a black jacket that was somehow fitted enough to show off his unfairly broad shoulders and seam-testing biceps. His boots were planted on the ground like the snow had personally offended him.

But it was his expression that nearly did me in. Not because he was looking at me, but because he looked... confused.

Not awkward. Not guilty. Not cocky like a man who'd told me exactly how to touch myself and watched me fall apart while wearing his hoodie.

No, this was so fucking much worse.

He looked at me like he had no idea. Like he was trying to place something. Like maybe he'd dreamed it.

My breath caught, and my heart stuttered to a screeching halt.

Oh.

My.

God.

He thought he'd *dreamed* it.

That low, gruff voice telling me to slip my hand between my thighs? Every hoarse command telling me exactly what to do?

He didn't even realize it had happened.

Meanwhile, I'd already replayed it enough times to short-circuit my vibrator. Twice.

Okay, three times.

But that was *it*. No more. I was done with that.

Because if he couldn't be bothered to remember the hottest thing that had ever happened to me, I was just going to pretend it hadn't happened too. Cut off my nose, spite my orgasm, and carry on like I hadn't come from his voice alone. If he could forget, so could I.

I lifted my chin and shot him a smile I didn't feel. And Emma—bless that girl—stole his scrutinizing attention from me.

"Daddy! Daddy, look! We made Captain Sparklepants!" She ran around our homely looking snowman, presenting it as if it were worthy of a medal.

Xander blinked away from me and focused on his daughter. "You named it?"

I huffed out a laugh and stood, brushing the snow off my pants. Pretending everything was fine. Totally normal over here. "Of course. He has a whole backstory and everything. Xander Steele, I'd like you to meet Captain Sparklepants, Secret Agent. He has glitter-based powers and a vendetta against anyone who doesn't think whipped cream and sprinkles belong on hot chocolate."

His lips twitched. Or it might've been a trick of the light.

It was probably most definitely a trick of the light because Xander didn't smile. "Sounds dangerous."

"Oh, he's a menace for sure." I gave Xander a quick once-over—in a strictly professional way, of course. His jacket and boots suggested he was out here to stay, but I needed to know what side of this snow war he was planning to be on. "You here to supervise or surrender?"

He narrowed his eyes on me. "Steeles don't surrender."

Emma took that as a green light and shrieked with the kind of glee only sugar and snowstorms could deliver. And then she promptly hurled a snowball at him.

With as bad as her aim had been all morning, I was shocked when it landed. A direct hit, right on the side of his head.

I snorted out a laugh and then slammed both mitten-covered hands over my mouth to hide the sound.

Xander glanced at me, sizing me up from head to toe, and then focused on Emma's giggling form. He brushed the snow from his beanie before bending down and scooping a handful of his own, his movements slow and ominous. "You sure about this, peanut?"

"*Yes!*" she yelled.

"Chief," I warned. "You're outnumbered, so maybe you should rethink this."

"You're assuming I play fair," he said with a smirk and a glint in his eyes that made my nipples perk up.

No. My nipples were no longer allowed to respond to this fuckhot man. Not when he didn't even remember the hottest night of my life.

He tossed a snowball at Emma, who shrieked with glee as I ducked behind Captain Sparklepants for cover, nearly falling on my ass at the sound of Xander's booming laugh. Something I hadn't once heard in the weeks I'd been staying here.

The snowball he lobbed my way missed me by mere inches, exploding in a puff of white against the tree trunk behind me. And even though it hadn't been a direct hit, I retaliated, gathering up a snowball of my own and hurling it at him.

It hit him in the shoulder, and he didn't even flinch, the smug, oversized, incredibly built bastard. But he leveled me with a look that had me slowly backing away.

"Oh, it's on now, chaos," he muttered.

It was pure pandemonium after that. Not to mention three direct hits to my ass and one suspiciously accurate shot that knocked the tiara off Captain Sparklepants, courtesy of Xander.

Emma gasped in horror like she was on an actual battlefield and had just witnessed her partner-in-arms go down.

"No, Daddy!" she shrieked, then rushed him, plowing into him at full speed.

It was actually more of a body slam to the knees, but he went down like he'd been tackled by a linebacker instead of a tiny four-year-old an eighth of his size. He landed flat on his back in the snow with a grunt and a grin that almost undid me.

Emma tossed back her head in cackles and climbed on top of him like a victorious Valkyrie. Xander tried so hard to maintain his grumpy firefighter dignity. Tried and failed spectacularly.

Through it all, I watched, flushed and breathless, laughing so hard my ribs hurt. And forgetting for a moment the utter humiliation that was last night.

Then he looked up at me, something calculated in his eyes, and gathered a fistful of snow, his determination clear.

"No," I said firmly, holding up my hands as I backed away. "The snowball war is *over*, Chief. I swear to God, if you throw that—"

He did, sending the snowball sailing toward me. It hit my chest with unerring accuracy, perfectly illustrating that every time he'd missed before had been on purpose.

I glanced down, huffing out an indignant breath as I brushed the snow from my coat. "You did not just do that."

He stood, gathered another snowball, and grinned. Full teeth. Pure evil. "Better run, chaos."

He didn't have to tell me twice.

Laughing so hard I could barely breathe, I sprinted across the yard, my boots slipping in the snow as Emma yelled encouragement from the sidelines. But my short little legs and firm stance to only run if zombies were on the loose were no match for the fire chief in his peak firefighter physique.

I glanced back once—just like every dumb heroine in a horror movie—and there he was, bearing down on me so fast I had no chance of dodging him.

I shrieked as soon as he was on me. But instead of pushing me into the snow like I assumed he would, he wrapped one strong, solid arm around my waist, hooked me into his side, and sent us tumbling into a snowbank, rolling us so he took the brunt of the fall.

I was laughing and breathless and...somehow straddling him, my hands on his chest, his on my hips. Completely frozen in a way that had absolutely nothing to do with the cold outside.

For several heartbeats, the world narrowed, everything else falling away. Including my resolve.

He was warm. *So* warm, I wanted nothing more than to sink into him. Wanted to rock against where I could feel him growing hard for me. He flexed his hands against my hips as he stared up at me, his eyes intense and unflinching, filled with something I didn't have the guts to name.

"Chloe," he murmured, soft and sweet. *Nothing* like the hoarse sound it had been last night.

A night he didn't even remember.

He reached up—slow, as if I might flee—and brushed a snowflake from my cheek with his thumb.

My heart didn't just stutter at the touch or his soft voice. It flatlined completely.

I opened my mouth to—*what?* Reply? Beg for a kiss? Confess that last night hadn't been a dream for him and, yeah, we actually had done all of that? Who knew? Sure as hell not me.

Thankfully, my short queen saved my dignity with another war cry, so I didn't have to find out.

"LoLee won!" Emma hollered from the porch, cackling with glee.

Scrambling off Xander, I slipped on the snow before standing and pretending I'd meant to do that.

"That was close. We almost corrupted the youth," I said, breathing out a forced laugh.

One Xander didn't return.

Instead, he just watched me. Slow and steady and intently, like I was a book with no title and too many torn-out pages to make sense of, but he was desperately trying to anyway.

The physical urge I had to flee was overwhelming. I wasn't at all interested in someone getting close enough to do that. And definitely not if that someone was my boss.

That was the moment I realized I wasn't just *avoiding* my feelings. I was actively trying to outsprint them.

And if Xander kept looking at me the way he was—all intent and disarming—I was absolutely going to lose.

CHAPTER TWENTY-ONE

XANDER

I THRIVED on order and structure, so that naturally bled over into my surroundings. Which meant I had always kept my house spotless.

That had shifted dramatically when Emma and her stuffed animals and toys and more hair ties than a four-year-old needed had moved in with me. But even my preschooler had absolutely nothing on the tornado of disorder Chloe had brought with her.

Since she'd moved in, there seemed to be a sheen of glitter on *everything*. Like a preschool rave gone wrong—or incredibly right, if it was her you were asking.

I pretended I didn't notice. Just like I'd pretended not to notice exactly how quiet it was in the house without her here tonight.

She was out with Quinn, Luna, and Sutton, probably giving them a carefully edited recap of our midnight encounter in the kitchen the other night.

Did I love that everyone would know I'd made out with

my nanny while grinding my cock against her like I was trying to start a fucking fire? Not particularly.

But it was fine. *I* was fine. Remaining calm. Mostly.

Or I *had* been anyway. At least until the lines between what I knew for certain had happened—the cookie dough, the kiss, the feel of her hands on me—and what I'd only dreamed—me catching her reading a spicy book and then telling her exactly how to make herself come while I watched—started to blur.

Because there were things I remembered that hadn't ever happened in my dreams, no matter how many of them she'd starred in.

For one thing, Chloe always *started* wearing my hoodie, but she ended completely naked. Every fucking time.

For another, she was never surprised or embarrassed in my dreams. She was all in from the get-go. No hesitation. Not a coy bone in her body.

Which was why the snippets that kept floating through my mind didn't add up.

Chloe in my hoodie, her pajama shorts hiding the sight of her playing with her pussy. Her cheeks flushing a deep red and her stuttered responses when she'd found me in her doorway. The way she'd said my name when she'd come, whispered into the dark instead of screaming it like I was used to.

But it hadn't been real. Couldn't have been.

Because if it *had* been, that meant I'd not only watched my nanny make herself come, but I'd told her how to do it. *Demanded* how she did. And then I'd gone on like nothing had happened.

Nothing *had* happened. Right?

Except I could still hear her moans and those soft little whimpers. Could still see every ounce of that hunger in her eyes as she stared at me—something that had been even more apparent during our snowball fight yesterday when she'd ended up on top of me.

I'd seen something else in her gaze as she'd stared down at me. Something that looked a hell of a lot like disappointment. Like she'd just realized I fucked up somehow... That I wasn't the guy she thought I was.

I didn't know what the hell I'd done to earn that look. And I didn't know why the hell it bothered me so damn much.

"Daddy, it's your turn," Emma said, pulling me from my thoughts. And not a moment too soon.

My daughter gestured to a dining chair as if it was a throne and she was two seconds from crowning me Glitter King of Starlight Cove.

Across the table, Atlas sat while Laurel had her head bent low over his hand as she painted his nails.

Painted *Atlas's* nails.

Atlas. As in six-foot-six former professional tight end and the man people around Starlight Cove referred to as "the big mean one." He sat with the resigned patience of a man waiting for his turn at the DMV while Laurel decorated his rough, scarred hands with a color called *Cotton Candied Clawz.*

My brows lifted at the sight. "You let her paint your nails?"

Atlas leveled me with a stare, his gaze unflinching. "Why wouldn't I?"

I held up my hands in surrender. "Absolutely no reason at all. Just surprised."

"This one"—he tipped his head toward Laurel—"can never pick a fucking color, so I'm always the guinea pig."

"That's a *whole dollar* in the swear jar, Uncle Atlas!" Emma cut in, eyes wide.

Keeping one hand steady for Laurel, he reached into his pocket with the other, pulled out a dollar, and slid it over to my daughter. "Worth it, little bean."

She grinned and grabbed the cash before running it over to the jar that was filling up far too quickly for my liking. But after living for thirty-eight years with absolutely no filter, I found it hard to suddenly turn that on.

"Can I paint *yours*, Daddy?" Emma asked, bouncing on her toes as she stood in front of me. She had her hands clasped together beneath her chin as she hit me with those eyes—the ones I'd figured out on day fucking one would have me hacking off my own arm if only she asked.

I blew out a heavy sigh. "Seriously?"

She stuck out her bottom lip, her shoulders sagging. "Uncle Atlas is doing it."

"And if Daddy Grump can do it, so can Fire Chief Growly Pants," Laurel murmured, her focus locked on the precise painting of Atlas's nails. "What's a little sparkle between family?"

I didn't know why that word felt like a knot loosening in my chest. It might have been the calm, offhanded way she'd said *family*, as if it was a foregone conclusion that that was what we all were. Or it might have been that family had felt ugly and poisoned for so much of my life but had suddenly shifted into something different in the past couple months. Not something softer, but something more alive.

Something I was a part of again after intentionally removing myself from it for more than a decade.

"Come on, Daddy Pants Growly Chief!" Emma said, earning a laugh from Laurel. And even my stoic, imposing older brother cracked a smile.

I blew out a defeated sigh and placed my hand on the table like the reluctant sacrifice I was. "Fine. But only because I love you."

Emma squealed and threw her arms around my neck, damn near choking me out with how hard she squeezed. She took the bottle Laurel had passed over and set to work on my nails, her tongue poking out between her teeth, her gaze laser-focused on the task at hand.

For all the good it did.

The first swipe of the brush across damn near the entire tip of my thumb looked like a unicorn bleeding out. The following swipes weren't any better, each finger somehow worse than the last.

By the time Emma was done, my hands looked like the aftermath of a glitter bomb exploding at a crime scene.

"You're beautiful," she whispered with awe. "Like a *fancy dragon.*"

Atlas choked on his beer, and Laurel snorted. And me? I didn't know whether I wanted to immediately wash it off or capture this moment so it was frozen in time forever—my daughter beaming up at me like I was Superman and her beloved stuffed unicorn all rolled into one.

Emma climbed into my lap and hooked an arm around my neck, gazing down at her work. "Promise not to wash it off until LoLee sees, okay, Daddy?"

"Yeah, gotta make sure Chloe sees that masterpiece," Laurel said dryly.

I grunted but otherwise didn't respond. Mostly because I was trying very hard not to think about that woman.

The one who'd bellowed taunts while lobbing snowballs my way, then went breathless and soft as she straddled me, as if we hadn't been at war seconds earlier.

The one who'd infiltrated the goddamn vents with her sunshine scent and who'd made the house feel too quiet without her narrating whatever domestic disaster she was about to unleash.

The one who'd gasped my name with her hand between her thighs, eyes wild and ruined as she came apart in front of me.

But I wasn't supposed to remember her like that last one. Not vividly. Not in detail. Because it hadn't happened...

Except, if it hadn't, then why were my memories of her like that in full Technicolor? Why did they play on a loop in my mind every time she walked into a room? Why did I keep catching myself looking at her like I already knew the way she sounded when she broke apart?

I didn't know what the hell that night had been. A dream? A hallucination? Just something I wanted so fucking desperately, I invented it entirely?

But if by some wild stretch of reality it actually *was* real and I was the only one pretending it wasn't? Then I wasn't the one in control anymore.

And that scared the shit out of me.

AFTER ATLAS and Laurel packed up the leftover Thai and headed out, I rested my hands on Emma's shoulders and marched her toward the stairs. "Bedtime."

"*Story*time," she countered, as if she were the world's greatest negotiator—a very tired, sleep-drunk negotiator, currently dragging her blanket behind her up the stairs.

"Deal, but only one. It's late, and you have school tomorrow."

She heaved a deep sigh, as if my stipulation was utterly exhausting, but she didn't argue. Telling me just exactly how tired she was.

After brushing her teeth and changing into pajamas, she climbed into bed, glancing up at me with expectant eyes.

"You want *Goodnight Moon*?" I asked, stretching out next to her on the bed and lifting my arm for her to snuggle into my side.

She scrunched up her nose, looking up at me with a horrified expression, as if I'd suggested boiled cabbage for a bedtime snack. "Not *books*, Daddy. I want a *you* story."

I raised my brows as I glanced down at her. "What's a me story?"

"You know, make-believe. LoLee pretends *so good*. Like the moonfish and the astronaut duck."

"The what now?"

"The moonfish and astronaut duck!" Emma repeated, excitement bleeding into her voice. "They had to 'scape space camp with a glitter bomb."

"Of course they did," I mumbled toward the ceiling before glancing down at her. "Are you sure you don't want to wait for another LoLee story tomorrow night?"

Emma shook her head, burying her face in my chest as she snuggled closer. "No, I want one from *you*."

I blew out a long, deep sigh and tucked her in close, warmth settling in my chest at her choosing me—not Chloe, not a story... Just me. "Okay, okay."

Emma squealed and kicked her feet, the hyperactive fallout of the cotton candy tub Laurel had brought over.

"But if I'm going to tell it, I need you to sit very still and be very quiet."

She stiffened her body as if freezing in place and mimed zipping her mouth shut and locking it tight before tossing the imaginary key over her shoulder.

"Okay. Well." I cleared my throat. "Once upon a time, there was a, uh...dragon."

Emma perked up, her eyes going wide as she glanced up at me. "Was he big?"

"Very big."

"Did he breathe fire?"

"Sometimes, but only when someone messed up his routines."

She grinned up at me, her eyes bright and curious as she hung on my every word.

"Anyway, this dragon lived in a cave. Alone. Far away

from his family. His cave was exactly how he wanted it—all the rocks just so and no glitter anywhere."

"That sounds sad, Daddy."

I huffed out a laugh. "Pretty sure only you and LoLee would think no glitter was sad."

"What about the dragon? Was he sad?"

"He didn't think so. Not then anyway. No one bugged him. No one moved his stuff. He was fine."

"But wasn't he lonely?"

My throat got tight, and I had to clear it a couple times before I could continue. "Yeah, he was. But he didn't know it. At least not until one day when a little dragon wandered into his cave. She looked like him, except she was way cuter and her scales shimmered in the sun. She was quiet but curious, and so full of questions, she talked through every one of the dragon's naps."

Emma grinned up at me, her eyes heavy. "What was her name?"

"Her name was...um, Doodle. She didn't mean to get lost, but one day, she was all alone. She didn't know much about big, grumpy dragons, but from the second she walked into that cave, she decided he was hers."

"Did the grumpy dragon like having her in his cave?"

"Very much," I said, hugging her to my side a little tighter and pressing a kiss to the top of her head. "Even though it was scary at first."

"That means the dragon was brave."

I hummed in acknowledgment. "*Both* of the dragons were brave. Very brave."

"Then what happened?"

"The big, grumpy dragon and Doodle moved caves to be closer to their dragon family. And not long after...a unicorn showed up at their cave entrance."

Emma gasped, glancing up at me with wide eyes. "A *unicorn*? Like Pinkie?"

"Yep, a unicorn with painted hooves and long pink hair and a horn that was so beautiful, everyone stopped to stare. She left a trail of glitter wherever she walked and turned the dragon's cave into a circus."

"A *real* circus? With clowns?"

"Not a real circus, but it felt like one. She built a throne out of mismatched shoes, painted every room with rainbows, and invited moonbeams in for sleepovers."

"Was she scared of the big, grumpy dragon?"

I huffed out a breath and shook my head. "Not even a little. She created a pillow fort in his cave and called it home. Just moved right in."

"Did the dragon like that?"

I brushed the hair back from Emma's face. "Not right away. At first, he growled a lot. But every day that passed, the unicorn made the cave a bit brighter and made the little dragon a bit happier. And every day, he growled a bit less."

"Did the unicorn stay?" Emma asked, her voice soft and sleepy, half there and already half gone.

I blew out a heavy sigh and stared at the ceiling. Did she stay? Fuck, I didn't know. The glittery unicorn from the damn story that made everything better wasn't real. Just like the idea of someone sticking around wasn't real.

People left—it was what they did. Hell, most of them didn't even say goodbye.

And this unicorn? She didn't do roots. She'd made that crystal clear. She was nothing more than glitter and mayhem and impulsivity. She was temporary.

Except I wasn't thinking about the fucking unicorn. I was thinking about Chloe.

I couldn't seem to *stop* thinking about Chloe.

If it wasn't remembering exactly what she tasted like, it was glimpses of her with my daughter. Laughing and singing and pulling my sweet, shy, *broken* girl out of her shell.

The mark she'd left on Emma and me and this house wasn't going to be temporary at all. Not when her scent still clung to the hallways, not when every room still echoed with the sound of her laugh, and sure as hell not when I could still feel her mouth against my neck, her lips against mine, as if I'd branded it there myself.

The worst part was she'd only been in my life for weeks, and already she had a lasting effect.

I wasn't supposed to want her like this. And I sure as hell wasn't supposed to notice how empty it felt in this house when she wasn't here. Or just how much she'd made it feel like a home.

But this undeniable draw I felt to her was only physical. Just my body needing something I'd denied it for far too long. My increasingly graphic dreams were proof enough of that.

Chloe was nothing more than a forbidden temptation. One that was getting damn hard to ignore.

CHAPTER TWENTY-TWO

CHLOE

BY THE TIME I got home, I was wine-flushed, disarmed, and emotionally whiplashed, all thanks to the tag-team therapy session I hadn't known I was signing up for.

Luna, Sutton, and Quinn had shown up and dragged me out of the house. Because I was being—and I quote—a whiny, emotionally stunted, and utterly avoidant *man* about the entire situation.

Apparently, they hadn't realized that was literally my entire personality.

And I also didn't think they realized just how much wine it would take for me to drop those walls. It hadn't been the four glasses they'd poured for me, in case anyone was keeping track. While they knew all about the entire make-out session in the kitchen with the cookie dough audience, I hadn't spilled one single word about my mortification from the other night.

When I'd come harder than I ever had before, all because

I'd thought Xander was in it with me, when in reality, he'd thought it was a dream.

Yeah, I wasn't interested in reliving *that* humiliation with my girlfriends. It was a big fat no fucking thank you from me.

With a threat—er, promise—to do this again next week, my girl gang had dropped me at Xander's place and went on their way.

I walked inside, dropped my keys on the table by the door, and kicked off the death traps I called heels, sighing in relief as my feet sank into the plush rug. After a night where I'd spent far more time avoiding—er, dancing—than I'd intended, my feet were absolutely throbbing and looked like a nightmare.

My soul? Maybe even slightly more so.

The main floor was quiet except for the soft hum of the refrigerator and the heat blowing through the vents. But the proof of an evening well spent was everywhere.

Nail polish bottles were scattered across the coffee table like confetti after a parade. A plastic pink tiara was half-hidden beneath a throw pillow. And an empty cotton candy tub sat on the dining room table.

It was a mess, yes, but now it was quiet and still. The aftermath of something exciting and fun.

Something I'd missed.

Honestly, I was used to missing things. It was basically the blueprint of my entire life. Of how I'd *designed* it to be.

So I wasn't jealous—not exactly. I just felt like I was outside looking in. Like the party had started and ended—the best part of the night having already happened—and I hadn't even realized I wanted to be here for it until it was too late.

But it was far easier not to feel left out if you bailed before someone forgot to invite you to stay.

My chest tightened, that all-too-familiar feeling blooming inside again. It was a sensation that had followed me like a shadow my entire life. It was why I'd leaned into my place as the opening act—fun, fleeting, forgettable.

I physically shook those thoughts away, rolling my eyes and mumbling to myself, "Your limit is *three* glasses before you get in your feels, Chloe. You know this. Remember it. Live by it."

When I was at the top of the stairs, I heard it—a voice, low and deep, soft but rough in the way that always made my belly tighten.

Emma's door was cracked, dim light spilling out into the hallway as Xander read a book to her. I paused in my trip to my bedroom and listened closer, my breath catching when I realized he wasn't *reading*.

He was storytelling.

His words were smooth and effortless, like he wasn't even thinking about them before they came tumbling out.

It was a story about a grumpy dragon who lived alone and was lonely without even realizing it, until a smaller, sweeter dragon stumbled upon his cave. And then came a unicorn that upended their lives.

Except, from the way he told the story, it didn't seem like he thought of the unicorn as an inconvenience or a disaster. Instead, he made it sound like the visitor was a gift.

And though he'd disguised this tale as one of make-believe with mystical beings, I had no doubt in my mind that he was telling *our* story. The story of him and Emma.

And me.

My breath caught in my throat, the sudden stinging behind my eyes immediate and completely irrational.

It was just a story. And I was drunk. Okay, I wasn't quite drunk, but I was definitely well past tipsy and had no business getting sappy in the hallway of my boss's home. So, I did what I always did when my emotions threatened to overcome me.

I ran.

Well, actually, I tiptoed down the hallway and fled to the safety of the guest room. I breathed a sigh of relief and quietly closed the door. Then I stripped out of my girls' night out clothes and swapped them for my favorite pajama shorts, a tank top, and, because I was a complete idiot as previously established, Xander's hoodie.

The one I'd come while wearing.

And no, I absolutely did not hold it up to my nose and inhale deeply as the lingering scent of Xander filled my lungs.

"You are a complete fucking weirdo," I said to my room, occupied by only me, myself, and I.

I should've just gone to bed. Should have stayed tucked away in my room and let the night end where the only mess involved the nail polish bottles strewn downstairs and not my emotional state.

Instead, I padded down the steps like a whole damn idiot, because apparently I had the self-preservation of a toddler barreling through a parking lot.

Once in the living room, I started collecting the polish bottles like my life depended on it—anything to distract me from the way my chest felt heavy and too tight. Like it was caving in on me. Like I'd sucked in too much air and there wasn't enough space to hold it all.

"Focus, Chloe. Just clean," I said to myself as I grabbed a bottle of Grape Escape, pretending I wasn't halfway to a self-induced menty B.

"You're not spiraling. You're *fine*. Totally, completely fine. And the reason you're fine is because you are absolutely *not* thinking about how the man upstairs saw you come and hasn't said a damn thing about it. And you're also not thinking about how he looked at you while you straddled him in the snow like he'd die if he didn't kiss you. And you most *definitely* are not thinking about the fact that he featured you as a star in a bedtime story he imagined for his daughter."

Thank god no one was around to hear my spiral because that was the last thing I needed. And I definitely did not need Xander Steele to grace me with his presence tonight when I was feeling like the frayed hem of those jeans I should've thrown out three years ago.

Because *that* was nothing but a recipe for disaster.

But since I'd crafted a damn good abundance spell that was still haunting me like my great-grandmother Edith, the object of my obsession—er, thoughts—stood at the bottom of the steps, hair damp from a shower. He was barefoot in gray sweatpants—and god*damn*, why was that so hot—and a well-fitted Henley that made my uterus glitch.

He swept his gaze over me from head to toe—my hair twisted up in a knot that looked like it lost a fight with a hand mixer, the borrowed hoodie he wasn't supposed to see (again), and bare legs—and swallowed hard. Froze as if the sight of me here knocked the air out of him. Shook something loose inside that had been caged too tight.

"You don't have to clean up my mess," he said, his voice that soft honey-gravel that made my pussy wet and my nipples tight and every ounce of self-preservation flee my body.

"It's fine. I didn't have any plans besides existential dread and an expired face mask."

"Is that thanks to girls' night or something else?" he asked, and from the way he was studying me so intently, it was clear he truly wanted to know.

"Oh, you know. Just another Monday night."

He hummed low in his throat, as if he didn't quite believe me but wasn't ready to call me out on it yet. He crossed the room slowly, his eyes on me the entire time. And I...collapsed onto the couch.

Obviously because my legs were tired and my feet were killing me from those shoes and not at all because Xander Steele literally knocked me off my feet. That would be ridiculous.

I didn't expect him to stalk toward me. I didn't expect him to crouch on the floor in front of me. I also didn't expect him to lift my foot into his lap, his thumb ghosting over the angry red welt left by my hot-as-fuck heels.

And I certainly didn't expect the way his brows slammed down as he glared daggers at my feet.

"What the hell is this?" he asked—demanded, really.

"Just a little female sacrifice in the name of looking good."

He turned his attention from my feet to glare at my shoes

instead. "Why do you wear those damn things if they hurt you?"

"Who said they hurt me?"

"I do. And these angry red marks are screaming about it pretty loud, too."

I lifted a single shoulder in a shrug and tried not to think about the press of his thumb against the arch of my foot. Or how easily he could toss my foot over his shoulder and let me feel that beard on my inner thighs. "They make my legs look great."

He lifted his eyes to mine, something hot and hungry in their depths. "Everything makes your legs look great."

My breath stuck in my throat, my heart seizing as his words played over again in my mind. I couldn't have heard him right...could I? He hadn't actually said that. Was *I* the one dreaming now?

"And if you break your damn ankle on those heels, I'm going to set the fucking things on fire."

Instead of giving in and reminding myself exactly what he tasted like and exactly the tenor of that low groan when I'd brushed my tongue against his, I breathed out a laugh that was too high, too fake, and pretended like everything was totally normal.

Totally, *completely* normal.

"You said that about my curling iron when I burned myself and about the mandoline slicer last week."

"You just about cut off your whole damn finger."

"It was barely a scratch, actually."

"It needed a bandage, didn't it?" He started rubbing slow

circles into the arch of my foot, his thumb ghosting over the red marks that were gradually fading.

I was gradually fading too. Into a puddle of goo right in front of him, and I needed to get back on solid ground. Immediately.

"For a fire chief, you sure do threaten to burn a lot of things."

Though my tone was playful and teasing, the look he shot back was anything but.

"Seems to me the only things I threaten to burn are ones that fuck with you."

And if I thought the air was thick between us before, it had nothing on what it felt like now. With my foot in his lap, his thumbs massaging away my aches and pains and that last shred of self-preservation I was clinging to, and his eyes locked on me, watching as if he didn't know how to stop...

As if he didn't *want* to.

He pressed his thumbs deeper into my arch, and I barely swallowed a moan. I curled my fingers around the couch cushion, just to keep from launching myself at him.

If I didn't focus on something else—literally *anything* else—I was going to do something stupid. Like mount him right here, amid the remnants of a riotous slumber party.

I darted my gaze around the space, looking at anything and everything. And that was when I noticed his fingers. Or rather, the massacre where his fingers used to be.

"Is there a crime scene somewhere we need to clean up?"

He snorted and shook his head, but he still didn't stop his delicious torture of my feet. "Just my nails. And now that you've seen them, I'm officially permitted to clean them up."

"Doodlebug got a little creative with her doodling?"

"Something like that," he murmured.

We sat there in silence—me reminding myself to breathe, all while he lavished spa-level foreplay on my feet with those hands that had starred in more than a dozen of my dreams and him carrying on as if this was all perfectly normal behavior. As if I wasn't sitting in his borrowed (stolen) hoodie, as if he hadn't seen me come apart days ago, as if I didn't know exactly what he tasted like.

In what felt like a scene from one of the books I loved to read, he set my foot down in his lap, reached for the bottle of Grape Escape polish I held, and unscrewed the lid. Then Xander—my scowly, gruff, emotionally constipated boss who'd demanded how I should get myself off—bent his head over my feet as if in prayer and carefully painted my toenails.

It was clear he was new to this—the initial crisscross on every nail before he painted over the top said as much. But he gave it as much attention as I imagined he gave fire truck inspections. He worked slowly. Precisely.

Like it wasn't just nail polish on toes, but something more. Like it mattered.

Like *I* mattered.

Every second that passed, that feeling inside me bubbled up more and more, rising through the butterflies in my stomach and the thudding beat of my heart and up my throat that was tight with an emotion I refused to name. And then it was spilling out of me, no hope whatsoever of catching it.

"This is dangerous," I said, a whispered oath in the silent room.

His hand stilled, and he glanced up at me, his voice just as low as mine. "You in my hoodie? Yeah, it just might be."

"You know that's not what I mean."

"Then what do you mean, chaos? What's dangerous?"

This. You. The way you touch me, and I forget how to breathe. You look at me, and it feels like the world disappears. The way this house has started to feel like a home—like the safest thing I've ever known.

The way I'm starting to want to stay, when all I've ever done is run.

But I didn't say any of that. I couldn't.

It was too much, too soon. And it definitely didn't belong in a space between a single dad and his nanny.

So instead, I just sat there—heart and hands trembling, my foot cradled in Xander's lap as if it were something precious. As if I were something he desperately wanted the privilege of taking care of.

CHAPTER TWENTY-THREE

CHLOE

I'D BEEN all over the world. But when I said small towns just did things differently, I meant it.

Because honestly, where else besides Starlight Cove would host an event whose sole purpose was to burn shit?

The Let It Burn Bash looked like the fever dream of a Hallmark executive after too many long hours and not enough sanity breaks. Lights hung between the lampposts, half a dozen tents were set up filled with refreshments and crafts and personal massagers—that woman would hawk her goods in the grocery store parking lot and actually had—and enough flammable supplies to catalog everyone's 3 a.m. mistakes.

Kids ran around wearing puffy coats and pelting each other with snowballs while teenagers lit sparklers under adult supervision that was mostly theoretical, and those adults laughed and gossiped and drank spiked hot chocolate.

And at the center of it all was the biggest bonfire I'd ever seen—roaring and wild, crackling high into the February sky as if it wanted to burn straight through the clouds.

Xander had already been here for hours by the time Emma and I arrived, and it took me all of three seconds to spot him in the crowd.

He stood sentinel near the flames, like some kind of brooding fire god. The only thing that would've made it straight out of that Hallmark exec's fever dream was if he'd been wearing flannel. His arms were crossed over his chest, his jaw locked, his gaze sweeping over the crowd in a way that was far too sexy for my own good.

As were most things when it came to Xander Steele.

A breeze kicked up, something in the fire snapped with a pop, and suddenly, his eyes were on me.

And I forgot how to breathe.

Just completely and utterly *forgot*.

Fortunately, before I could make a fool of myself by attempting to hurdle the bonfire just to get closer to him, Emma gasped and squeezed my hand, eyes bright as she stared at the raging inferno in front of us. "It's *huge*."

"That's what she said." Mabel popped up on my other side like a vibrator-selling ninja. She handed Emma a s'mores kit and gave me a quick once-over. "Look who finally showed up—Starlight Cove's newest and most requested pleasure party host, the hot fire chief's favorite temptation, and the only woman to have ever survived the pre-K pasta night without crying in the broom closet."

I dipped my head. "Flattered, truly. Do any of these accolades come with a crown?"

"They should. If not them, then the Most Influential

Newcomer Award. I don't think we've had someone this entrenched in Starlight Cove after mere weeks since... Nope. You're it."

"Really? That seems like an awfully low bar." Especially because I wasn't what people would call *involved*. I kept to myself, stayed on the edges, really tried to—

"Well, now you're just being modest. You're decorating the St. Paddy's Day Parade float, helping set up for the spring book fair, and hosting whatever the hell this new yoga and goat cheese pop-up is next Tuesday with Luna."

I raised my brows. "Did I agree to all that?"

Mabel shrugged. "You posted an emoji in the group chat. That's consent as far as we're concerned."

Honestly, that tracked. I'd probably done it when I'd been four glasses deep after girls' night. But I wasn't thinking about that. Or the night before it. Or the night before that.

"Also," Mabel added, as if she were reading off a grocery list, "Christie says thanks in advance for helping with the fairy garden remodel in her backyard. Her kid beheaded two gnomes, and she swears you're the only person who can bring it back to life."

"Cool, cool, cool. Gnome triage. I'm on it."

"Knew you would be." Mabel flashed me a smile, then stepped aside and swept an arm out in front of her. "Now, allow me to be the first to welcome you two lovely ladies to Starlight Cove's finest fire-fueled purge. We've got glitter, booze, and emotional exorcisms that should probably be done by a licensed professional, but sometimes a little fire is all you need."

"Sounds dangerous."

"Come on now, you know the Chief won't let *anyone* get injured," she said, a teasing note to her voice that I absolutely refused to acknowledge. "The theme of the night is letting go of whatever no longer serves you—winter gloom, bad habits, ex-boyfriends. Your dignity if you stand too close to Lincoln's drink table—or maybe that's just me."

I snorted. "I'm pretty sure he's heavy-handed with your pours just to see what you'll do."

"Well, last year, I burned my bra, so I guess I've gotta figure out something to top that..."

"Not your panties, Mabel. *Promise me* it won't be your panties."

"I will do no such thing."

Emma tugged on my hand with both of hers, bouncing on her feet like a pixie hopped up on an energy drink. "Can we do the crafts now? I want to draw things on the paper logs and burn 'em. Daddy said we can only do it here because he's spoofervising."

Mabel snorted and leaned close, whispering out of the corner of her mouth, "Yeah, supervising your ass in those leggings."

"Mabel," I hissed, pinning her with a glare.

I was still mad she'd ratted me out to my girl gang, but she just shrugged and shot me a smile as I allowed Emma to drag me in the direction she wanted to go.

We made our way toward a pair of folding tables set up under a canvas canopy. One was marked DECORATE YOUR LET GO LOGS and the other—clearly thought up by Lincoln—DRINKS THAT BURN. Declan sat behind the first, expression flat as half a dozen children crowded the space. Lincoln handled the drink station beside him, shaking something violently in a mason jar while wearing an apron that said *Hot Cocoa Daddy* across the front.

He shot Emma and me a wide grin. "There're two of my favorite ladies!"

Declan dipped his chin in acknowledgment. "Welcome to the pit of emotional doom."

Emma dropped my hand and dove straight for the art supplies, yanking markers from the bin with the ferocity of a trash panda on crack. "Can I draw on you after I finish my log, Uncle Dec?"

He heaved a sigh as if he had the weight of the world on his shoulders, but he pushed up his sleeve and offered his tattoo-covered arm to her like a sacrificial lamb. And I definitely saw his lips twitch when she beamed up at him in response.

Lincoln leaned over the space separating the two stations and slid a hot pink concoction toward Emma. The cup was rimmed with crushed candy canes, something neon pink practically glowing from inside, and it was all topped with enough whipped cream to drown a giant.

I narrowed my eyes. "What's that?"

"My specialty," he said with a wink. "Made just for the little glitter gremlin in our midst."

"Should I be scared?"

"Depends." He pursed his lips. "Do you like sleep?"

Before I could answer, Emma giggled and grabbed for the drink with both hands, bringing it to her mouth without hesitation. She took one sip, her eyes going wide as she practically vibrated in her seat. "*Yummy!*"

"It should be." Lincoln leaned a hip on the counter and grinned. "I call it the Sugar Coma. The base is strawberry soda, then I add two shots of marshmallow syrup, a whipped cream mountain, a candy rim, and enough grenadine to make it glow."

I blew out a sigh, knowing exactly how this was going to affect our little glitter gremlin. "Xander's going to kill you."

Lincoln winked. "Not if we don't tell him."

"Not if you don't tell him what?" The voice came from behind me. Low and rough, like secrets and sex, and the air around me shifted. Crackled.

My body—on account of its hating me—reacted immediately.

Intensely.

Involuntarily.

I turned around slowly, trying not to betray the flutter in my chest that always seemed to be present around Xander Steele and took him in.

He stood there in boots, all six foot four inches of glowering, broad-shouldered perfection wrapped in a black coat stretched tight across his chest. The gray Starlight Cove Fire Department hoodie I'd definitely been wearing while he'd told me how to make myself come peeked out beneath it. A charcoal beanie was pulled low over his dark hair, and his eyes—God, those eyes—drank me in, sweeping over me from head to toe.

It was a second, really. Just a fleeting moment of time. But that one glance from him made me feel more cared for than I had any right to.

Especially when it came courtesy of my boss.

Thankfully, before my body could literally combust from just that look alone, he turned his attention to his daughter, locking his gaze on the drink in Emma's hand as if it was a bomb seconds from detonating.

"Linc," he said, voice sharp enough to cut through four layers of denial and my reinforced no-feelings policy. "What the hell did you give my daughter?"

Lincoln grinned, completely unrepentant. "Don't worry about it. It's a secret between an uncle and his nieces. I'm going to give one to Laurel too as soon as that trio gets here."

"Laurel is sixteen and the size of an adult. Emma is four and weighs all of thirty-five pounds. Jesus Christ, man. Do you want her vibrating through the ceiling?"

Lincoln rolled his eyes. "*Relax.* This is her version of Mardi Gras. Let the kid live."

"Yeah, Daddy! It tastes like a party in my mouth!" Emma took another huge gulp before running circles around Declan.

"I swear to God..." Xander muttered, then pivoted his stare away from his brother and toward me.

And I felt it—just like I always did—that full-body shiver that was as delicious as it was unwelcome.

Especially when he clocked it immediately.

"Why the hell aren't you wearing a coat?" he barked—part reprimand, part concern he was trying and failing to hide.

"I have layers," I said defensively, gesturing to my puffy vest, long-sleeved thermal, and knee-high snow boots. "And these leggings are fleece-lined."

If I thought his quick glances set my body on fire, that had nothing on the slow perusal he gave me now.

He started at my boots and dragged his gaze—lazily, deliberately, no doubt making sure I felt that trek along every inch—back up to my eyes. "And yet, you're still cold."

"I'm f-fine," I said. Except the second word was garbled as a frigid gust of air kicked up, and a shudder swept through me.

Without a word and without looking away from me, he shrugged off his coat, yanked off the hoodie underneath, and tossed it over my shoulders like it was pure reflex.

Like he hadn't just rewired my entire fucking brain from that alone.

Meanwhile, all I could do was stand there, wrapped in his scent, and use every ounce of my feminine willpower not to swoon.

Because, this? This should not have felt as good as it did.

"You think I should be wearing your hoodie out here?" I asked.

He looked at me for a long moment, his gaze falling briefly to catalog the garment on my body, before lifting to mine once again. "What? You think you should only wear it in the privacy of your room?"

Ice shot through my veins, my entire body locking up at the insinuation beneath his words. The only time he'd seen me wear that hoodie in my room had been the night he'd made me come. The night he'd been avoiding ever since. The one he might be starting to realize wasn't actually a dream...

Then, as if he hadn't cracked my reality in two, he said,

"Linc. Make me a white hot chocolate—two pumps raspberry syrup, whipped cream and sprinkles on top."

Lincoln saluted without a word, while all I could do was stare at this man. My boss. The guy who—apparently—wrapped me up in his hoodies that smelled deliciously like him and ordered me my favorite drink as if it was no big deal.

"What?" Xander asked.

"Since when do you know my secret fancy drink order?"

He pinned me with a stare, those eyes heavy and intense. He leaned in, just close enough that I could feel his warm breath across my lips. "Since when do you think I'm not paying attention?"

And...what?

No, seriously, *what?*

All I could do was stare at him and blink, my mouth opening and closing as if preparing to say something, but god only knew what it would be. Because while he was tossing hoodies over my shoulders and yelling at his brothers for giving his little girl too much sugar and ordering my secret fancy drink exactly how I liked it, I was over here with my heart tap-dancing in my chest, my knees ten seconds away from buckling under the weight of his stare.

Not to mention the unspoken promises I saw in those eyes, just daring me to do what I'd sworn I wouldn't.

Because I didn't *do* whatever the hell this was—a slow-burn forbidden romance and shared hoodies and bosses who glared at anyone or anything that fucked with your peace.

I didn't do *this.*

Fortunately, before I made a complete ass of myself, Xander's and my little stare-off was interrupted as Atlas,

Sutton, and Laurel strolled up. There were greetings all around before Laurel headed straight for Emma to create a log of her own.

Atlas, Xander, and Lincoln started talking about improvements needed at the bar, and Sutton just stared at me—her arms crossed over her chest and one brow raised.

"What?" I asked far too defensively.

"Nice hoodie."

"He made me wear it."

"Uh-huh."

"He did! It's...warm."

"Sure." Her eyes sparkled, her lips twitching into a smirk that very loudly proclaimed, *girls' night wasn't that long ago, and I remember everything you said—and most definitely what you didn't say.* "Don't think I won't be bringing this up at the next girls' night."

"Can't wait."

She didn't say anything else, just bumped my shoulder with hers before hooking an arm through Laurel's as they headed toward the bonfire, Emma perched on Atlas's shoulders following behind.

I should have followed too.

Instead, I stood there, drowning in a hoodie that smelled like a man who wasn't mine and overcome by a heartbeat that wasn't slowing down.

Xander had gone back to his post, but even from across the fire, I could feel his gaze on me—something weighted and warm. And if I wasn't careful, I could get used to this.

Not just him looking at me like that, but everything.

This town, with its ridiculous festivals and the horny old

woman I loved with my whole damn soul and these girlfriends whom I'd all but just met—save for one—yet felt like we'd been friends for a lifetime.

And then there was the family I'd found—not just Lincoln and Declan and Atlas and Holly—but Emma and Xander and our little house that was starting to feel a hell of a lot like home.

A home in which I never intended to stay.

My chest tightened, my palms growing sweaty even in the cold February air. It was all too much, and I needed just a second to breathe.

Knowing Atlas and Sutton were taking care of Emma, I headed in the opposite direction, fleeing to god knew where. But I didn't get far before a hand on my elbow stopped me.

"Chloe. Hey." Eli stood there, wearing a letterman's jacket from high school and a smile that was a little too sharp to be sincere. "I was hoping to run into you."

"Hey, Eli. How are you?"

"Good. Just tying up some loose ends before I head out next week."

"Right. You mentioned you were leaving."

"Just for a while. But I was hoping to have a little fun before I had to go." He slipped a hand into his pocket and shot me a grin. "I was thinking maybe you, me, a couple drinks, and trivia night at One Night Stan's... Are you free Monday?"

I swallowed thickly, knowing there was a safe answer and a stupid answer to this question.

The safe answer was saying yes. Hell yes. A thousand times yes. Because Eli was temporary, just like I was. He wasn't going to stick around, and he wasn't going to give me his hoodie to wear, and he wasn't going to memorize my favorite drink order. He sure as hell wasn't going to make me feel one iota of what I felt in the presence of the fire chief.

The stupid thing would be turning Eli down and allowing this—what, *crush?*—I had for my boss to fester and grow into something that overtook me completely. Something that made those feelings stick. Made *me* stick.

So I did the safe thing.

I offered Eli a closed-lipped smile and nodded. "Sure. That sounds fun."

Except as he rattled off details about Monday night, the pit that had settled in my stomach had me second-guessing if this was *really* the safe option.

And the look in Xander's eyes as I met his gaze across the fire, his jaw tight, body tense, had me wondering all over again.

CHAPTER TWENTY-FOUR

XANDER

Group text with Atlas, Xander, Declan, and Lincoln

4:04 p.m.

LINCOLN:

We've got a problem.

Trivia night was rescheduled to tonight because of a goat thing. Don't ask.

We're short-staffed. I need a body behind the bar because I can't run this by myself.

DECLAN:

I've got back to backs booked till midnight

ATLAS:

I've got a thing.

XANDER:

I've got Emma. Chloe has a date.

LINCOLN:

brb

Group text with Atlas, Xander, Declan, and Lincoln

4:17 p.m.

LINCOLN:

Got it handled. Atlas and Sutton are taking Emma to a movie and she's sleeping over there.

Xan, I'll see you at 7

XANDER:

Why the hell can't Atlas just save us all this back and forth and take the shift?

ATLAS:

Because I don't fucking want to.

DECLAN:

That's fair

XANDER:

That's not even an excuse.

ATLAS:

You're right. It's a boundary.

XANDER:

When tf did you start setting boundaries?

ATLAS:

Love does crazy things to a man.

LINCOLN:

Don't be late, Xan.

And if you want to rake in the tips, the theme tonight is Save a Horse, Ride a Cowboy

XANDER:

I'm not dressing up as a fucking cowboy.

LINCOLN:

Suit yourself. More thirsty women for me.

DECLAN:

Didn't know Little Miss Farmer had plans for trivia night

LINCOLN:

What's that? You want to work a TRIPLE next week, Dec? Done.

I SHOULD'VE KNOWN that text was a fucking trap. Lincoln was nothing if not a shit-stirrer. Anything to get his mind off things he didn't want to be thinking about—namely, his best friend's little sister who had his balls in a vise and didn't even know it. And since he'd seen my reaction to Chloe the last time she'd been in One Night Stan's, he was like a dog with a fucking bone.

And I was going to kill him.

Because now, I had to stand here for who the fuck knew how long and watch Chloe while she was on a date with another man.

She and that shithead Eli were sitting at a high-top table next to the bar, which meant I had a direct line of sight straight to them. And to what she was wearing.

I'd been hard since the second she'd walked in carrying her summer scent with her, but her outfit sure as fuck hadn't helped. A sweater that dipped low enough to show just the shadow of her tits and one of those flirty, flouncy skirts that swished around her thighs as she walked. As if that wasn't bad enough, she also wore those knee-high boots and fishnets again.

The ones I wanted to rip off her.

The ones I wanted to fuck her straight through.

With one foot propped on the rung of the stool, her leg crossed over the other, she leaned toward Eli with a smile he didn't deserve. The ass clown didn't deserve the laughter she tossed his way either. Didn't deserve to even be able to *look* at her, let alone be on a date with her.

They were talking and joking and having a great fucking time like she hadn't come apart against her hand with *my* name on her lips just last week.

Like she hadn't kissed me back as if she was starving for it.

Like she hadn't begged me to instruct her exactly how to make herself come.

Motherfucker.

I clenched my hands into fists at my sides, fighting the urge to stalk over to them, pour that asshole's drink in his lap, and drag Chloe straight home where she belonged.

With *me.*

Because that wouldn't help anyone, I busied myself

behind the bar. Lined up glasses. Wiped down surfaces that were already spotless. Any-fucking-thing to keep myself from staring at them or doing something I'd later regret.

But then Eli leaned closer and said something in her ear, and I saw red. I slammed a pint glass down loud enough to draw Linc's attention from his end of the bar.

He glanced at me with raised brows. "You good, man?"

"Fine," I bit out.

I was not fucking fine. I was losing my mind, and I didn't know what to do about it.

Before I had any chance of getting my shit together or escaping to the back so I didn't punch that stupid look off Eli's face, he and Chloe strode straight for the bar.

Straight for me.

He had on that smarmy grin I fucking hated, and I consoled myself with the fact that Chloe's smile wasn't genuine. And it slipped entirely when she caught sight of me behind the bar.

"Xander Steele," Eli said with unwelcome familiarity. "Been a while. Didn't realize you still pulled shifts here."

I braced my hands on the bar top and shot him a look. "Didn't realize you still wore that much product in your hair."

Chloe sucked in a breath, clearly sensing what was coming.

But Eli was about as sharp as a box of marbles, so he grinned like we were all good. "Still got that sense of humor, huh?"

"My sense of humor and your weak chin are two things that've stuck around, I guess."

Chloe sputtered and covered it up with a cough, while Lincoln whistled under his breath. I just stared down the douchebag who thought he was good enough to go out with her. He wasn't good enough to take out the goat who'd been tied up at the station's flagpole, so he sure as fuck wasn't good enough for the equivalent of sunshine in human form.

"Well, uh..." Eli chuckled awkwardly and rapped his knuckles on the bar top. "We wanted to put in an order for some wings and—" His words cut off at the sound of a phone ringing, and he pulled his cell from his pocket.

What a piece of shit. He was out on a date with Chloe fucking Bradshaw, and he was taking a goddamn phone call? I wasn't sure I could glare any harder at this cheesedick, but I was willing to try.

"Sorry, Chloe," he said. "I've gotta grab this."

Chloe nodded and tucked her hair behind her ear. "Sure, no problem."

"Be right back," he said, already walking toward the door.

I stared at her for a long beat. Long enough that the silence felt like a physical being between us. Long enough that she finally turned to walk away.

Before she could get far, I said, "That's the kind of guy you want?"

She stopped in her tracks and turned around, lifting a brow in my direction. "What?"

I tipped my head toward the front door wankstain just walked out of. "You think a guy like that has any idea what to do with a woman like you?"

Her spine stiffened as her mouth dropped open, shock written on her face. "Excuse me?"

"You heard me." Bracing my elbows on the bar top, I leaned toward her, our gazes locked, and dropped my voice so it stayed between us. "You think he'd be able to get you off with just his words? Think he'd even know where to start if you begged him to tell you what to do?"

Her eyes widened a fraction, and color bloomed across her cheeks. But her words didn't hold a single ounce of embarrassment, only venom and steel. "Since no one else is stepping up to the plate, I guess I'll take my chances."

The commotion of the bar echoed around us as she stared at me for a second. Two. Three.

Waiting...

Wanting?

It didn't matter.

Clenching my jaw, I tightened my hands into fists and forced myself not to move. Not to do exactly what I wanted to and drag her into the back room. Fuck her like I'd been dying to since the first day I'd laid eyes on her in those stupid fucking fox slippers and one of those hoodies I couldn't get out of my goddamn mind.

She huffed out a breath and shook her head. "That's what I thought."

Without waiting for a response, she headed toward the bathrooms in the back, her spine straight, head held high.

Five goddamn seconds hadn't even passed before I followed. Of fucking course I followed. I couldn't do anything else. I was a prisoner to her gravitational pull.

"Why'd you go out with him, chaos?" I asked into the otherwise unoccupied hallway. Unable to stop myself. "Why did you say yes after everything?"

She glanced back at me and breathed out an incredulous laugh. "What's 'everything,' Xander? The kiss you ignored? The night you're pretending never happened? Or is it something else?"

When my only response was another tick of my jaw, she nodded. "Right. I can't keep doing this with you—this back-and-forth, hot and cold. And Eli might not be who I want, but he's the safe choice."

I stepped toward her, not stopping until she was sandwiched between me and the bathroom door, focused on the single part of her sentence that made my chest tighten. "Who do you want?"

"You don't have the right to ask me that." She darted her gaze over my face, assessing me more intently than I was comfortable with. "And I don't think you're ready for the answer anyway."

With that, she slipped into the single stall bathroom and let the door swing shut behind her, the sound of the lock clicking like a gunshot in the space between us.

I braced my hands on the doorframe and hung my head between my shoulders, staring at the two-inch piece of wood separating us. Staring at it like it held the answers to everything I'd never allowed myself to even ask for.

What the hell was I *doing*? Chasing after her. Ruining her date. Acting like I had any kind of claim over her. She was my nanny, and that was it.

And yet, I couldn't move.

I couldn't walk back out there, serve drinks, and pretend like everything was fine. Couldn't watch her toss her head back with that manufactured laugh and not die a little more inside.

Minutes later, when she opened the door, I was right where she'd left me. Hands braced on the doorframe, head hanging, rib cage in a vise...squeezing, squeezing.

She startled and jerked to a stop, her eyes snapping to mine. Where those eyes normally sparkled with playfulness, now anger and uncertainty and desire all fought for dominance. But it was the hope I saw brimming there that made me swallow down every ounce of my reservations and throw caution to the wind.

I was so tired of fighting this. So tired of pretending I didn't want her with every goddamn breath.

So fucking tired.

"Fuck it," I muttered before cupping her face and kissing her like I was going to lose her before I'd even had the chance to *have* her.

I walked her backward into the bathroom and kicked the door shut behind us, and then all I could focus on was her lips under mine.

The kiss wasn't slow or sweet. It was hunger and desperation and need. It was weeks of deprivation with nowhere else to go.

It was a man at his fucking breaking point, tired of holding back.

Chloe gasped into my mouth, met my tongue stroke for stroke, her hands fisting in my shirt and tugging me closer. Closer. Even though we were already pressed together, it still wasn't enough.

I wasn't sure it'd ever be enough.

I hoisted her up, guiding her legs around my waist, and slammed her against the tile wall, every ounce of my self-control gone. Snapped like a twig.

"*God*, Xander." She hooked her ankles at the base of my spine and tightened her grip, as if she wanted me closer too.

"Are you going to say his name when I make you come?"

A spark of challenge lit in her eyes. "I don't know. Are you going to pretend like this never happened tomorrow?"

"No." I shook my head, darting my gaze over her flushed face and those kiss-swollen lips. "But I can promise you I'm going to dream about it. I can't fucking stop dreaming about you."

"You should maybe work on not sounding so pissed off at the girl you're trying to fuck."

"I *am* pissed off. You want to know why?" I gripped her hips, digging my fingers into her flesh as I pinned her against the wall. Nipped at her jaw. Scraped my teeth down the column of her neck. This fucking wet dream come to life.

"Why?" she breathed, her fingers in my hair, holding my head to her.

"Because I haven't been able to stop thinking about you since you stumbled out of that fucking shack. Every night when I close my eyes, you're there. Every morning when I wake up, you're there. And every goddamn moment in between, you're on my mind. I can't *stop* thinking about you, Chloe. And that's a fucking problem."

"It only became a fucking problem when you decided to hold yourself back." She tightened her legs around me and ground her pussy down against my cock, a whimper slipping past her lips. "So, are you ready to stop holding yourself back, Chief?"

A growl tore from my throat as that last thread restraining me finally broke. I unhooked her legs from around my waist, set her on her feet, and dropped to my knees in front of her.

"Wha—"

Before she could even get the word out, I had her leg over my shoulder and nothing more than a scrap of lace standing between me and her cunt. The holes of the fishnets were wide enough that all I had to do was reach up and slide that little piece of purple fabric to the side. And then there she was, just as pretty as I'd known she'd be. That perfect little pussy, so pink and wet and ready for me.

Unable to wait another second, I dove in, licking a path straight through her slit before fixing my mouth to her. I groaned as soon as her taste hit my senses. She was sweet and tangy and every-fucking-thing I'd imagined she'd be.

She slid her hands into my hair, her hips rolling against my questing tongue, and I groaned into her flesh as I slipped two fingers inside her.

"*Fuck.*" Surprise was laced in her tone as she stared down at me, her eyes darting over my face as I feasted on her like a starving man. "I'm gonna come already. Don't stop. Don't stop. *Don't*—"

She let out a soft cry then, her fingers tightening in my hair as she held me firmly against her. I groaned as her taste flooded my mouth, and she rolled her hips, her pussy squeezing my fingers in a way that had me aching to feel it on my cock.

I didn't even wait for the aftershocks to work their way

through her body, too desperate to be inside her. To finally fuck this need that hadn't waned a bit out of me.

Standing to my full height, I undid my fly and pulled out my cock, already leaking at the head for her. And then I lifted her up and pressed her against the wall again, her legs automatically going around my hips as I slid my dick through her slit and slammed home.

I captured her sharp cry with my mouth, sealing my lips over hers as I thrust inside over and over and over. Desperate to get closer. Desperate to make her come undone. Desperate to satisfy this unwavering need inside me.

Desperate for it to never end.

"You want to know why I didn't talk about that night I watched you come?" I asked, our lips brushing, eyes connected as she clung to me. "Because I thought it was a dream."

She inhaled sharply and dug her fingernails into the back of my neck, her eyes locked on mine.

"Because I'm *always* dreaming about you. I've fucked you a hundred different ways in my fantasies."

"Tell me..."

"You want to know all the different ways I've been inside you?"

Not even a moment's hesitation before she nodded, her bottom lip caught between her teeth.

"Of course you do, my dirty girl. You love when I talk to you like this, don't you?"

"*Yes.*"

"I've had you bent over the kitchen counter. I've had you riding me on the couch. I've had you laid out on my bed. I've feasted on your cunt so much there were some mornings I swore I could taste you when I woke up."

I slammed into her, trying to focus on anything but the overwhelming bliss that was her pussy. She was so wet, so tight, so fucking hot, I was going to lose my mind if I didn't get a handle on myself.

"So, yeah. I thought I was dreaming because that's the only place I ever allowed myself to have you." I scraped my teeth along her jaw, nipped her ear. "But not anymore. Isn't that right, chaos? Now that I've tasted your sweet little pussy, sunk inside this tight cunt, there's no stopping me now, is there? I fucking *knew* you'd have me addicted with one goddamn taste. And I was right."

"Xander, *please...*"

A groan rumbled in my chest at hearing her say my name while I was settled deep inside her. While her pussy was fluttering around me, already seeking release. "I remember what you need. You want me to tell you exactly what to do, don't you, dirty girl?"

She tightened her hold on me, her ankles locking at my back, her nails scoring my flesh as she nodded rapidly.

"Reach down and rub that needy little clit. Make yourself come for me."

Without hesitation, she did as I asked, reaching down between us, her fingers flying over her clit as I pounded into her.

"*God.* I'm so close."

"Do it. Come for me." I gripped her hips, digging my fingers into her flesh as I split my gaze between her wrecked and ravaged expression and the sight of her little cunt wrapped so tight around me. Taking me in again and again. "Be my dirty girl, and come on my cock in the bathroom while you're on a date with another man. Show me exactly how much you love it when I fuck you."

She cried out then, her legs locking tighter around my hips as she shattered, her pussy milking every bit of sanity straight from my soul. I had no hope of doing anything but following her over the edge. I settled deep and exploded, my vision blurring as my cock spilled inside her.

I stayed like that for a beat too long, still pulsing, still catching my goddamn breath—like my body hadn't gotten the message that it was over. That I'd already fucking come. When I finally pulled out of her, slow and shaky, the slick drag of it—of us—nearly made me groan again.

And that was when it hit me.

Skin. No barrier. Just her, wrapped tight around me, and the mess I'd left behind.

Jesus fucking Christ, what the hell was wrong with me? I didn't fuck without a condom—ever. And the fact that I had a surprise four-year-old daughter even after that rule should've been enough to keep me on my goddamn toes about it.

But that was what Chloe did to me—made me lose my fucking mind.

My cock jerked at the realization that I'd been inside her bare. And it made me some kind of bastard that not only had I fucked her while she was out with another man, but I was going to smile at that asshole when she went back to their table, knowing her thighs were wet with our mixed come.

CHAPTER TWENTY-FIVE

CHLOE

I HADN'T MEANT to make eye contact. Had told myself no fewer than 17,000 times that I was absolutely *not* going to make eye contact.

I'd repeated it to myself this morning as I made Emma's breakfast.

I'd recited it on the way to the school and the bus ride over here.

I'd said it multiple times on the walk up to the fire station. Because I knew the second I locked eyes with Xander, everything about the other night in One Night Stan's would come rushing back.

Be my dirty girl, and come on my cock in the bathroom while you're on a date with another man.

Show me exactly how much you love it when I fuck you.

Well. Obviously, I'd been right, because now I was standing in a sea of four-year-olds, remembering what it felt like when Xander pinned me to the wall, shoved my panties to the side, and fucked me while I was still wearing my fishnets and my boots. To say nothing of the fact that I was on a date with *another man*.

And the worst part? I liked it.

I didn't just like it. I fucking *loved* it.

I thought he'd made me come hard when he'd told me exactly how to touch myself. But that had *nothing* on how hard I'd come while he'd been inside me. While he'd whispered every filthy thought he had, like he couldn't help himself. Like the dam had finally broken.

And it had, considering he and I'd had to have a conversation about birth control—IUD for the win—and test records—all clear on both sides—since we hadn't used a condom. Since I'd been able to feel his come spilling out of me while I'd ended the date with Eli.

That was why I wasn't supposed to make eye contact. And why I was currently fucked.

Because now, I was feeling all...all...*this*...while Xander stared at me from across the fire station like there weren't a bunch of munchkins surrounding us, having the time of their lives. And it wasn't just any Xander giving me his full attention...

It was Xander. In. Uniform.

Why the hell had I thought it would be a good idea to volunteer for this field trip in the first place? I should've remembered that the Starlight Cove Fire Department wasn't just a quaint little building at the edge of downtown—it was *his* domain. And I sure as hell should've remembered what he looked like in turnout gear.

Spoiler alert: like sin and safety had a very hot, very off-limits baby.

He hadn't looked at me at first. Not really. He'd been busy wrangling fifteen tiny humans, explaining how the hoses worked and why they couldn't stick crayons in the emergency radio. But then he'd glanced up—just once—and our gazes locked. Immediately. My stomach did a traitorous little somersault, and I pretended not to notice the way his eyes heated as soon as they landed on me.

He had no right looking at me like that.

Like he knew exactly what was going through my mind.

Like he was remembering it too.

Remembering *everything*.

The way I'd moaned against his mouth, clung to his shoulders, locked my legs tight around him, and pulled him deeper. Begged him not to stop.

But this was fine. Totally, completely, absolutely, one hundred percent *fine*.

"Miss Chloe! Miss Chloe! When do we get to go on the truck?" one of the kids shrieked, tugging at my sleeve with the patience of a...well, of a four-year-old at a fire station.

I blinked down at her, plastering on a smile. "Soon, kiddo. Listen for the instruction from Chief Steele, okay?"

And while she did that, I was going to be trying to *forget* all that glorious instruction from Chief Steele.

She nodded rapid-fire before scampering off toward a group of kids currently trying on the way-oversized firefighter gear.

I blew out an unsteady breath and grounded myself in the pandemonium. I just needed to focus on the kids. That was safe. That was manageable. That didn't involve thinking about how Xander had fucked me like he couldn't get enough and looked at me like I was already his.

The trouble was, he was positively magnetic, standing over there looking all capable and in charge. He always held himself with a confidence that was unmatched. But here? He moved through the station like he *owned* it. Not in an arrogant way. This was competence, pure and simple. The way he hoisted a hose with casual ease, knelt to tie a kid's shoelace without missing a beat in his safety spiel, and answered a question about fire poles without even looking winded.

But *I* was winded. I was over here losing my damn mind, and I hated it.

Hated how every cell in my body was still humming from the memory of him inside me. Hated that I wanted *more* when I'd never, ever been interested in that.

"Okay, everybody, line up," Xander called, clapping his hands once. "Who's ready to climb into the big rig?"

The chorus of squeals and cheers was deafening. It was complete mayhem as kids surged toward the engine, their excitement palpable. But it only took one look from Xander and a firm reminder about safety for everyone to line up like little soldiers and wait their turn.

He stood at the open door of the cab, offering a steadying hand to each child as they climbed up. He calmly explained what every button did and how the truck worked—not a watered-down version for them because they were kids. Instead, he explained it just as he would to any adult, assuming their capability and gently correcting any misunderstandings.

And why the hell did I find that so fucking hot?

When it was Emma's turn, she climbed up, but Xander didn't just steady her—he lifted her effortlessly, setting her in the seat with a gentleness and familiarity that made something twist behind my ribs.

She immediately took hold of the steering wheel, face lit with awe. "Is this where you sit, Daddy?"

"Sometimes. But sometimes other firefighters drive."

"Do you get to turn on the sirens?"

"Sometimes."

"Can *I* turn on the sirens?" she whispered, a soft, pleading note to her voice.

"You have to be officially certified to do that."

Emma sat up a bit straighter. "I *am* certified."

Xander arched a brow at her. "Oh really?"

She nodded fiercely. "I passed LoLee's bravery test this morning. So that means I'm certified, right?"

His mouth twitched the tiniest bit as he looked at me over his shoulder. "Is that true?"

I gave a casual shrug, like having his attention on me wasn't undoing me. "It *was* pretty rigorous. Required bravery, kindness, and finishing her pancakes so she had fuel for the day."

He turned back to Emma. "And did you do that?"

"I did, Daddy!" She glanced at me, eyes wide. "Tell him, LoLee! Tell him I did it."

"She did. Finished all three."

The same girl who'd eaten half the top on a muffin when I'd first arrived had slammed down three blueberry pancakes like it was no big deal. And yeah. I was feeling pretty great about that.

Xander locked his gaze on mine, and it was clear he was thinking the same thing. While the heat that'd been in his stare earlier had had me nearly combusting on the spot, it was the gratitude shining there now that had me almost melting into a puddle at his feet.

He dropped his voice as if he were sharing a secret with Emma. "Then I guess that makes you qualified."

She squealed, then settled immediately when he began instructing her on what to do, his voice patient and sure.

I should've been focused on the kids. Should've been making sure everyone had what they needed and no one was causing a catastrophe.

Instead, I watched him.

Watched the way he didn't just handle this, he *owned* it. Watched how steady he was, how natural. Like being a hero to this group of preschoolers didn't require anything more than showing up, knowing what to do, and being exactly the man he already was.

God help me, I wanted to climb him like a fire ladder, but I was pretty sure the preschool teacher and other chaperones would look down on that.

So instead, I took a breath and kept my distance. All while watching the man I wasn't supposed to want act like the father he never thought he could be.

"Are you guys married?" The question came out of nowhere. Innocent, unapologetic, and far too loud in the way all questions from four-year-olds tended to be.

Xander froze mid-sentence, his hand braced casually on the side of the truck. Meanwhile, my heart plummeted somewhere south of my stomach for absolutely no reason.

"Um…what?" I asked, trying to laugh, like the idea was *so ridiculous* my heart hadn't just flung itself into a wall.

The little boy shrugged. "You live with them. Are you married?"

"We're a fire family!" Emma said, loud and proud and beaming.

Xander glanced over at me, a million unspoken things in that look. But before I could dissect what exactly that meant, another boy chimed in.

"But she's not your real mom."

My heart that had been thundering wildly in my chest halted. Just stopped completely as I watched Emma's smile falter. Watched her brow crease. Watched her shoulders slump. She glanced up at me with something new in her eyes. Something fragile and questioning, and I suddenly couldn't breathe.

And if *I* couldn't breathe, I knew she wasn't going to be faring much better.

So I pushed aside the urge to tell that little shit that Santa didn't visit assholes, and I crouched beside her, brushing a wayward strand of hair behind her ear.

"I think our fire family is the coolest family around," I whispered, instilling as much confidence in my voice as possible. "Maybe you can draw a picture of us at the take-home station?"

"Okay," she said, but her voice was small. Those cracks that had seemed to be healing busted wide open again, all because of one little jerk.

If I thought capable Xander was hot, it had nothing on protective Xander. After checking in with Emma, he turned his attention to the kid, his eyes locked on the boy for a second too long. Not glaring. Not speaking. Just enough to remind everyone in a ten-foot radius that he was not one to mess with. And, by extension, neither was his daughter.

And I was over here being the victim of emotional whiplash. Honestly, a girl could only take so much in one day.

By the end of the tour, I was fraying at the edges. Xander had hung close to Emma's side since that comment, his unrelenting gaze focused on the instigator as if daring the boy to say something again.

When Emma was engrossed in the art station and creating her take-home trophy for the day, Xander headed in my direction. He allowed his gaze to rake over me—just a quick glance, but one I felt deep in my bones.

Arms crossed, he stood next to me and stared out at the kids scattered around the station. "You okay?"

"Fine," I said too quickly. Too brightly.

Something he noticed immediately.

He turned his head, giving me his full attention, and I was absolutely not ready for *that*.

"I'm fine," I repeated, then swallowed, glancing once over at Emma. "But I think you might want to bring this up with Emma's therapist next week."

He dipped his chin. "Already on the list."

Of course it was. Because while macaroni crafts were out of his wheelhouse, he was a pro at protecting Emma.

"Daddy! LoLee! *Look!*" Emma called, skipping over to us, a piece of construction paper flying along beside her.

She held up the paper between us. She'd colored three

stick figures, all holding hands. One was huge with brown hair and a beard, one was smaller with wild yellow hair clear down to her waist, and the smallest one held what looked like a stuffed unicorn.

"It's our fire family!"

I didn't speak. Couldn't. Because what the hell was I supposed to say to that? I'd chosen to insert myself into this little family knowing damn well I wasn't going to stay.

Knowing damn well I never, ever stayed.

And now I was supposed to tell her that? This little girl who'd already lost so much? Absolutely not.

So instead, I just smiled and pretended like I wasn't slowly falling apart on the inside. Because if the thought of leaving was this hard now, what was it going to be like in a few weeks when it was really time for me to go?

CHAPTER TWENTY-SIX

CHLOE

IT WAS ALMOST one in the morning, and I was elbow-deep in banana bread batter. Which, by the way, was totally normal behavior.

It was just a craving. A whim. A sudden domestic urge that had absolutely *nothing* to do with the fact that Xander's bedroom light had turned off a little over an hour ago, or that mine had stayed on while I stared at the ceiling and pretended not to hear his voice echoing through my head.

Be my dirty girl...

Yeah, well. That dirty girl was currently stress-baking in his oversized sweatshirt, barefoot, with her hair piled on top of her head like a Pinterest fail, because lying in bed meant thinking. And thinking meant spiraling. And spiraling meant *remembering*.

Remembering exactly what it felt like to be pressed between Xander's body and the cool tile wall of the bathroom at One Night Stan's, with him so thick and hard inside me, his hands everywhere, his voice rough and low in my ear—

I dropped the spoon with a clatter, muttering a curse as batter splashed over the bowl. "Jesus, Chloe. Get it together."

I turned around to grab some chocolate chips—because banana bread was objectively better with them, and also because it gave me something to focus on that wasn't the ache in my chest or the throb lower down that I was absolutely *not* acknowledging. But instead of finding what I was looking for, I found *him*.

Xander stood in the doorway to the kitchen like a goddamn vision of regret and temptation. He leaned against the frame in a plain white T-shirt, his shoulders and biceps testing the limits of the seams, and gray sweatpants that certainly thought a lot of his junk.

Honestly, same.

His hair was mussed, and his eyes were locked on me like *I* was the temptation and he was ready to sin.

My mouth went dry. "You're supposed to be in bed."

"I could say the same to you." His gaze dropped to my feet, then slowly traced up my bare legs, to the hem of his sweatshirt, his attention lingering briefly there. When he lifted his gaze to once again meet mine, his was molten. "Why are you baking at 1 a.m.? Do you need someone to tuck you in?"

A dozen images of him *tucking me in* flipped through my mind, and my knees almost buckled. I had to grip the counter just to keep from collapsing.

So. This was going well.

I breathed out a forced laugh and turned my back to him, focusing once again on the bowl of batter. "I had a craving for banana bread. You want some?"

"I want something," he said, his voice low and rough.

My breath caught at his husky tone, and I couldn't do anything but stand frozen, heart thudding, while I stared down at the batter like it held all the answers.

"What's that?" I managed through a tight throat.

He didn't answer right away, but suddenly, he was behind me. No warning, just heat and muscle and *him* bracketing me against the counter, his hands on either side of my hips. He was so close, his broad chest pressed against my back, my ass nestled into him, his cock unmistakable and not even pretending to be subtle.

He dipped his head, bringing his lips close to my ear. "What I want is to know how long you plan to keep avoiding me."

I swallowed hard. "I'm...not avoiding you."

"Uh-huh." He nosed along my neck, his voice like gravel and smoke. "So that wasn't you sprinting out of here this morning like your ass was on fire?"

"I had to be at the school early for the field trip," I said defensively, heat rising in my cheeks at the utter lie. "You didn't expect me to be late, did you?"

"I bet *you* didn't expect to keep running into me," he murmured. "First at the bar, then at the fire station. Now the kitchen."

I glanced at him over my shoulder. "The kitchen is a shared space. And the others were clearly coincidences. Your family owns the bar. And you're the fire chief—of course I'd see you at the station when I volunteered for the tour."

"I don't know. Sounds like a hell of a lot to be a coincidence."

I scoffed, trying to keep my voice steady. "Yeah? Well, what about all those late-night run-ins when I first started? You didn't say anything about those."

He was quiet for a moment, but I felt him lean closer. Felt the heat of his body bracketing me, felt his breath against the shell of my ear, sending a shiver skating down my spine. "Because I was the one who kept making them happen."

I exhaled a sharp, shocked breath and tightened my fingers on the counter. He'd said it so easily. Like it wasn't a confession. Like it wasn't a goddamn wrecking ball aimed straight at my carefully constructed walls.

"Are you ready to stop pretending, chaos?"

I parted my lips, but no sound came out. Because yes, I was ready. I was *so* goddamn ready. But admitting that meant admitting everything else too—that I wanted him. That I couldn't stop thinking about him. That I was in over my head and worried I wouldn't land on my feet when the inevitable fall came.

And it would come. It always did.

So I did the only thing I could. I lost myself in the moment.

I lost myself in Xander.

Turning in his arms, I grabbed a fistful of his T-shirt and pulled him down to my mouth. He came without hesitation, falling into the kiss like he was starving. Like he'd been underwater for too long and I was his first breath of fresh air.

I didn't know how to do anything but kiss him back with the same urgency. The same desperation. The same need.

It was all teeth and tongues and roaming hands. He shoved up my—*his*—sweatshirt, growling low when he found nothing but bare skin underneath. And then he descended on my breasts, sucking first one nipple then the other into his mouth. Feasting on them as if they were every one of his fantasies come to life.

"Been dreaming about what these perfect little tits looked like. How are they even better than that?" He sucked hard, tugging one nipple with his teeth as he stared up at me. "How is the real you better than my dreams, chaos?"

He didn't wait for me to answer—and thank god for that because my speaking capacity was somewhere in the range of *mmphf*. He just yanked down my shorts, lifted me onto the counter as if I weighed nothing, and laid me out on top. Then he stood in front of me, his gaze raking over every naked inch he'd uncovered, while he stood there, fully clothed, something dark and hungry in his eyes.

"You better be sure about this, because as soon as you say yes, I'm going to eat this sweet little cunt until you forget your own name."

Oh. My. *God*. Just his words made my clit throb, my pussy pulsing around absolutely nothing. So damn desperate for him.

I bit my lower lip and nodded, needing him to give me *everything*.

He braced himself on either side of my shoulders and leaned over me until our faces were inches apart, his eyes dark and intense. "What did I tell you about giving me the words?"

"Yes. I'm sure."

"There's my dirty girl," he said, satisfaction ringing in his tone. A stool scraped across the floor as he pulled one closer and sat down, his face directly in line with my pussy. "Now, spread those legs, baby. Let me taste what's mine."

Sweet sparkling Moses, I just about came from that claim alone. And for some reason—for some *unknown* reason—I did exactly as he told me to. I parted my thighs, making room for the wide breadth of his shoulders as he hooked his arms under my legs and dove in.

He swiped his tongue through my slit. Slowly. Deliberately. Like he had all the time in the world to savor me. It was so at odds with that first time. And why did it feel like he was trying to commit the taste of me to memory? Like he'd waited too fucking long for this and wasn't about to waste a second?

"Fuck," he groaned, the sound vibrating against me, sending pleasure straight to my core. "You taste so fucking good. You better hold on, chaos, because I'm about to make a mess."

He flattened his tongue and licked a broad path from entrance to clit, then circled it once...twice...before capturing it with his lips. He sucked it into his mouth like he fully intended to drag every single moan out of my throat whether I wanted to give them to him or not.

It didn't matter what I wanted because I had no hope of staying quiet. Not with Xander's mouth on me. Thank god Emma was a deep sleeper so she wouldn't hear my whimpers. Wouldn't hear me repeating her daddy's name while he drove me halfway to ecstasy with just his tongue.

I threaded my fingers through his hair and tugged hard, trying to anchor myself to something—*anything*—as he devoured me like a man starved. He didn't stop. Didn't ease up. Just kept eating me out like my pussy had personally wronged him and the only way to punish it was with pleasure.

"Xander... Oh my god, this feels so good." I gasped, then moaned low and deep, my hips rolling, seeking, as I held him to me.

He pulled back just enough to rasp, "There you go, baby. Ride my face just like that. Show me how bad you need to come."

And Jesus, I did. Needed it desperately.

So I rocked against him like I was possessed, chasing that white-hot high as he fucked me with his tongue, his nose bumping my clit with each thrust. Then he replaced his tongue with his fingers, sinking two deep inside before sucking my clit into his mouth and pushing me that much closer to the edge as my pussy pulsed, so desperate for release. But it was the growl against my flesh—that low, animalistic sound that set every nerve ending I had on fire—that sent me flying.

I shattered, coming apart against his mouth and crying out his name like it was the only word I knew...the only word I remembered.

But even as bliss overcame me, he didn't stop. Didn't pull away. Didn't let up.

He licked me through that orgasm and straight to the next. Adding a third finger and making me so wet, I felt my pleasure dripping down my thighs and my ass, no doubt making a mess on the counter beneath me.

Just like he'd promised.

He held me down and kept licking, coaxing a third

climax from me, my body trembling and boneless. Completely wrecked as I lay panting on the counter, like a girl who'd just had her entire world turned inside out.

As he sat back on the stool, his lips coated in my pleasure, his beard wet with me, he looked absolutely feral. And I knew.

He was only getting started.

CHAPTER TWENTY-SEVEN

CHLOE

XANDER STOOD SLOWLY, brushing his mouth over the lotus flower on my hip, the cluster of stars just below my breast, the scripted *wanderlust* below my collarbone. My body felt like a live wire, still sensitive, still buzzing. And somehow, still needy for him.

But thankfully, from the way he looked at me, I knew we weren't done. Not even close.

There were a thousand unspoken promises in his gaze, and I certainly wasn't going to complain if he wanted to fulfill every single one.

"You gonna run again?" he murmured against my throat, dragging his lips down my neck.

I gasped when he ground his cock against me, the friction of his sweatpants against my bare pussy enough to make my eyes roll back in my head. Enough to make me focus on something other than his words. "You gonna stop me?"

He grazed my collarbone with his teeth. "Try me."

"Right now, all I want to do is fuck you."

"Is that right?" He pulled away and glanced down at my pussy, flushed a deep pink and so wet it was obscene. "Tell me what you need."

"You," I whispered, hating how the word caught in my throat. Hating how vulnerable...how *exposed*...I felt right now.

He tutted and shook his head. "You need more than that."

To prove his point, he ghosted his thumb over my clit, the touch featherlight and doing absolutely nothing to slake this need inside me.

I lifted my hips, seeking more pressure. "If you know what I need, then give it to me."

"I am, dirty girl." He covered my pussy with his hand, grinding the heel of his palm against my clit. "What you need is someone to tell you what to do. And right now, I'm telling you to ask for *exactly* what you need. Tell me, in explicit detail, and I'll give it to you. Whatever you ask for."

My heart pounded so hard I was sure he could hear it. But it wasn't fear swamping me—it was anticipation. *Need.* The heavy, all-consuming kind that unraveled all my defenses and left me stripped bare.

"Use me," I whispered, eyes locked with his. "Take whatever you want. Whatever you need. Just let me give it to you."

Something dark and primal flickered in his gaze, and I wanted to revel in it. Wanted to bask in the feeling of lust pouring off him. Of worship. Of ownership.

All directed at *me.*

"Fuck," he muttered, his voice thick as he skated his gaze

over me, settling once again on my pussy. "My dirty little girl wants to be used, is that right?"

Oh my *fuck*. Why did it sound so hot when he said it like that? If I had any uncertainty about whether this was something I really wanted, my tight nipples and the throbbing of my clit were proof enough that I didn't just want it. I was *hungry* for it.

I nodded, shakily, my lip caught between my teeth as I stared up at him. At this imposing man, so stoic. So reserved.

But right now, he looked like a man on the edge of breaking.

He wrapped his hands around my hips, his grip firm and possessive as he yanked me closer to him. "Then that's what I'm going to do." He dragged his sweatpants down just far enough to free his cock, thick and glistening with precome and so damn hard for me. For *me*. "Gonna fuck you like I've been fantasizing about since that first night. Gonna ruin you for anyone else."

My stomach flipped at his words, my breathing growing rapid at the thought of what was about to happen. That he'd take everything he wanted from me and give me what I needed in return. Not just the sex—though, *god*, I needed that too. But being used in the way he meant—not carelessly. Not cruelly. But with purpose. With possession.

He shoved my thighs wide, making room for himself between them. He tapped his thick cock against my clit, the unexpected contact making me gasp, and I shifted my hips, wanting him inside.

"What do you need?" he asked again, circling my clit

with the head of his cock before tracing it down my seam and pressing the barest inch inside.

"You. I need you inside." I reached for him, hooked my legs around his hips. Attempted to tug him closer. "Fuck me, Xander. Use me."

His jaw ticked once, his eyes going positively molten, and then he was there, sliding deep in one unrelenting, unyielding thrust.

"*God,*" I choked out. Without my permission, my back arched off the counter, my mouth dropping open as he filled me... As he *kept* filling me.

"Say it again," he rasped, breath hot against my mouth. He stilled as deep as he could get, his eyes locked with mine. "Say it while I'm buried inside you."

I knew what he was asking for. What he wanted me to say. And I was all too willing to give it to him.

"Use me," I breathed, stretching my arms out above me on the counter. Offering myself to him in the only way I knew how. "However you want. *Use* me."

My low plea was all it took.

With a rough growl, he pulled his hips back before snapping them forward, dragging a ragged moan from my throat as his cock filled me to the hilt. Again and again and again.

He built up a steady, punishing rhythm that was pure instinct. Restraint unraveled. His hands were everywhere—gripping my hips, ghosting over my thighs, cupping my breasts. It was like he couldn't get enough—wanted to touch all of me all at once.

He lifted one of my legs up onto his shoulder, allowing him to sink farther inside.

"God, yes," I moaned, wrapping my other leg around his waist, trying to pull him deeper. Harder. Closer. "Don't stop."

"I'm not going to. You wanted me to use you, and that's exactly what I'm going to do." He leaned forward, wrapping one hand around my throat—not tight, just there, just present. A reminder of the power I'd willingly handed over to him.

A reminder that had my pussy clenching around him, so fucking close to exploding all over again.

He hummed low in his throat. "My dirty girl likes that, doesn't she? You like that I'm using you. That I can't fucking help myself. That I've tried to hold myself back, over and over, and I can't do it anymore. You fucking love that you've made me desperate for it. For *you*."

I didn't know if it was his words or the way he moved inside me, dragging the head of his cock against my G-spot with every thrust, or the way he looked at me—like he was *wrecked* for me—but I cried out as the orgasm slammed into me. Sweeping me away before I even realized it was on the horizon.

"Oh, fuck me," he muttered under his breath as he ghosted a thumb over my clit, extending every ounce of my pleasure. "God*damn*, you feel so fucking good. Like you were made for me. This little pussy was made for me, wasn't she?"

I wanted to tell him yes. God, yes. But I couldn't speak. I couldn't do anything but lie there, spread out on the counter,

Xander's thick cock filling me, his hands everywhere as he stared down at me like I was everything...*everything*.

When I'd always only been nothing.

"You feel that?" he murmured, brushing his lips over my ankle. He slid his hand down my leg that was still propped on his shoulder and settled it low on my belly, his thumb circling my clit. "Every inch of me inside you, just like you begged for? Your perfect little pussy is going to make me lose my goddamn mind. But that's exactly what you wanted, isn't it? Wanted me lost to this cunt."

The idea that this man—this stoic, unflinching, unmovable man—would be lost to anything, let alone me, was ridiculous. But I couldn't deny my body's reaction to his words. My pussy fluttered around his driving shaft, goose bumps skating across my skin as I ached for another release. Desperate to pull him with me this time.

I nodded, unable to speak. Unable to do anything but feel him...*everywhere*. His hands, his mouth, his teeth. He gripped me like he couldn't get enough. Pounded into me relentlessly like he was trying to etch himself into my very bones. Fucked me like he never, ever wanted to stop.

I wasn't sure I wanted him to either. And that was a fucking problem.

"Look at you," he said, his gaze caught on the sight of himself disappearing inside me. He pressed his palm flat on my lower stomach, making me feel every thrust. "Taking me so deep. Your little cunt is squeezing me like you never want me to leave."

"I don't," I whispered, the words spilling out of me without any conscious thought.

He leaned down, bending my leg toward my chest, his eyes molten as he filled me over and over. As he owned me with his body. "Say it again."

"Don't stop. Please don't stop."

"Not even if you run. No more avoiding me, chaos. No more hiding. You hear me?"

I nodded, sure I would've agreed to sell my soul to him at this point. I was so lost to the pleasure he was coaxing out of me, my body on the precipice, teetering on the edge of oblivion.

"That's it, baby." He groaned low, glancing down between us. "Give me one more. Come on my cock like the filthy girl we both know you are."

"*Oh fuck*," I breathed as everything in me tightened... tightened...and then broke all at once. Fireworks burst behind my eyelids as waves of euphoria rushed over me. Nothing but bliss blanketing my body.

And through it all, Xander was there, his low grunts and moans, his filthy words telling me how perfect I was, how *good* I was. Before the last wave washed over my body, he cursed and settled deep, his cock pulsing as he spilled himself inside me.

We stayed like that for long moments, panting against each other, our bodies still tangled. Him, half dressed. Me, completely naked and utterly wrecked. I should've felt exposed and raw. But all I felt was his warm breath on my skin, his body covering mine, and the echo of his cock claiming me.

Making me feel like I finally belonged somewhere, even if just for a moment.

CHAPTER TWENTY-EIGHT

XANDER

IT WAS midafternoon on Saturday when I carried Emma into the living room, both of us exhausted. She had pink glitter smeared across her cheek, a mostly empty juice box squished under one arm, and the telltale wobble of a kid who'd burned through all her emotional regulation hours ago.

It had been a fucking day.

Chloe was out with Luna, Sutton, and Quinn, which meant I was on solo dad duty, and Emma was one minor inconvenience away from total meltdown.

She'd lost her favorite scrunchie somewhere between the couch cushions and the seventh circle of hell. She'd tripped over her shoelaces at the library, taken a tumble, and cried like the world was ending. And the snack tantrum after I'd offered her the wrong-colored apple slices? It was one for the record books.

But we'd survived it. No yelling. No bribes. Just her and me and some deep breaths, silly voices, and more than one mermaid bandage.

She was still off-kilter, and I was exhausted but determined to end our day together on a high note.

"Okay, peanut." I set her in front of the couch before dragging over the box I'd brought in from the garage. "I was thinking maybe you and I should tackle this bookcase LoLee found for your room. How's that sound?"

"We can build it?" Emma asked, eyes wide and voice filled with awe.

"We sure can. What do you think?"

"We can do it, Daddy!" Emma stood tall, her ponytail askew, and propped her hands on her hips, just over her tutu-and-leggings combo she'd insisted on that morning. "LoLee said we were gonna have *so* much fun!"

"What else did she say?"

"That *I'm* the boss, and you're Chief Growly, and that if we work together, we can do hard things."

I stared at my daughter—the little girl I hadn't even known mere months ago—so overcome that she was...*mine.* "Well, you're definitely the boss, so everything else she said must be true too."

I opened the box, glancing at the instructions and immediately regretting my decision to tackle this. Going by the clusterfuck printed on this paper, I could've built this from scratch without a blueprint for less hassle.

But my daughter was right. When we worked together, we could do hard things.

While Emma climbed on the coffee table and shouted demands that had nothing to do with the instructions I was looking at, I focused on the musings of what appeared to be a deranged squirrel and attempted to build something that resembled a bookcase.

It wasn't perfect. And it wasn't without challenges—including a splinter and a buttload of money tossed in the swear jar—but we were doing it. And through it all, I couldn't stop watching my little girl. How she furrowed her brow as she placed the special stickers Chloe had gotten for decoration *just so*. How she made up silly songs and danced around, a rendition of something I'd seen her and Chloe do a hundred times. Her laughter was easy now—even after a day of struggles—and that made me feel lighter than I had in a long time.

Lighter than I could ever remember being.

All because Emma was blooming. Right here, in this house, with me.

With Chloe.

Once the bookcase was standing—and I had only one extra screw I couldn't find a purpose for—I filled the empty box with the trash, ready to take it outside, when a pink Post-it Note stuck to the back caught my eye.

> For Chief Growly and The Boss—
> I can't wait to see the magic
> you make together!
> xoxo LoLee

It wasn't long. Wasn't fancy. Just that bubbly handwriting I could now spot a mile away, but my throat went tight anyway.

I stared at the note for a second too long as Emma sang a song about the moonfish and astronaut duck. And then I folded it up and tucked it into my wallet, right behind Emma's preschool picture. A reminder of what Emma and I could do together.

A reminder of what an important part Chloe was in our little family, even though she was trying so hard to stay on the edge. But it didn't matter how hard she tried—she was already here. Woven into everything.

"Can we add books to it now, Daddy?" Emma asked, standing next to our masterpiece like we'd built the Eiffel Tower.

I gave a short nod. "As many as you can fit on it."

Emma beamed at me, glancing down at our bookcase, before running over and throwing her arms around my legs. "We're builders."

"We sure are," I said, voice low as I brushed a hand over her hair. "We're a team."

"You, me, and LoLee!"

ONE NIGHT STAN'S was packed, though that wasn't surprising for a Saturday night. It hadn't been my first choice to take a four-year-old who'd just discovered the echo properties of her Velcro sneakers and had decided to demonstrate every five seconds, but it was where she wanted to go.

Emma ran through the throngs of people and straight behind the bar like she owned the place.

"Bean!" Lincoln yelled as he picked Emma up. "You came to visit me?"

"We came to cebrelate!"

Lincoln cocked a brow and glanced at me as I took a seat at the bar. "What are we celebrating?"

"Me and Daddy built a bookcase and I decrated it with stickers LoLee got me and now all my books have a 'pecial place to live!"

"Well, that *does* sound like it's worth celebrating." He hoisted Emma over the bar and sat her on the stool next to me as she giggled with glee. "You sit right there, and I'm gonna whip you up something special."

I eyed him warily as he began mixing up something obnoxiously pink and fizzy. "You gonna feed my kid sugar?"

Lincoln shot me a grin. "Please. I'm a professional. I balanced it with fruit."

"Those are gummy bears."

"Yeah, and the red ones are cherry. See? Fruit." He passed it to Emma with a flourish. "I call it the Sugar Rush. Sprite, pink lemonade, splash of grenadine, and a gummy bear floater."

Emma's eyes widened. "It's for *me?*"

Before I could snatch it away from her and tell Lincoln water would do just fine, thank you, she grabbed it and took a huge drink.

She let out a hum and danced in her seat, her grin a little unhinged. "It tastes like *fireworks!*"

"Jesus Christ," I muttered, grabbing the glass halfway through her second chug. "Easy there, champ, or you're gonna be hyped up enough to shoot straight to the moon."

Lincoln chuckled under his breath and shook his head. "What?"

"Nothing. Just thinking about how lost you were three months ago, and now look at you." He lifted a chin toward me, where I was setting up a place mat for Emma to color on. "Being a dad and shit."

He wasn't wrong. Three months ago, Emma and I had both been fumbling, trying to find our way. She'd been a lost little girl, and I hadn't been anyone's daddy, just a guy trying not to drown.

And now? It no longer felt jarring when she called me that. Now, it felt like it had always been true.

Emma was halfway through her order of chicken fingers and fries when the back door opened hard enough to bounce off the wall, and Lincoln's entire body tensed.

I glanced at him with a raised brow as Willa marched up to the bar, eyes stormy, expression stormier. She set a pallet of jars filled with honey on the bar top hard enough for the cocktail shaker to jump.

"Here's the last of your order," she said without preamble. "Now where's my money, jackass?"

Lincoln just shot her a smile, that cocky grin firmly in place. "Nice to see you too."

"You know what would be *nice*? If you paid your damn bill. I've texted you. I've sent you *four* invoices. I even left Post-it Notes on the mirror in the office because I figured you'd look there at least seventeen times a day—"

"Are you saying you think I'm handsome?"

"—and still *nothing*. So this is me escalating." She held

out her hand, palm up, and made a *gimme* motion. "Pay up, or you're cut off."

Emma was too entranced in her drawing of a unicorn and a spaceship to pay any attention to the bickering in front of us, but I couldn't take my eyes off the two of them.

"You always threaten people over artisanal honey, Willa?" I asked.

She didn't remove her glare from Lincoln. "Only the ones who think it's cute to call it 'bee juice' and try to pay me in expired bitters."

Lincoln chuckled under his breath. "That was a *joke*."

"I'm not laughing." She really, really wasn't.

He sighed, pulled out some crumpled bills, and handed them over. "There. Paid in full."

Willa huffed and rolled her eyes but grabbed the money, stuffing it into her pocket. "You still owe me for emotional damage."

"Just put it on my tab," he called after her as she strode out the way she came, not looking back.

I sat there for several long moments, watching my brother watch the back door. Finally, I said, "You wanna tell me what that was all about?"

That snapped him out of whatever trance he was in, and he glanced at me with a brow raised. "You wanna tell me what's going on with your hot nanny?"

I stared at him and he stared back and neither of us said a word.

At least until I couldn't keep it in anymore. "Don't call her hot."

He barked out a laugh and knocked twice on the bar top. "Yeah, that's what I thought."

Before I could tell him he didn't know *what* he thought—mostly because *I* didn't and I was living the damn thing—the front door opened, and in walked Chloe. She looked windblown and flushed and fucking gorgeous, her eyes bright and smile wide as she said hello and chatted with people who stopped her on her way toward us.

And there I sat, watching her the entire time. Watching as she charmed people just by breathing, her infectious laugh making everyone smile a little brighter. Making me *feel* a little brighter. But it had nothing on what happened when she glanced my way and spotted Emma and me.

Her grin widened, her shoulders relaxed, and she looked...content.

She looked like mine.

"Hey," she said once she reached us, brushing a hand down Emma's hair. "You survived."

"Without you, chaos?" I said. "Barely."

Chloe's smile faltered—just a little, but I saw it. The surprise and disbelief written plainly on her face. I didn't know why either of those were there, but I hated them both. Yeah, Emma and I had survived today on our own, but it hadn't been without Chloe's help. Maybe not there, in the moment, but in all the other times behind the scenes. In her gentle parenting of Emma and in her encouragement of creativity and curiosity, and in her confidence in me.

Before Chloe could reply to that, Emma spun around on her stool and launched herself into Chloe's arms, babbling a mile a minute about our entire clusterfuck of a day and ending with the masterpiece that was her bookcase.

"And me and Daddy did it all by ourselves! We *made* it, LoLee!"

"I knew you could," Chloe said, splitting her gaze between Emma and me. "I can't wait to see it."

"It's there," I said. "Waiting for you when you get home."

The word came easily...effortlessly. But it landed like a bomb. Chloe's entire body jerked as if she'd been electrocuted, and she breathed out a shaky laugh, once again giving Emma all her attention like nothing was amiss.

But I'd seen it. Seen how she'd flinched at the single word. As if it didn't belong to her.

CHAPTER TWENTY-NINE

XANDER

Group text with Atlas, Xander, Declan, and Lincoln

9:18 p.m.

LINCOLN:

Hey, remember earlier tonight when Chloe
called Xander "Daddy" at the table and I
choked on my roll?

DECLAN:

unfortunately

ATLAS:

It's more info than I need to know about
whatever's going on over there, so I've
blocked it out.

LINCOLN:

idk how you can. It's burned into my
memory for all time. I'll be telling my
grandkids about this.

XANDER:

You're all jackasses. She was obviously talking about me to Emma.

LINCOLN:

Was she, though? Because she looked RIGHT at you when she said it.

ATLAS:

She did.

XANDER:

I thought you were staying out of this?

DECLAN:

Xan froze like his whole mainframe was being rebooted

LINCOLN:

Went into full statue mode while the proverbial record scratch could be heard on the other side of town. Mabel actually posted a Live asking if anyone knew what it was from.

XANDER:

Are you done?

LINCOLN:

Is that what Chloe says when you play Daddy at home?

XANDER:

Shut the fuck up. I mean it, Linc.

LINCOLN:

Uh oh. Daddy's mad.

ATLAS:

I'm drawing the line. Stop being shitheads.
And do NOT call him that. It's fucking weird.

LINCOLN:

Too late. I'm having an apron made. BDE:
Big Daddy Energy. It'll go great with the I
love DILFs mug I'm getting Chloe.

XANDER:

I swear to god, if you make her feel
uncomfortable at family dinner, it will
become my personal mission to make your
life a living hell. Starting with whatever the
fuck was happening last night.

DECLAN:

What was happening last night?

XANDER:

I'll let Linc fill you in. I'm muting this chat for
72 hours so I don't not-so-accidentally
murder one of you.

LINCOLN:

So Daddy's putting himself in a time-out?

DECLAN:

You're gonna pay for that

LINCOLN:

Worth it

CHLOE

Group text with Chloe, Sutton, Luna, and Quinn

9:22 p.m.

SUTTON:

Just so everyone's on the same page,
Chloe definitely called the Chief "Daddy" at
family dinner over at Holly's tonight.

LUNA:

WAIT.

BACK UP.

The Chief?

As in Xander???

Daddy as in SEX DADDY???

QUINN:

Please tell me she moaned it by accident.
PLEASE.

CHLOE:

Oh my GOD

No one moaned anything!

It was just a reflex! I was talking to Emma
about Xander. It wasn't a big deal.

SUTTON:

Uh-huh.

QUINN:

I hear the skepticism in that uh-huh

SUTTON:

She looked Xander *dead in the eye* and
said "Tell Daddy thanks."

He froze for so long, I thought he short-
circuited.

Silence descended on the table like we
suddenly found ourselves in The Quiet
Place.

QUINN:

Tell us he said something. Tell us he
corrected you.

LUNA:

Tell us he GROWLED.

CHLOE:

He didn't say anything because it's not a
big deal! I call him that all the time at home.

LUNA:

Oh, I just bet you do…

CHLOE:

OH MY GOD. NOT FOR SEX STUFF.

LUNA:

But you DID actually call your hot firefighter
boss Daddy at family dinner with his mom
in attendance, yes?

CHLOE:

Please stop talking about it. I'm begging
you.

QUINN:

Where's the fun in that?

LUNA:

Hear me out…

What if you did it again?

But on purpose this time?

In the bedroom?

CHLOE:

I'm NOT calling my single dad boss Daddy while he's fucking me.

QUINN:

But he IS fucking you…?

CHLOE:

You are all menaces.

MENACES.

LUNA:

Maybe. But you're the girl who called the Chief DADDY in front of his mom

QUINN:

A true legend.

SUTTON:

Iconic.

CHLOE:

I hate you all.

SUTTON:

No you don't, Daddy's Girl 😊

CHAPTER THIRTY

XANDER

THIS SHIFT FELT like it was never going to end. I had things under control and was no longer fumbling my way through the days, but right now, I'd give anything for a night of full moon mayhem. Hell, I'd even take another visit from the snack-raiding raccoon. Something—anything—to keep my mind occupied because this quiet was driving me insane.

I couldn't stop thinking about Emma and Chloe and the two of them at home without me when all I wanted was to be *there*. With them. Watching *Frozen* a-fucking-gain and eating pizza for the twelfth time this month and staring in amusement as my two girls danced around the house to made-up, gibberish lyrics.

And just when the hell had *that* happened?

I had a little less than an hour left on my shift when a text from my mom came in.

MOM:

Emma's staying with me tonight. Girls' night
with unicorn jammies, a movie, and
popcorn. Chloe looked a little pale when
she dropped off Emma.

I didn't even finish reading before I texted Chloe.

XANDER:

Everything okay at home, chaos?

It took an eternity for a response to come in. As soon as
my phone buzzed with an incoming text, I snatched it off my
desk.

CHLOE:

Just my uterus being a complete asshole
and doing its monthly death spiral.

Nothing some Midol and a little blanket
burrito action won't fix.

Should be human again by morning in time
to grab Emma if you get called in.

Like that was why I asked. Like I was checking because I
might need her on deck for Emma and not at all because my
brain had been stuck on a constant Chloe loop all damn day
—all damn *month*—and the thought of her hurting made my
chest tight.

XANDER:

You need anything?

CHLOE:

Nah. I'll survive. Don't worry about me,
Chief.

As if there was any realm of reality where that was possible.

Hell, I wasn't so sure I hadn't been worrying about her every fucking day since she'd stumbled out of that smoke-filled shed and blazed her way into my life.

The next hour felt like an eternity as I waited for my shift to end, all while knowing Chloe was at home, alone and miserable, and I couldn't do anything about it. Since it was an exceptionally quiet day, I used my time to do some research and make a list of items to grab on the way home.

When my shift was finally over, I tore out of the station so fast, several people shot me double takes, but I didn't care. They could draw their own conclusions about what I had going on. I needed to focus.

I hit the drugstore like I was prepping for a natural disaster—but from how Chloe sounded even over text, I was pretty sure that was exactly what I was doing.

Midol. Ginger and chamomile teas. Peppermint and lavender essential oils. Five different kinds of bath bombs. Epsom salt. Microwavable heating pad. Chocolate-covered almonds. Fuzzy socks with foxes on them. Anything I saw that I thought Chloe would remotely enjoy went in the basket.

Once I was done there, I picked up her favorite noodles and dumplings from The Lucky Chopstick and swung by the bakery to grab one cupcake. Instead, I bought one in each flavor because I wasn't sure which she'd like best. Better to be overprepared than under.

By the time I got home, it was just after seven. The house was still and dark, with only the blue glow from the TV illuminating the space. Chloe was on the couch, wrapped up like a burrito, the hood of my sweatshirt pulled up over her head.

She glanced from me to the overstuffed bags I carried and raised a brow. "Did you rob a CVS?"

"Needed a few things." I toed off my boots and headed toward her, my gaze assessing every inch I could see.

Even in the dim light, her skin looked pale, her normally sunshiny disposition AWOL, and that bright smile that felt like a sucker punch every time she aimed it at me was nowhere to be found.

I unloaded the items I'd purchased on the coffee table in front of her, her brows inching up with each item I pulled out of the bag.

"*You* needed a few things, huh?"

"Yeah."

"Uh-huh." She reached over and grabbed the package of Midol, giving it a shake. "You use these for your mantrums?"

"Sutton taught you that, didn't she?"

"Please, *I* taught *her* that. And don't avoid the question."

"You mentioned it in your text, so I grabbed some."

She hummed, her lips pursed to the side as she eyed everything else. "You hate tea."

I shrugged. "It was on sale."

"Right," she said, skepticism heavy in her tone. "And

you're suddenly into essential oils now? And how many bath bombs does one person need?"

"Can never have too many."

"And you just so happened to grab *these* chocolate-covered almonds?"

"Those are actually for me." I grabbed the package out of her hand.

She stared at me, her mouth hanging open in shock. "Seriously? Those are my favorite..."

I opened the package before handing them back. Then I stood, pressed a kiss to her forehead, and murmured, "I know."

"Oh, you're good," she mumbled as she grabbed a handful before tossing them into her mouth.

"Gonna change. Eat your noodles and dumplings before they get cold."

"Noodles *and* dumplings?"

"Don't forget the cupcakes."

I didn't know why her gasp made me feel ten feet tall, but I wasn't going to question it. I was tired of questioning things when it came to Chloe.

After I changed, I headed back downstairs to find the couch empty and the door to the bathroom closed. While she was in there, I tossed the heating pad in the microwave and prepped her a cup of chamomile tea.

By the time she came out, the heating pad and tea were ready for her, along with her dinner, and I was sitting in her spot.

She froze as soon as she saw me. "What are you doing?"

I eyed her from head to toe, noticing the subtle hunch to

her shoulders and how she couldn't seem to keep her hand from her lower abdomen. Then I patted the spot between my legs. "C'mere."

She narrowed her eyes at me, as if she couldn't quite figure me out, then she grimaced, her face creasing in pain, and shuffled over. With a sigh, she dropped into the space between my legs, and I wrapped the blanket around her. Then I grabbed the heating pad and tucked it under her blanket, directly over her stomach, and settled my hand on top. Firm. Anchoring.

Slowly, her body melted into mine until her back was pressed flush against me, her head resting on my chest. "You're being dangerous right now."

"Noted." With my other hand, I reached for the noodles and held them in front of her, the chopsticks poking out of the container. "Eat something."

"Bossy," she murmured but accepted the container.

She ate slowly at first, but once the first bite hit, her whole body sighed like it had been waiting for it all day, and I ignored the warmth that settled in my chest at being able to give her that.

I found her favorite reality TV show and let it play in the background. Chloe ate her dinner, gathering noodles on the chopsticks and passing some back to me every couple bites.

With her eyes on the screen, she said, "You couldn't pay me enough money to go on national television and expose all my shit. All while hoping someone picks me."

"Yeah," I murmured. "Feels like emotional Russian roulette. But with a lot more crying into wineglasses."

She huffed out a laugh and passed me another bite. "The

part that always gets me is how *loud* this is without actually saying anything. Sure, they choose the other person, but that's out of obligation. It's expected. It's the whole purpose of the show. But I always wonder if there are any quiet moments where they choose each other too. When no one's around to see, no one around to perform for."

There was something in her tone that had me instantly on alert. Something soft and mournful...full of yearning.

"You probably think that's ridiculous," she said, her voice low. "It *is* ridiculous."

"No."

The firmness of my single word seemed to surprise her, if the look she shot me over her shoulder was any indication.

"No?"

Chloe didn't share much about her life or what led her here...what led her everywhere. And if this was my chance to learn a bit more, I was going to take it.

"If you're feeling it, it's not ridiculous."

She huffed out a surprised breath, her gaze darting over my face before she set the empty noodle carton on the coffee table and settled back against my chest again. "I was the oops baby, you know? My brother—the middle kid—was in college to be an astrophysicist before I hit kindergarten. My sister got a PhD in, like, everything. They were exactly what my parents wanted. And then I came along, this...well, *me*...and upended their world."

"You mean brightened. You *brightened* their world."

Shaking her head, she blew out a humorless laugh. "That's not what they'd call it. They had this full life that I didn't fit into." Her voice dropped, and she murmured, "They didn't even try to fit me into it."

"You were alone?" I asked, my voice sharper than I'd intended because she sure as hell didn't deserve my anger. But her shitty family did.

"Not alone. I was included. But it was obligatory, you know? I was just rarely noticed the rest of the time." She shrugged against me, her fingers tracing over my hand still palming her stomach. "So I got really good at being me. Loud, quirky, and chaotic. Because if I couldn't be important, I could at least be entertaining, right?"

"You *are* important," I said, my voice harsh. Harsher than she needed right now, but I couldn't seem to stem it.

She went still for a moment, her entire body frozen. Then she glanced back with a teasing smile. "For sure...whatever would you do without the shoe orphanage?"

"Don't," I said firmly. "Don't do that. Don't discount what you are. You're not just important to Emma."

You're important to me.

I didn't say the words. I didn't know why, just that they sat frozen on the tip of my tongue, and I swallowed them down before I could admit something I couldn't take back.

Quiet settled around us then, and we sat like that through half another episode where Brantley and the woman he was on a date with were in a hot tub in the mountains, spilling all their childhood traumas.

"This is dangerously close to intimacy, you know," she murmured.

I pressed a kiss to her temple and lowered my face until

my lips brushed her ear. "Not quite, but the bath I'm going to run you just might be."

"A bath, huh? Are you going to add one of those fancy bath bombs, or are we savages?"

"Bath bomb and some lavender oil. Maybe we can summon a demon while we're at it."

She tipped her head back to stare up at me, something soft and vulnerable in her gaze. "I've never had anyone do this for me before."

That made my chest tighten with an uncomfortable emotion I couldn't quite name. I hated the fact that she'd never had anyone look after her. Look out for her. And I wanted to do shit like this for her every day until the surprise in her voice was gone.

Until she began to expect it.

CHAPTER THIRTY-ONE

CHLOE

THE BATHWATER WAS a deep shade of purple—like something a unicorn would bathe in—and the scent of lavender hung in the air, thick and sweet. It should've felt over the top and ridiculous, but it didn't. Not the unicorn water. Not the candles flickering on the windowsill. Not even Xander standing in the doorway, arms crossed, shoulder propped against the frame as if he was guarding something sacred while he watched me lower myself into the tub with a sigh.

"This is gonna give a girl ideas," I murmured, voice low, teasing, as I rested my head back and steam floated up from the water.

"About time."

My heart stuttered at his immediate response, and I shifted in the water, having no idea what to do with all his attention focused directly on me. Especially when I looked like *this*.

I ran my hand through the water and glanced at him. "So

this is what does it for you, huh? Cramps. Puffy eyes. General emotional instability. Real sexy stuff over here."

He allowed his gaze to trace over me—to the hair piled on my head and the aforementioned puffy eyes and the rest of my body hidden in the deep purple water—before locking his eyes with mine again. "It's still you."

I stared at him, mouth parted, and could only blink while my stomach flipped over itself and something sharp tugged in my chest. I wasn't lying when I'd said he was going to give a girl ideas. What was concerning was *this* girl didn't usually have *those* kinds of ideas.

"You going to stand there and watch the whole time, or do you want to join me?"

There was that slow drag of his gaze again, as if he was trying to clock everything I didn't say in every subtle tic of my body, every twitch of my expression. "You don't want to enjoy your bath alone?"

I gave a slow shake of my head, my eyes locked with his, and sat up, scooting forward and giving him a place to slip in behind me.

Xander didn't even pause. Just reached back and pulled his shirt over his head before shoving down his sweatpants and boxer briefs. And then he strode toward me like a man on a mission, and I... Well, I enjoyed the show, to be honest.

A naked Xander Steele was a sight to behold. But a naked Xander Steele with his attention and focus locked on me?

That was enough to steal every ounce of my breath straight from my lungs.

He stepped into the tub behind me and sank into the

water with a hiss. "Jesus Christ. It's like the seventh circle of hell in here."

I snorted. "You fight literal fires for a living. I think you're fine."

"I'll probably survive." He circled my waist and palmed my stomach low, just over the incessant ache that refused to calm down. "Now, lean back and relax."

I did as he'd instructed, exhaling a deep sigh and melting into him. The solidness of him behind me and the weight of his palms against my front felt like the most wonderful, comforting cocoon, and I wasn't sure I ever wanted to leave.

Especially not when I rested my head against his shoulder, and he dipped his face to kiss a path up my neck, across my jaw, and along my hairline. And especially not when he tucked his face in close, his beard brushing my temple, his breaths ghosting over my skin.

"Does it still hurt?" he murmured, his thumb brushing a soft path along my abdomen beneath the water.

"Unfortunately."

"What can I do?"

I hummed and shook my head, closing my eyes as I rested my hands on top of his. "Tell me something to get my mind off it."

He was quiet for a long while, and I thought for a minute he wasn't going to say anything. And then, quietly, like he was scared to say the words aloud, he whispered, "I'm afraid Emma's going to hate me for not being there."

I froze for a moment, my body going stiff as his confession sank in. And then I had the overwhelming urge to reassure him, and I couldn't hold back. "No, Xander. She won't. You're here now, and that's what matters."

"Is it? Because if my dad came back right now—left that brand-new family he abandoned us for—I'd tell him to get fucked. Him finally stepping up wouldn't rewrite the years he'd been gone. My dad left when I was old enough to hate him for it, and now I worry Emma's going to feel the same about me."

Jesus. We were quite a pair. I'd thought Xander's family was picture-perfect—rowdy, yes. Weird and wonderful and obnoxious, yes. But that was the family here in Starlight Cove. His dad? Well, he was an asshole. And I'd had no idea just how much Xander and I would have in common, thanks to our shitty parents.

"It's not the same." I squeezed his hand. "You have to know that."

"Do I?"

"*Yes.*" I shifted, turning around to face him and straddling his hips. "You were there for her the second you knew she existed. You changed *everything* for her. You're here."

"Now I am. But I wasn't. For four years, I wasn't. Not for her first word or her first step or her first day of preschool. I missed all of it."

Darting my gaze across his face, I catalogued his features, tight with guilt and regret. Guilt that wasn't his to bear and regret that wouldn't help anyone. "You didn't *miss* it. That time was stolen from you both. But you're making up for it now. You didn't run. You showed up. Moved your life for her. Became the dad she needs. That's not abandoning her. She sees it. *I* see it."

I reached up and cupped his face, his beard scraping my palms. He met my gaze—his so full of guilt and grief and hope and so much damn love. No doubt for his daughter and this little life they'd built.

"She knows you now. And she adores you."

A muscle in his jaw ticked as he stared at me, as if he didn't know what to do with the weight of my words. Like maybe they were too much.

Or maybe they were exactly enough.

He didn't respond. Didn't speak at all. Instead, he pressed his forehead against mine, his eyes closing for a beat as he breathed me in. And I couldn't wait. Couldn't sit there unmoving. Couldn't do anything but shift the tiniest bit and press my lips to his. Softly. Just a lingering touch, really, but there was so much wrapped up in it—*thank you* and *please* and *don't let go* all rolled into one.

My pleas were silent, but he seemed to have heard them anyway, because he kissed me back. He slid his hand around to cup my neck, his thumb brushing along the curve of my jaw and then using it to guide my mouth open. Allow him deeper.

He slipped his tongue between my lips—soft and claiming—and I moaned at the first taste of him. The sound seemed to crack something in us both, the tether holding us back snapping all at once. He tightened his hold on me as I shifted forward, grinding against his cock before I even realized I'd moved.

With a low groan, he shifted his hold and gripped my hips, tugging me closer. Holding me tight, as if I was the only thing keeping him anchored to earth. And it felt so good—so fucking good to be here with him, like this. To feel wanted and needed and...cherished.

I wanted to feel *everything* with him.

I rolled my hips against him again, just a slow drag of our bodies together, but the result was anything but soft. He groaned into my mouth again, but it was needier this time. Desperate. Both of us aching with something we couldn't say aloud. I needed his hands everywhere—needed him inside me, filling me up and reminding me I was his.

At least for this brief moment in time, I was his.

But the reality of the moment caught up to me—why I was here in this bath in the first place—and I stilled, my breaths coming out in pants as I rested my forehead against his.

"Sorry," I murmured against his lips, shifting my hips back, away from him.

He didn't allow me to get far, his grip tightening on my flesh, holding me steady. "Why are you sorry?"

"Because of...this." I bit my lip and gestured vaguely to my midsection. "Hell-spawn uterus and whatnot."

"Are you saying that because *you* don't want to or because you think *I* don't?" He skated his gaze across my face, dipping briefly to where my breasts peeked out over the top of the water, his fingers tightening...tightening against my skin. "Because I can promise you it's not the latter."

"No?"

He gave a slow shake of his head, wrapped one large palm around my hip, and tugged me toward him in the water. "No."

I rested my hands on his bare chest, loving the feel of him

under my seeking hands. Loving the feel of him everywhere. "It might get messy."

"I don't mind."

I huffed out a short laugh. "Please. You hate messes."

He didn't look away. Didn't even blink. "Not anymore."

Maybe it didn't mean anything. Maybe it was just the steam and the relaxing bath and the way he was touching me like I wasn't too much and instead like I was exactly enough. But god...in that moment, I wanted it to mean *everything*. Wanted to believe it wasn't just tonight...wasn't just *this*. Wanted to believe that maybe—*maybe*—this was something else. This was something more.

And those thoughts terrified me most of all.

With his hands bracketing my hips, he pulled me forward, guiding my hips against him in a slow, steady grind. Both of us moaning at that first contact. He felt so good—it *always* felt so good with him—that I couldn't stop. I gripped his broad shoulders for leverage and rolled my hips over his hard cock, grinding my clit against him, desperate to satisfy this burning need that always simmered between us.

But that was a lost cause. I wasn't sure it would ever be satisfied. Not with the desire and want he brought out in me. Not with how much I craved him even when he wasn't around.

I rocked against him, building a rhythm between us as his mouth found my throat. He kissed down the column of my neck and across my shoulder, brushing his lips against me, softly, reverently, before dipping his head to my breast. His touch was featherlight—just a whisper of breath against me— until, all at once, it wasn't.

He took my nipple into his mouth and sucked hard, deep, pulling a gasp from my throat. Controlling my body with nothing more than his lips and tongue as I arched against him, my hands flying to his head to hold him steady. Hold him close.

"You feel that?" he rasped, his lips brushing against my nipple. "You feel how much I want you? That pussy gets wet, and I want it in my mouth...want it wrapped around my cock."

"Oh god," I choked out, my release so close, I could taste it. But I didn't want to come like this—empty and aching for him—so I reached between us, gripped his shaft, and guided it to my entrance.

And then I sank down on him, our groans mixing together in the otherwise quiet space as I took him inside. Took him deep.

"Xander..."

"That's right, baby. Just me who gets to feel this perfect cunt, isn't it? Just me who's filling you up so well."

I rolled my hips against him, chasing that high he always gave me. He dug his fingers into my flesh, guiding me, anchoring me, until I wasn't sure where I ended and he began.

On his next deep thrust, my head fell back, a broken moan spilling from my lips as he hit that spot every time I sank down.

"Look at you... Riding me like this. Sitting on my cock like you were made for it. Made to be filled up by me," he rasped against my skin, his voice laced with something I couldn't quite name. "Gonna keep filling you until you believe it too."

I whimpered, digging my fingers into his shoulders, working my hips faster, faster, chasing that release I always found with him. He kissed my breasts, up my chest to my collarbone, my neck, my jaw, then the corner of my mouth. Like he couldn't get enough. Couldn't stop tasting me.

Like he didn't want to.

"I've never wanted anything the way I want to stay inside you," he murmured.

And *god*, I wanted to believe him. Wanted to live in a world where a man like Xander Steele wanted me that completely. That desperately. That reverently.

My cheeks were flushed, my body burning up from the inside out as I rode him with a gnawing hunger I was all too familiar with around him. I kissed him then, because I didn't trust my mouth. Didn't trust myself not to say something I couldn't take back. Something that gave him the power to break me.

"I dream about the way your pussy feels around me. Wake up hard and aching every fucking day, thanks to you. Because nothing—*nothing*—feels as good as this. As you." He dropped his hand into the water between us and found my clit with his thumb, rubbing quick, tight circles around it in a way that had my legs tightening, my thighs trembling.

"There you go," he said, low and rough and laced with a need that made my chest ache. "I can feel you, dirty girl. Can feel you squeezing my cock, that little cunt begging to come. Let me give it to you. Let me be the reason you fall apart every fucking time."

"Xander," I choked out, sure I would've collapsed on him if he weren't guiding me. If I weren't so starved for the release I knew he could give me.

"You think I care about a little blood, baby?" He moved his thumb faster against me, dragging his lips up the column of my throat to my ear. "I'd fuck you in a goddamn war zone if it meant being inside you."

That was it—that was all it took. Just that broken plea, that low growl proving just how desperate he was. How desperate he was for *me*.

I shattered—wrecked, ravaged, ruined as I shook in his arms, my body contracting around him as he filled me up. As he sank deep and spilled inside me with a groan. With my name on his lips and something soft and silent between us.

I had no idea how long we stayed like that, tangled up in each other, the water cooling, the candlelight flickering.

All I knew was, in that moment, neither of us let go.

CHAPTER THIRTY-TWO

XANDER

WE'D BARELY WALKED through my mom's back door when the noise hit us full force.

"You touch that roll, and I'll stab you with a butter knife," Sutton said, pointing a finger at Lincoln.

He froze, hand hovering an inch above the bread basket. "I was testing for warmth."

"You were testing my patience," Mom said, not even turning from the stove.

Declan, seated on the counter like he was fifteen, smirked. "He's carb-loading to flirt with Farmer Girl later. Needs the stamina."

"Says the guy still trying to recover from the hot librarian's sudden interest in getting a tattoo from someone else," Lincoln shot back.

Declan's brows slammed down, that Steele glower sliding into place. "Don't start, Linc."

"How about you both shut the hell up?" Atlas stood like a

bodyguard next to Sutton, his arms crossed over his chest, his scowl as deep as the ocean. "You're being shitheads."

Emma gasped dramatically as she toed off her boots. "That's a dollar in the swear jar, Uncle Atlas!"

"I actually think he owes about twenty," Laurel murmured from her perch at the breakfast nook as she scrolled on her phone.

Sunday dinners were always so fucking much—basically, the aftermath of a tornado—but from the very first one I'd brought Chloe to, she'd slid into the mayhem effortlessly.

Just like now, as she slipped straight into the fold as if she'd always been here, guiding Emma toward Laurel before sidling up to Lincoln, a smirk on her face.

"Hey, warmth-tester. What level are they?"

"Uh...level *perfection*," he said. "Cool enough to eat but warm enough to basically melt in your mouth."

"Grab one. I'll distract them."

"Marry me," Lincoln said, and I couldn't stop the short growl that rumbled from my chest. Thankfully, it was quiet enough that only one person heard it. Unfortunately, that single person was my idiot youngest brother who shot me a smirk and stepped closer to Chloe just to piss me off. "We could go down to town hall tomorrow."

She popped half a roll into her mouth before tossing the rest to him, then spun around. "Linc's been a bad boy, ladies. He swiped a roll."

Lincoln gasped and held a hand to his chest. "That was cruel."

Meanwhile, something close to a laugh rumbled out of

Declan, but it came to a screeching halt when Chloe smacked him upside the head.

"Jesus, what the hell did I do?" he grumbled, rubbing a hand on the back of his head. "I'm just sitting here."

"Please." Chloe rolled her eyes. "You egg him on like you get paid to."

"Do you blame me? He's a pain in my ass."

"You're all a pain in my ass," Mom said. "Now, either help with dinner or get out of my kitchen."

Everyone stayed right where they were, hovering in the hub of the house, the conversations spilling into each other, just like always. Lincoln was teaching Emma a card trick while Laurel and Declan heckled him. Sutton and my mom were discussing whether one of the sex scenes in their latest book was physically possible or strictly fantasy fodder, while Atlas supervised the entire thing.

And then there was Chloe, wearing a sundress in the middle of March as if she could usher in summer with her will alone. She stepped up next to my mom, seamlessly took over gravy duty, and jumped into the debate about the book.

And all I could do was stand on the outside looking in.

Sunday dinners weren't new...they were tradition, which meant I was used to this. Used to my brothers bickering and Sutton multitasking and Emma playing games and Laurel roasting people twice her age. All of that was familiar. But Chloe?

She was the piece I hadn't even realized was missing.

Unfortunately, that didn't matter because she wasn't supposed to stay. The plan was for her to leave at the end of March. That had *always* been the plan.

So then, why did it feel like someone had hollowed out my chest as I watched her stir gravy and talk with my brothers and laugh with my mom and shoot a secret wink at my daughter, all while knowing it could never last?

After dinner, I was standing in the kitchen, grabbing a glass of water. Taking a much-needed break to catch my damn breath.

"Chloe fits, doesn't she?" Mom said, following me in as if she knew I needed the company. She tipped her head toward the sunbeam currently shining brightly in the family room—laughing with Sutton and teasing my brothers and absent-mindedly braiding my daughter's hair.

Like she belonged.

"Doesn't matter. She's not staying."

Mom turned to look at me with raised brows. "Has she actually said that?"

"She's said she's leaving, so yeah. Pretty much." I kept my voice even, refusing to allow even a crack to show. "At the end of March. She made that clear."

"She made it clear *then*. Things have changed."

"Have they?" I asked because, yeah, I'd been hoping.

Hoping maybe Chloe would change her mind. That whatever this was between us meant something real to her. But she hadn't said a word. And I wasn't going to be the idiot who asked, just to hear her say no. Not when she was born to fly and spread her chaos everywhere she went.

"*Haven't* they?" Mom bumped her shoulder against mine, her attention on the side of my face while I was trying valiantly to keep my attention off the one woman I couldn't seem to get out of my mind. "You look at her like she's everything. And I think maybe she could use a bit of that in her life."

"She's my nanny. Nothing more."

Mom hummed in that way that said she knew I was full of shit. "You've always been the steady one, Xander. But even anchors deserve to get swept away once in a while."

I didn't respond to her. I couldn't. So instead, I just watched from the periphery while Laurel played DJ for Chloe and Emma, the two of them spinning in clumsy circles, dancing and laughing, and my heart fucking ached watching it.

Because I wanted it so goddamn badly.

Wanted Chloe. Here, at Sunday dinners. Here, dancing with my daughter and bullshitting with my brothers. Here, in my town and in my house and in my bed.

But I'd learned a long time ago that wanting didn't mean keeping. And Chloe? Wild, beautiful, radiant Chloe?

She was never mine to keep. And she sure as hell wasn't meant to stay.

CHAPTER THIRTY-THREE

XANDER

THE SECOND we stepped inside after getting home from Sunday dinner, I knew Chloe was going to run. Hide. Try to do what she did best.

I'd known it as soon as Emma had asked to stay with my mom tonight and Chloe had realized she wouldn't have a four-year-old buffer keeping her safe.

The trouble was, neither of us was safe. Not with this inevitable end we were careening toward.

She didn't even bother to turn on any lights as she slipped off her shoes and walked upstairs, her body stiff in a way that told me she was trying like hell to ignore my presence. As though if she didn't acknowledge me, I'd just go away. Leave her to hide in her room. Spend the night out of my bed when I had only a handful of nights left when she'd be by my side.

At the doorway to her bedroom, I hooked an arm around her waist and tugged her back against my chest. She stiffened before slowly melting into me, just like always, her hands resting on my forearm.

Lowering my head, I settled my lips against her ear and murmured, "Where do you think you're going?"

"To sleep?"

Shaking my head, I made a low noise of disagreement. "You sleep in *my* bed."

I guided her toward my room, loving how easily she came. Like she didn't want to fight it anymore. Like she knew it was exactly where she belonged.

"I'm afraid I have some bad news, though," I said once we were tucked away inside, the sliver of moonlight the only illumination in the room.

"What's that?"

I traced along the low scoop neck of her dress, brushing my fingertips over her skin. "We're not going to sleep for a while."

"No? What are we going to do instead?"

"Make sure you can't hide."

"I wasn't—"

I nipped her earlobe, cutting off her words. "You don't get to lie to me. Not here. Not like this. Not when I'm about to have you spread out, dripping and begging for me. Not when I'm going to give you everything you need."

She parted her lips, no doubt in an effort to challenge me or say something funny or clever or distant—slot that armor she loved so much right into place—but I didn't allow it to come.

Instead, I kissed her. Not slow or sweet. This was a claiming, pure and simple. I captured her lips with mine, tasted her tongue, and breathed her in, sure she was the only oxygen I'd ever need.

As soon as the backs of her knees hit the mattress, I reached down, gripped the hem of her sundress, and tugged it straight over her head. Then I rid her of her bra and panties before pushing her flat on the bed and standing back to take her all in.

Fucking stunning. Hair spread out around her like a halo, her tits tight little handfuls, nipples pointed directly at me, her pussy—pink and smooth and already wet, just from my kiss.

But it was her eyes that got me. Dark and pleading—confusion and hope and trepidation all swirling in their depths.

And I was right there with her, feeling all of that and more.

I couldn't tell her to stay. Couldn't tell her any of these thoughts buzzing through my head, mostly because I couldn't even admit them to myself. But I could do this—I could be this for her. Could use my body to tell her everything I couldn't with my words.

I tugged off my shirt and tossed it to the side before going to work on my belt. "You know what you look like, lying here and spread out on my sheets like a fucking wet dream?"

"What?" she asked, her gaze tracking my movements as I slid off my jeans and boxer briefs, eyes zeroing in as I wrapped my hand around my cock and gave one firm tug.

"You look like mine." I started at her feet, kissing my way over her ankles, up her calves and knees, brushing my lips along her inner thighs. "You look like every inch of you belongs here—right here. Just waiting for everything I want to give you."

Her breath hitched as I swiped my tongue through her pussy, her hands flying to my hair as I feasted on her like she was my last fucking meal. "Xander."

"See?" I murmured against her flesh, rubbing her clit with my beard and reveling in her answering moan. "It's *my* name you're saying tonight, isn't it? My name you're going to be crying out when I eat this delicious cunt. My name you're going to moan when you ride my fingers. And it'll be my name you scream when I make you come all over my cock and beg for more, won't it?"

"Yes." She tightened her fingers in my hair, attempting to tug me closer to her pussy. To give her exactly what she wanted.

"Because even though my dirty girl likes to be used—likes to know I can't hold myself back anymore—I make sure that perfect little pussy is nice and ready to take everything I give, don't I? I don't stop until you're dripping with your need."

I didn't give her time to respond since we both knew it was true. Instead, I dove in, licking a line straight up her seam and groaning at her taste. I slid two fingers into her, curling them inside and stroking that spot that had her hips arching off the bed, her fingers tugging harder at my hair.

"Oh fuck," she breathed, her hips rolling beneath me as she rode my face from below, fucked herself with my fingers like she couldn't help it. "God, you're gonna make me come."

I hummed a self-satisfied sound directly against her pussy, the vibrations shooting through her and sending her straight over the cliff. She cried out my name as her cunt squeezed my fingers, her hips rolling as she moaned and gasped and came apart beneath me.

There was no sound in the world like Chloe coming undone. I wanted to make her do it again and again and again, just like that. With my mouth on her pussy and her thighs wrapped tight around my head. Wanted to drink down every ounce of her pleasure, but I needed to be inside her just as badly. And from the way she tightened her fingers in my hair and tugged me up her body, that same desperation was beating like a drum inside her too.

I covered her body with mine, sucked one of her nipples into my mouth, and then cupped her face and captured her lips. I kissed her like I'd never get enough. Like I never wanted this to end.

Settling into the cradle of her thighs, I hooked one of her knees over my elbow, spreading her wide for me as I sank inside the hot fist of her cunt. Everything in me easing the second I was as deep as I could get. The second she was filled to the fucking brim with me.

"You feel that? That pressure? The way your little pussy stretches so fucking tight to take me inside?"

She nodded, her eyes wild as she stared up at me, her fingers digging into my sides, my ass, pulling me even deeper.

"That's what you do to me. No one else gets me this hard. No one else takes me this deep."

"God," she choked out, her pussy fluttering around me, already desperate to come again.

"But my dirty girl can take it, can't she? You can take every fucking inch of my cock because I make sure of it. I make sure this sweet cunt is satisfied, don't I?"

"Every time," she breathed, her hips rolling beneath me, meeting my every thrust.

"That's right. Every fucking time. And you love it, don't you? Love how I take you. Like you're *mine*."

"*Yes.*"

"You think anyone else knows how to touch you like this? You think anyone else knows exactly what you need?"

She arched off the bed, her back bowed, hips rolling and chasing a release I wasn't yet ready to give her.

"Answer me," I growled, sinking deep and grinding my pelvis against her, basking in the sharp gasp that fell from her lips. "You think anyone else could make you fall apart like this?"

"No," she whispered, her words barely more than a breath, but I heard them. "Only you."

"That's right," I murmured into her neck, my cock jerking at her admission, my hips driving into her a bit harder. "Just me."

She raked her nails down my back, her hips restless beneath me as she whimpered and moaned, desperate for whatever I could give her. "Xander, I need you."

On a groan, I dropped my face into her neck and sank as deep as I could. I knew she meant this, here, now. That she needed me to make her come, make her fall apart and be stitched back together all at once. But in my mind, I let it mean something else. Something more.

A life. Here. With me and Emma and this home that had just been a house until Chloe set foot in it.

I rested my forehead against hers and fucked her slow and deep. Every thrust was a confession, every stroke a wordless plea I couldn't bring myself to say aloud, every kiss against her lips a promise I couldn't voice.

She gripped my shoulders, her nails digging into my flesh as if anchoring herself right here, in this moment. To me.

"Come on, baby. Give me one more. Let me feel this sweet little cunt milk my cock while I fill you up, while I give you everything."

Her whole body shook, her legs tightening around me as she stared at me with wide eyes. And then, all at once, she broke. She sobbed out a moan, her eyes fluttering closed as she shattered beneath me.

I couldn't do anything but follow her over the edge, a groan so raw torn from my throat that it felt like a confession all on its own.

Even after the last ounce of pleasure had seeped out of me, I didn't move—couldn't. I just stayed right there, settled on top of her, her heartbeat hammering against mine, her fingers curled into my hair as if she wasn't ready to let me go just yet.

She didn't say a word, and neither did I. But every breath we shared was a plea I was both desperate and terrified to utter aloud.

Stay.

CHAPTER THIRTY-FOUR

CHLOE

THE VAGINA-SHAPED CAKE perched on the front table like a centerpiece wasn't even the weirdest part of the night. Neither was the lube tasting station or the lacy thong toss Mabel had set up like the ringtoss game—winner to take home a basket full of bad decisions. Nope. The weirdest part was that this sex-toy-and-sass-fueled extravaganza actually felt...*normal*. Like it was just another Thursday night in Starlight Cove.

The *Love Yourself* evening was in full swing at Wicked Little Things, and I was, somehow, in charge of it all. Me—the girl whose résumé was a mile long and who couldn't even commit to shampoo for more than a month was running things over here. And not just running them, but absolutely *nailing* it.

I'd managed to get people in the door who'd never so much as looked sideways at one of Mabel's displays. But more than that, I got women laughing and joking and talking and bonding and *loving themselves*, which was the whole damn point.

"I've got some Screaming Orgasms coming through!" I weaved my way through a group of giggling women, a tray of cocktails perched on my hand.

Willa snagged one, sniffed it, and downed it in one gulp before scrunching up her nose. "Could be better, but it's not the worst thing I've swallowed by the same name," she murmured.

"That belongs on a shirt," I said, handing her a condom that glittered like a disco ball and sparkling lube to match. "Compliments of Mabel."

"If these don't come with a matching vibe, what are we even doing here?"

I snorted and shook my head. "You gotta talk to the woman in charge. I just throw the parties."

"And you do them so well," Sutton said, sidling up to me and grabbing a Screaming Orgasm off my tray. "This turnout is amazing. How did you get Hot Librarian to come?"

"You know we're actually going to have to use her name when we speak to her, right?"

"Obviously." She rolled her eyes and downed the shot. "Now, what's your secret?"

"Wasn't me." I glanced over to where Penelope was sitting, stiff as a statue and trying desperately not to make eye contact with the ten-speed monstrosity to her right. "Holly dragged her over straight from work. Didn't even let the poor girl go home and change."

"That's because she would've *stayed* home," Luna said, grabbing the last Screaming Orgasm off the tray. "I've lived here for a couple years, and I rarely see that girl outside the library. It's good Holly pushed her."

"Maybe." I glanced in Penelope's direction again, taking in her rigid posture. Her arms were folded over her chest, her cardigan buttoned all the way up like it was the only shield she had access to. "But maybe pushing her to sit directly in front of the large display of monster peens was a bit much."

"Oh, come on. Everyone loves an obscene tentacle dick." Sutton glanced between us, her brows raised. "Am I right?"

I snorted and shook my head, doing a quick survey of the space. Mabel had turned the boutique into a sparkly, lace-draped den of sin where women were free to be...well, free. The music was thrumming, the conversation was flowing, and everything was damn near perfect.

Luna linked her arm through mine and tipped her head toward me. "Look at what you did, Chloe. You got all these women here and convinced them there's no such thing as a guilty pleasure—it's just *pleasure*. That's pretty amazing."

I smiled, because that was the whole point of all this ridiculousness—of the glitter and lube and the vulva cake proudly displayed in the front window. This was meant to be a night about pleasure without apology. About women claiming space without saying sorry. About them not feeling guilty for their wants or their needs and, instead, just going after them.

But my smile felt a little too tight as I glanced around. Because while, yes, it did feel amazing to have a hand in that, it was also a harsh reminder.

It was easy to teach everyone else how to be soft and open

and brave. But it was a hell of a lot harder to have faith that I could do the same.

"You're out of Buttery Nipples," Quinn called from the front of the store, where she was keeping inventory.

"On it!" I hollered, grateful for that interruption. I made my way toward the back, tossing Sutton a quick thumbs-up as she coached Penelope on proper vibe technique before slipping into the back room.

The door shut behind me, dimming the music and the laughter and all the noise, but that only made me want to get back out there quicker. I'd always been a people person—loved getting lost in a crowd—but there was something special here, tonight. Watching women who'd been scared of or scared away from pleasure seek that for themselves was so damn empowering. And I loved that I'd had a little something to do with it.

Well, me and the orgasm fairy, Mabel.

As I loaded my tray with more shots, my phone buzzed in my pocket. I reached for it, expecting a text from Xander or a directive from Mabel, but instead, I found a calendar notification.

Get ready! Sedona reset in 10 days.

The phone screen dimmed, but the tight, hot feeling in my chest didn't fade. If anything, it spread until it beat like a drum through my veins, impossible to ignore.

It was the same notification that had been popping up every year for the past decade. The one I was usually desperate to see. The one that filled me with hope and excitement and happiness about everything that was on the horizon.

Tonight, all it filled me with was dread.

Raucous laughter floated in from the other room, reminding me that all those women I brought together were out there finding freedom through something as simple as frilly lingerie and battery-operated boyfriends. They were realizing it was okay to want more, and they were choosing themselves on purpose.

And me? I was standing in a stock room with foreboding drowning out the happiness that had been echoing through me while staring at a reminder that I had one foot out the door.

I always had one foot out the door.

Leaving was safe. It was easy. It was all I knew.

But part of me—the part who believed every word Xander had ever whispered against my ear while he was inside me and read something into the smiles and laughter his little girl shot my way every day—started to wonder what it might feel like if I stayed.

CHAPTER THIRTY-FIVE

CHLOE

VOLUNTEERING in a pre-K classroom sounded fun and easy. Clearly, I was an idiot. And clearly, I wasn't familiar with the havoc that reigned when fifteen kids were armed with glue sticks, pipe cleaners, and enough glitter to make the New Year's Eve ball in Times Square sparkle.

Emma stood behind the craft table, absolutely glowing in her *Art Queen* smock, her cheek streaked with purple paint. "LoLee, look!" She held up what I thought might be a paper cat and beamed at me.

"Now, *that* is a masterpiece. We need to book it its own gallery showing."

Emma giggled and thrust it toward me, flapping it around in the air like a wind sock. "I made it for you! For being the best LoLee in the whole *world*!"

I took it with a slight bow. "I've never been more honored."

She laughed at my awful British accent and turned to

help a classmate glue feathers on a paper crown while I glanced around for anyone who needed a little assistance.

The day had been frenzied and sweet in the way that only existed in preschool. It was messy and loud, but I was so grateful I was here to experience it with my little doodlebug.

"My mom said you're not Emma's *real* mom."

The statement came out of nowhere, the little boy's voice cutting through the laughter and shrieks like a needle popping a balloon.

I turned to find that same little asshole from the fire station looking up at me, his mouth full of Goldfish crackers.

"She said you just get paid to be nice 'cause you're her babysitter, and that's what babysitters do." He shrugged like he hadn't just punched a hole through my soul with his words.

I shot my gaze to Emma, hoping—*praying*—she hadn't heard him because she didn't need to deal with this again. But of course, she was staring right at him, her smile collapsing in slow motion.

Then that little shit walked off, unaware or uncaring of the bomb he'd just dropped in the middle of the arts and crafts station. Sounds started up again, kids squealing and laughing and fighting, but all I could focus on was Emma.

She glanced up at me, her eyes sad and worried. "Is that why you're nice to me, LoLee? Cause Daddy gives you money?"

"Bug," I said, my heart breaking right along with hers. I squatted down to her level and reached for her hand. "I'm nice to you because I *love* you. Not because it's my job to look after you or because I get paid to. I think you're the most amazing little girl in the whole world, and *that* is why I'm nice to you. Not because I have to be."

She stared at me for a beat, her gaze assessing in a way that should've been reserved for someone ten times her age. Then she nodded like she accepted my answer, but I'd already watched the light fade from her eyes. Watched her shoulders slump a bit, that bottom lip quivering like she was trying so hard not to cry.

It almost broke me.

I wrapped an arm around her and squeezed her into my side. "I think we deserve matching sparkle crowns. What do you say?"

"Okay." She smiled at me, but it wasn't her usual beaming grin. It was thinner. Sadder.

Like she wanted to break so badly but had to hold it together for just a bit longer.

XANDER WAS WORKING LATE, so I put Emma down that night. I lay stretched out on her bed, and she was tucked under my arm, curled into my side like always. Instead of clutching Pinkie to her chest, she gripped the hem of my sweatshirt like if she let go I might float away.

I told her a story of a brave little princess who was teased that her favorite star only shone because the queen demanded it to. But the princess knew better because that star showed up every night, just for her, even when no one was looking.

Bedtime was usually full of laughter and stories and too

many *just one more* drinks of water, but tonight, it was eerily silent, a heaviness having settled in the house the moment we'd stepped through the door after preschool.

"When you leave, will you say goodbye first?" Emma asked, her small voice breaking through the stillness.

My throat squeezed tight, my eyes and nose stinging, hands shaking as if my whole body rejected her words. She was smart—probably the smartest four-year-old I'd ever met. And, somehow, she knew not to ask me if I was staying. And she knew not to ask me not to leave.

She was only asking for a goodbye.

Blinking away the tears, I swallowed down the lump in my throat and held out my pinkie toward her. "Pinkie promise."

She tipped her head back and glanced up at me before hooking her finger around mine. Then she snuggled deeper into my side, and I stroked a hand down her hair, pressing my nose against the crown of her head and inhaling deeply.

Emma was asleep within minutes, her little body going limp against mine, but I lay next to her for a long time, not ready to leave just yet. Because I knew the second I moved, this would all be real.

So instead, I stayed right there, my arms wrapped around her as if I could shield her from this wreckage I'd built with my own hands.

I shouldn't have stayed this long. Should've left before she needed me. Before she loved me.

And I definitely should've left long before I fell in love with either of them.

CHAPTER THIRTY-SIX

XANDER

THE LIVING ROOM was quiet when I stepped inside after my shift. The flickering blue light from the TV cast a soft glow over Chloe where she sat on the couch. Her knees were tucked up to her chest, Emma's unicorn blanket wrapped around her as she stared, unseeing, at the screen.

"Hey, chaos." I dropped my keys on the table by the door, my gaze tracking over every inch of her, brows drawing down. "You good?"

She turned to face me, resting her head on her knees, and blew out a deep breath. "Emma had a rough day."

My entire body stiffened, every molecule in me on high alert, ready to go to war if my little girl needed it. "What happened?"

Chloe huffed a humorless laugh and settled her forehead on her knees, hiding her face from me. "That same little asshole from the fire station tour told her I only love her because you pay me to."

"*What?*"

"I talked to her about it. Said it wasn't true. Tonight, I told her a story about a brave princess before bed." She swallowed, glancing up at me with sadness heavy in her eyes. "And then she asked me to say goodbye before I leave."

Fuck.

I'd known it was coming. The entire time Chloe had been here, this had been the inevitable end. It was also exactly what I'd wanted to prevent. Exactly what I swore I wouldn't let happen.

I wasn't supposed to let Emma fall in love with her.

I wasn't supposed to fall in love with her.

"I pinkie promised I would," she said. "It's the least I can do, right? I mean, I *am* leaving. That was always the plan."

"Plans change," I said roughly, the words like gravel.

The corner of her mouth twitched, and she glanced at me with amusement in her eyes. "Says the man with the color-coded routine on the fridge."

"Says the man who used to follow it." I met her gaze, mine steady and unflinching. "Things change."

She tightened her fingers on the blanket as she shifted her gaze to the side, staring at nothing. "I've never stayed anywhere this long. Not since I turned eighteen and got the hell out of my parents' house." She traced the outline of a unicorn on the blanket, not meeting my gaze. "Sedona is my reset. I've done it every year. We talked about it when I first started. When you said this was all temporary."

I *had* said that. Back when I was a fucking idiot.

"Like I said, things change."

"Like what?" she asked, her voice barely more than a whisper.

"You let her fall in love with you," I said, unable to keep the accusation from my voice.

She jerked as if she'd been shocked and snapped her gaze to mine. "You think I *wanted* her to?"

"Doesn't matter what you wanted. She did. And now she doesn't think of you as temporary." I cleared my throat, hoping to hide the gruffness in my voice, but it was no use. "She thinks of you as hers."

Chloe's eyes glassed over, a subtle sheen illuminated by the flickering light from the TV.

"You think she's going to understand when you leave?" I asked.

She rolled her lips inward and wrapped her arms around her knees, shaking her head. "No."

"You think I will?"

She stared up at me, unblinking, her eyes shiny and haunted. She wasn't the only one. It felt like someone had reached into my chest, gripped my heart, and ripped it straight out of my body. Took my soul right along with it.

But I'd walked right into this, hadn't I? I'd known this was coming the whole time.

"She thinks of you as home, you know. You'd better decide if she's wrong."

"And what about you?" she asked, her voice thin. "Do you think of me as home?"

I met her gaze, trying to put everything I could into that single look. "If you don't already know the answer to that, then I haven't been doing my job."

CHLOE

IT WAS WELL AFTER MIDNIGHT, and the house was quiet, filled with the kind of stillness that was suffocating.

I stood in the hallway just outside Xander's bedroom, bare feet silent against the hardwood and hand resting on the doorknob. I should've stayed in my room. Should've gone to sleep and let this day end without poking at the bruise that was only spreading over my heart, but I couldn't.

Without knocking, I turned the knob and pushed open the door, the floor creaking as I stepped inside. I cringed at the announcement of my presence, but it didn't matter anyway.

Xander's eyes were already locked on me, as if he'd been staring at the door, just waiting—*hoping?*—for me to walk through it.

He tracked my movements, his eyes following each slow step I made toward him. He allowed his gaze to sweep over me, his eyes heating when he took in the Starlight Cove Fire Department hoodie I'd stopped pretending I hadn't stolen from him.

I stood next to the bed, close enough that he could touch me. Could slide his fingers up the outside of my thigh, tell me to climb in next to him. And my entire body ached for that very thing with a desire so visceral it was staggering. "I'm not here to talk."

There was a beat of silence. Two. Three.

And then he murmured, "Good," just before hooking an

arm around my waist and tugging me into bed until I straddled him. He rested his hands on my thighs, his callused fingertips creating goose bumps in their wake as he stared up at me with something I wasn't ready to acknowledge.

"Don't look at me like that," I whispered, placing my hands on his bare chest and rolling my hips over where he was already growing hard for me.

"Like what?" he asked, hands anchored on my hips, guiding my movements over him.

"Like this means something."

His eyes hardened, his jaw clenching as he stared up at me. "It doesn't."

It was a lie. I knew it was, but it still broke my heart in two. From the lie or the truth I couldn't bear to hear, I wasn't sure.

It didn't matter anyway. Not when he cupped my face and tugged me down, capturing my lips with his. Not when he kissed me like he was drowning. Kissed me like I was the only thing he'd ever wanted in his whole life. The only thing he'd ever need.

Our clothes came off in a blur—everything but his hoodie. That, he'd just shoved above my tits, descending on them with his mouth as soon as he sank inside. He stared down at me as he thrust deep, one hand wrapped around my throat, the other gripping my hip and tugging me to him again and again. His gaze skated over me, his eyes boring into his name printed over my heart like he needed the reminder that I was his.

Even if I never said the words, I was always, always his.

He fucked me hard and rough, his hips slapping against

mine and his grunts filling the air like this was only about release. Only about getting off and not about this undeniable connection tethering us together. A connection I'd never once felt with anyone else.

A connection I was sure I'd never feel again for as long as I lived. Not like I did with Xander.

He bent over me, resting his forehead against mine as he sank deep and gave a slow grind of his hips, just like he knew I loved. Just like he knew I needed to come.

"This was supposed to be just sex," I whispered, as much for myself as for him. Like if I said the words aloud, they'd somehow, miraculously, be true.

"It's never been just sex, chaos," he said, firm and unyielding as he slipped a hand between us and thumbed my clit. "And you fucking know it."

My pussy clenched around him, my body tightening at his touch, already knowing where he was taking me. Ready to follow him anywhere.

"You think I touch anyone else like this?" His voice was just a low growl against my ear, his hips grinding into me like it was the only thing keeping him sane. "You think I *want* to?"

"Xander," I breathed because I didn't know what else to say. There was no realm of reality where I could tell him it was the same for me. That I felt it too.

Because while he confessed all these wild, broken claims of me, he always said them while he was buried deep inside me, half gone to the pleasure. But in the real world? In our real lives where shitty little boys said mean things to our girl and we'd both sworn this was only temporary? He'd been silent.

"I can't fucking breathe when you're not near me." He dragged his mouth down the column of my neck, his tongue tracing the tattoo below my collarbone, then sucking the skin hard enough to brand me. "And when you are? I want you just like this. Spread out and begging. That cunt dripping for me. Because that's the only time it feels even *close* to enough."

He shifted his hips, pulling nearly all the way out before slamming into me again, deep and deliberate. Punishing. "This pussy? Mine. All your little fuck-me sounds when I tongue that cunt or sink deep inside? Mine. That look in your eyes when you come so hard you forget your own fucking name? That's all *mine*, Chloe."

His words shouldn't have made my body come alive. Not with how he growled them in my ear, not with the possession laced into every syllable. And sure as hell not when I knew it could never be true.

"Say it." He squeezed my throat, a reminder of exactly what I'd asked for.

"It's yours. I'm yours," I breathed, unable to stop the words. Not even trying to.

What was the point? Why bother when he had me spread out like this, wrecked and ravaged and, yes, completely, utterly *his*.

"That's what I fucking thought. Every inch of you, isn't that right? Try to tell me again," he demanded, his thumb a relentless force against my clit, his other hand gripping my throat, forcing me to look at him. "Tell me it's just sex."

I shook my head, fighting against...everything. Falling apart in his arms and coming undone and admitting what we both already knew.

"You think I can't tell when you're close?" he asked, gripping my face and making me look up at him. He slammed his hips against mine, his cock hitting that spot inside me that had me seconds from coming all over him, and he fucking knew it. "You think I can't read your body and give her exactly what she needs?"

As if to prove his point, he pressed down hard on my clit and bent to take my nipple in his mouth, tugging it with his teeth until I shattered beneath him, his name the only thing spilling from my lips.

"*Fuck.* You think you can come on my cock like you fucking own it and pretend this isn't real?" He pressed his forehead against mine and sank deep, filling me to the brim as my release still echoed around him. "Lie better, baby."

I tried. I tried so fucking hard, but no matter what I did, my body told the truth with every aftershock that rocked through me, every fluttering pulse around his cock.

"You think this is just fucking?" He drove into me again. Deep. Hard. Like he wanted to sink inside and never leave. "I don't fucking believe you. Not when you come like your whole body's begging me to stay. Not when every inch of this pussy feels like *mine.*"

I couldn't deny it. Couldn't do anything but get lost in the pleasure he was wringing from my body, already sending me straight for another climax.

"Say it again." He slid his hand up my throat to cup my jaw, his thumb brushing against the corner of my mouth.

Tender now, even while his hips pistoned against me, his cock a relentless force thrusting inside. "Say you're mine. Or are you gonna try to lie to me one more time?"

I arched beneath him, my body clenching tight around his shaft, so close to falling, and breathed the only words that mattered. The words I wished fiercely were true. "I'm yours."

He groaned, long and low as he brought his mouth to mine, our lips touching, breath shared between us. "That's right. You've been mine since the second you stumbled out of that fucking shed. And you'll be mine even when you leave, won't you?"

Sobbing out a moan, I closed my eyes against the tears I couldn't stop, and I kissed him. Desperately. Reverently. Drowning out everything else but the feel of him against me, inside me, his heart beating wildly against my own.

Like they were both trying to rewrite this ending.

Maybe that was why I clung to him harder. Why I rocked my hips up to meet each one of his brutal thrusts, needing to lose myself to him again. Needing him to lose himself in me.

Needing him to need me, period.

"There's my dirty girl," he said against my ear, his voice a low rumble as he worked his thumb faster against my clit. "Let me feel that greedy cunt take what she needs. Come on my cock and show me who you belong to."

I couldn't hold back even a second more, my body bowing off the bed as I shattered around him, legs shaking, hands trembling, heart breaking.

Because I knew.

Even as he settled deep, burying his groan into my neck,

his cock pulsing inside me, I knew. I felt it in my bones. Felt it all the way down to my soul.

I'd gone and done the one thing I swore I never would.

I'd fallen in love.

Me—the girl who never stayed. The girl no one ever *asked* to stay.

And now, I wasn't sure I'd survive what came next.

CHAPTER THIRTY-SEVEN

CHLOE

ATLAS'S PLACE was huge and gorgeous and...not at all what I expected for a former professional football player. Fairy lights decorated the mantel and the bookcases around it, illuminating the space with a soft glow. Half a dozen blankets were tossed over a sectional that looked like a cloud, and the room had enough lit candles to hold a séance.

Luna tossed me a knowing smirk as soon as she saw me. "You're late."

I shrugged and slipped off my jacket. "Wasn't sure I was even gonna come, so consider yourself lucky."

"And you consider yourself lucky you decided to show up," Sutton said, grabbing my coat and hanging it by the door. "You wouldn't have liked the other option."

I eyed the three of them warily. "What was the other option?"

Luna handed over a glass of wine filled to the brim and smiled. "We were going to kidnap you and make you watch *The Notebook* until you cracked."

Quinn raised her glass. "No one can hold it together through that heartbreak."

"Better drink up, babe," Sutton said, sinking back into the couch and propping her feet on the coffee table. "You've got secrets that need prying, and we're not feeling particularly gentle tonight."

"What, this wine is supposed to be my lube?"

"Or we have *actual* lube." Sutton tipped her head toward a package by the front door. "A whole box of it that Mabel dropped off because the packaging was wrong, but she figured I could use it, 'what with Atlas's *size* and all.'"

I snorted and shook my head. "Oh my god, that woman is a *menace*. Didn't anyone tell her what you should and shouldn't say out loud?"

"Oh, please." Luna rolled her eyes before pinning me with a look I was very familiar with coming from her. "You love it. And her."

I pressed my lips together, my attention focused on my wineglass because I was afraid if I met any of their eyes, I'd just burst into tears. Because, yeah, I loved that ridiculous old woman, and I loved this town and these people and my friends who felt like missing pieces of my heart and the little girl who looked at me like I was her whole world and the man who was the other half of my soul.

But I couldn't *say* any of that.

I'd learned a long time ago, it didn't matter how much I loved something or someone or how badly I wanted to be a part of it. That didn't mean it would be mine to keep.

"What's that face all about?" Quinn asked, eyes narrowed on me, doctor mode fully engaged.

Smiling brightly—falsely—I shook my head. "Nothing. Just been a long week."

"Uh-huh." Sutton pinned me with a look that said not to test her bullshit meter because I'd fail every time. "And would that long week have anything to do with the fact that we're watching your heart break in real time?"

I blew out a forced laugh. "I'm *fine*."

"You're not fine," Luna said, her voice soft but firm. "You're unraveling. And we're not going to let you do it alone."

"She's right." Sutton grabbed a cube of cheese and popped it into her mouth before pointing a finger at me. "Time to spill, babe. Tell us what's going on in that pretty, chaotic head of yours."

I glanced around at the three of them, all of their attention focused on me. Nowhere for me to run. Nowhere for me to hide. And I realized...I didn't even want to. Not from this. Not from them.

These women *saw* me. Not the bright and breezy surface-level Chloe that the world got, but the mess underneath it all. The aching contradiction of a girl who'd never stayed anywhere long enough to need anyone or be needed back, while yearning for that kind of belonging.

I swallowed down half my glass of wine because I'd definitely need the liquid courage. "Emma made me pinkie promise to say goodbye when I leave. Not if—*when*."

Without even glancing up, I could feel their gazes on me. Could feel their hearts breaking along with mine even in the silence.

"Are you?" Quinn asked, her voice gentle.

"Am I what?"

"Leaving?"

There was that pit in my stomach again, gnawing and relentless and widening with every second that passed.

"Sedona's next week."

"What's in Sedona?" Sutton asked.

"It's her reset." Luna lifted her wineglass to her lips and took a sip, her gaze locked on me. "The only place she's ever allowed herself to return to."

I lifted a single shoulder in a shrug, searching for the normal weightless feeling I usually got when thinking about that place. Instead, I came up empty. "It was where I landed after I left home. I drove until I couldn't anymore and ended up there. Found a part of myself I'd been missing my whole life." I smiled like I hadn't ripped open my chest and flashed them all my trauma. "So now I go back every year on my birthday. My personal little reset button."

"Sounds nice," Sutton said.

"It sounds lonely," Luna cut in, not pulling her punches.

Quinn tipped her head in agreement. "She's not wrong."

I didn't say anything in reply. Because...yeah. That was exactly what it was. My entire life had only ever been lonely.

But I'd found if I ran far enough and fast enough, that loneliness couldn't catch up to me. Couldn't suffocate me if I didn't let it.

And if I *chose* to be alone on my birthday, it wouldn't hurt when no one else remembered the day.

"It's just safer this way."

"Safer for whom?" Quinn asked.

"Me." I gave her a forced smile and shrugged. "I've

always been the girl who leaves before anyone can ask her to."

Quinn stared at me with something that looked an awful lot like kinship, and Luna gave me that soft, sad smile she'd been sending my way for years.

"But what if no one's asking you to leave?" Sutton leaned forward, her brows raised. "What if we're asking you to stay?"

My breath caught in my throat, my eyes burning and my nose stinging for some stupid reason. As if I'd been waiting my whole life to hear those words.

"Not just us," Luna added, pressing her foot into my thigh. "But everyone in this whole messy, quirky, amazing town. It's been making room for you since you showed up with glitter trailing behind you."

I pressed a hand to my chest, attempting to rub away the ache that had settled beneath my breastbone and shook my head. "I don't know how to stay."

"I'm pretty sure you can learn." Sutton tipped her glass of wine toward me. "You're smart and stubborn and resourceful. Aren't you the girl who coached a group of middle schoolers through their first roller derby tournament?"

Among other ridiculous things, yes.

"You've built something real here, Chloe," Sutton said. "People are clamoring to get on the wait list for you to host their pleasure parties."

"You talked the town council into approving a winter dog fashion show and turned it into a coat drive for the shelter," Quinn added.

"And you got the library to replace small overdue fees with acts of kindness." Luna raised her brows. "Not to mention the four-year-old who thinks you hung the moon and her daddy who'd give his left nut—and probably his right too —just to call you his. And don't even try to deny it."

A lump the size of Arizona lodged itself in my throat, and I attempted to swallow it down. Attempted to shove back those tears threatening to spill over too, but neither was budging.

"And you've got us," Luna said, bumping her shoulder into mine.

For the first time in my life, I felt like maybe I actually did have something.

"I'm just gonna say one more thing, and then I'll drop it." Sutton set her glass on the table and leveled me with her no-bullshit stare. "Sometimes the thing you think will trap you ends up being exactly what you need to hold you steady. And I'm saying that as someone who also spent her entire life running. At least until I found a reason to stay."

CHAPTER THIRTY-EIGHT

XANDER

WEEKLY COUSIN DATES were something my mom had suggested when Emma and I had first arrived in Starlight Cove, and it had stuck. Emma and Laurel did something different each week—sometimes it was a movie or shopping or a dance party in the kitchen. And sometimes it was crafts that included—what else?—glitter.

I was just glad this week's glitterfest was happening at Atlas and Sutton's place because god knew I had enough sparkly shit in my home to last a lifetime.

Or at least I would for the next five days.

I sat at the kitchen island while my mom and Sutton chatted about something I wasn't paying attention to, Atlas's deep voice cutting in every so often.

Sutton knocked on the island in front of me until I met her raised brow. "What's with the face?"

"What face?"

She circled her finger in the general direction of my head. "*That* face. You good?"

"Fine."

"You sure?" Mom asked. "Because you don't seem fine."

"Well, I am," I snapped, harsher than necessary.

"Watch it," Atlas barked right back.

"Sorry." I blew out a heavy sigh and scrubbed a hand down my face. "It's just childcare logistics. I need you to watch Emma next week, Mom."

She raised a brow and brought her tea to her lips like I wasn't having a full-blown meltdown in front of her. "We've been over this. I'm full time at the library again. That's why you hired Chloe, remember?"

Yeah, I fucking remembered. And it was both the worst mistake and the best decision of my life. If I hadn't, I wouldn't be stuck in this clusterfuck of emotions, not knowing up from down and left from right.

But if I hadn't, I would've never experienced the force of nature that was Chloe Bradshaw.

"Chloe's leaving," I said without preamble. Best to rip off the bandage. "She's heading to Sedona in a few days. Some yearly thing she does."

Silence fell in the kitchen until only the sounds of Laurel and Emma talking and giggling filled the space.

Then, quietly, Mom asked, "Is she coming back?"

I glanced at my daughter, knowing how badly this was going to hurt her. Knowing because I was living it too.

"I don't know." Because I didn't ask. I was a coward who was afraid of the answer, so I just...didn't ask.

"Do you think maybe you should find out?" Sutton asked, though the correct answer was obvious from the *you fucking idiot* in her tone.

Before I could answer, Emma flew past us toward the bathroom in a rush of tulle and glitter, muttering something about a poop parade that was about to start.

Laurel abandoned the glitter and strolled over, teenage petulance pouring off her in waves, and shook her head. "What is it with you Steele boys and your deep-seated need for a dramatic come-to-Jesus moment before you pull your heads out of your asses?"

I blinked at her. "Excuse me?"

"She's talking about me." Atlas shrugged. "I had a little... issue."

Laurel snorted. "Your head was *so* far up your ass."

"It usually is with him," I said. "But I still don't know what this has to do with me."

Mom reached over and patted my arm. "Laurel's referring to the time I had to talk some sense into your brother when he and Sutton were having some issues."

"And thank God for that because he would've lost the best things that ever happened to him otherwise." Sutton raised a brow at Atlas. "Isn't that right, big guy?"

"Right, trouble." My brother hooked an arm around her waist and tugged her into his side, bending low to press a kiss to her temple. "And all it took was a custom-built library filled with all her favorite books."

"Oh. Is that all?" I deadpanned. "Let me just go grab my pro-footballer money and get right on that."

Sutton swatted Atlas's chest and rolled her eyes. "I already told him, and I'm going to tell you—I didn't need the library. I needed the words."

"She's right, honey," Mom said. "Chloe doesn't need a library."

"Then what the hell does she need? Because I don't know."

"That girl has wanderlust in her soul. What she needs is an adventure."

"Well, I guess I'm fucked because I can't exactly give her an adventure in Starlight Cove."

"Can't you?" Sutton asked, her head tipped to the side. "Because I was a runner too, but I found a reason to stay. Found all the adventure I needed right here."

"I mean, seriously," Laurel cut in. "Have you heard about the time Mabel chased a goat through the town meeting, trying to grab a buzzing vibrator from its mouth? Doesn't get much more adventurous than that."

"Somehow, I think Chloe needs something a bit more than that," I said, shaking my head.

"To help with that 'something a bit more,' let me just add that Chloe wouldn't say no to some glitter. And maybe a party? Did you know the reason she heads to Sedona is to celebrate her birthday? Alone." Sutton leveled me with a look that I felt all the way to my gut. "Because I'm pretty sure no one's ever made it a priority to remember her special day. So she figures it's safer to disappear."

Sutton's words hit me like a sucker punch, nearly knocking the wind out of me. Not only did I not know it was Chloe's birthday next week, but I had no idea she disappeared for it every year, and the thought made my stomach churn. The image of her, all alone in a rented cabin or a hotel room, pretending she didn't care that no one showed up and no one remembered, because that meant it would hurt less.

And all this time—all this fucking time—I'd been letting her think this thing between us was temporary. Letting our ending hang over us like a guillotine all because I was too chickenshit to admit how fucking wrecked I'd be when she left.

Every night, I pulled her into my bed and took her apart piece by piece with my mouth and my hands and my cock, reminding her exactly who she was in the way that was safe for me.

And every night after I'd made her come and wrung every ounce of pleasure from her body, she settled against me like I was the only home she'd ever need.

The only one she'd ever known.

Mom hummed into her mug of tea. "Wonder what that amazing girl would do if someone built a life custom made for her right here and asked her to stay?"

I had no fucking idea. And as much as that terrified me, it didn't scare me nearly as much as watching her walk away would. So I had to figure this out. Had to figure out how to make her want to stay. Not just for me or for Emma or for the rest of this town. But for her.

Because if anyone deserved to call someplace home, it was the girl with sunshine in her soul.

CHAPTER THIRTY-NINE

XANDER

*Group text with Mom, Atlas, Xander, Declan, Lincoln,
Sutton, and Laurel*

5:18 p.m.

XANDER:

Final check. Everyone sound off.

SUTTON:

The girls and I are grabbing Chloe at 6 and
swinging by ONS for "just one drink"

If she shows up in sweatpants, that's not
on me.

LAUREL:

lbr if anyone can make sweatpants look
good it's Chloe

LINCOLN:

Bar's set. Lights are on. Glitter is…not at all contained, and I'm not the one in charge of cleaning this shit up. Mabel's pregaming in the green room.

DECLAN:

Jesus, she has a green room now?

ATLAS:

It's the mop closet.

LINCOLN:

But we hung a velvet curtain, so it's official.

XANDER:

Mom?

MOM:

Emma is prepped and ready! She's got a crown, a wand, and six pounds of pink tulle!! You can't miss her!!!

DECLAN:

Is anyone bringing earplugs for when Mabel inevitably sings? And can you hook me up?

LAUREL:

How dare you

Mabel has the voice of a frisky angel

DECLAN:

Drunk already? Aren't you a little young for that?

LAUREL:

idk what you're talking about

I'm a sparkly ray of innocence

ATLAS:

You better not give her even a drop of
alcohol tonight, Linc.

She's 16 goddamn years old

LAUREL:

Relax Daddy Grump

I'm just fucking with you

LINCOLN:

Who's bringing the slideshow?

XANDER:

What slideshow?

SUTTON:

Don't worry about it

XANDER:

I AM worried about it

DECLAN:

Good, you should be

MOM:

Everyone play nice!! This is a very special
night for a very special girl, and I'm not
going to have the four of you screwing it
up!!!

XANDER:

Why am I lumped in with those assholes? It was my idea!

SUTTON:

Ahem.

XANDER:

Fine, it was Sutton's idea, but I pulled it all together.

SUTTON:

Ahem x2

ATLAS:

Seriously?

DECLAN:

wtf

LINCOLN:

HELLO???

LAUREL:

Please, you'd be lost without us

MOM:

What they mean to say is we're happy to help!!

LINCOLN:

Stop distracting me. I'm still finessing the LoLee Sparkletini's vodka content to find that fine line between Mabel singing karaoke into a dildo microphone and Mabel dancing topless on the bar.

DECLAN:

You better not fuck that up, Linc. I mean it.

LINCOLN:

XANDER better not fuck this up. He's the
one with everything on the line.

> XANDER:
>
> Thanks for the pep talk.

MOM:

You're going to do great, honey!! And
Chloe's going to just love it!!!

CHAPTER FORTY

CHLOE

I SHOULD'VE KNOWN something was up from the looks the girls kept shooting me in the car. And by how dressed up they were—like, full makeup, hot-as-fuck clothes, not a ponytail or messy bun in sight.

"What are we doing again?" I asked from the back seat of Sutton's car. Because surely they had something more planned than what they'd already told me, which was one drink and then all-we-could-eat carbs at whoever's house was closest.

"Grabbing a drink at the bar," Luna said. "Then we'll see where the night takes us."

I could've sworn I heard Quinn snort, but when I glanced her way, she was staring out the window, not even a smirk on her lips.

"Hmm. And why do you all look hot as shit while I'm over here looking like I just got off a bender?"

"You look perfect." Sutton glanced at me in the rearview mirror and shot me a smile.

"Uh-huh," I said, skepticism heavy in my tone because I had working eyeballs, and what I looked like was a hot mess.

And that was because I hadn't had the desire to get out of Xander's hoodie in far too many days. I was definitely smuggling that thing into my suitcase when it was time for me to leave.

Just the thought of my inevitable departure had that ever-present ache throbbing a bit harsher in my chest. I was mere days away from my official disappearing act, and I still hadn't figured out how to say goodbye to this weird little life I'd built here in only a couple short months.

The truth was, I didn't *want* to.

By the time we pulled up in front of One Night Stan's, my radar was screaming that something was off. It could've been the line of cars parked out front or the music blasting from inside or how the girls dragged me to the front door, their smiles infectious, their bodies practically vibrating with excitement.

"Seriously, *what* is going on?" I asked, glancing between the three of them, my eyes narrowed.

"Just a little Chloe celebration." Luna shot me a grin and opened the door.

Before I could ask her to clarify just what the hell that meant, we stepped inside, and the whole place erupted in a chorus of "*Surprise!*"

Confetti cannons went off from every corner, raining colorful flecks of paper into the space. A pink-and-purple balloon arch framed the hallway leading to the back room. And Mabel—bless her sequined soul—stood on a makeshift stage, holding a sparkly pink microphone and shooting me a wink.

My mouth hung open and I glanced around, taking in everyone as people swarmed me. People I'd met at a preschool event or one of my many adventures around town. People I'd laughed with and sold lingerie to and hosted pleasure parties for. People I'd grown to love.

They were all here. For me.

"Told you she'd be speechless!" Mabel said into the microphone before doing a little shimmy. "Now, someone get the birthday girl a LoLee Sparkletini, and let's get this party started!"

I breathed out a laugh and accepted the martini glass filled with something pink and delicious and didn't shrug off the plastic tiara Sutton placed on my head.

"You okay?" she asked, her hands on my shoulders as she darted her gaze over my face.

I swallowed hard, glancing around the room filled to bursting, and nodded. "Yeah. I just...didn't expect this."

She grinned, wide and beautiful, and hooked her arm in mine. "That was kind of the point. He went to a lot of work to make sure of it."

I froze and stared at her, my mouth dropped open in shock. "*He...?*"

Instead of answering, she just gave me a soft, knowing smile and tugged me into the crowd. From there, the night blurred together in the most beautiful way—friends pulling me to dance with them, shouting over the music to toast me with smiles and heartfelt words, and hugging me so tight, I felt it in my bones.

Hugging me like they didn't want me to leave.

My girls were all here, along with everyone from the *Love Yourself* evening and every pleasure party I'd ever hosted. Atlas and Declan and Lincoln were running things behind the bar like they...well, like they owned the place. Holly brought Emma over to me, and the three of us danced and laughed, and it felt so *good* to be in the middle of all this love.

And through it all, I felt him. Even in the commotion. Even through the noise.

Xander leaned against the far wall, his body half in shadow, arms crossed over his chest, his eyes locked on me. Every time I laughed, he watched, his gaze skating over my wide smile and my tipped-back head like he wanted to memorize the shape of me. Wanted to take every bit of me inside himself and never let go.

It was all too much and not enough, and I needed a damn breather.

I told the girls where I was headed and slipped away into the back hallway, the sounds fading the farther I went. The bathroom was open, thank god, and I stepped inside, locking myself away.

Leaning back against the door, I closed my eyes and took a deep breath. Then another and another, hoping, somehow, it would abate this ache that had set up camp in my heart.

Because while this night was beautiful and wonderful and so, so sweet, it was only temporary.

The problem was, I didn't want it to be.

I'd let all these people in, and I'd fallen in love with this town. Worse? I'd let *Xander* in, and I'd fallen in love with that structured, rule-following, color-coded-schedule kind of man.

Me—chaos in a hoodie—fell in love with the one person in the world I shouldn't click with but somehow did.

I shook my head and wiped under my eyes, blowing out a deep breath to get myself together. Then I smiled into the mirror like my heart wasn't breaking and turned to head back into the party.

I took one last deep breath and opened the door, and then I stopped short before I could step out into the hallway.

Xander stood there, leaning against the frame like he had every right to be there. Every right to wait for me. Like he knew exactly where I'd be. Just like the last time he'd found me back here.

"You planning to fuck me in the bathroom again?" I asked, going for light and flirty, except my words came out shaky and frayed around the edges.

His eyes darkened as he ran his gaze over me, hunger and intent clear in his expression.

"Actually..." He gripped my waist and stepped forward, backing me into the bathroom before shutting and locking the door behind us. "I was hoping to do that tonight. In our bed. In our room. Once we get home."

I could only stare at him, my breath freezing in my lungs, lips parted and heart racing like a thoroughbred. I swallowed, attempting to impart some moisture into my too-dry mouth, and croaked, "Home?"

He nodded, slow and sure, his gaze never leaving mine. "Home."

That wasn't the first time he'd said that word to me, but I'd always laughed it off. Swatted it aside. Assumed it didn't mean anything. But I couldn't do that now. Not with the way he was looking at me. Like I was everything he'd ever wanted —everything he'd ever need—wrapped up in one hurricane of a package.

Before I could say anything, he handed me a slim, wrapped box. "Happy birthday, chaos."

"What's this?"

"Open it and find out."

With trembling fingers, I took the gift and unwrapped it, peeling back the paper and lifting the lid. Inside were two beautiful silk scarves—not at all like the ones I'd lost in the fire, but somehow even better.

"I couldn't pop over to Marrakesh to replace the ones that burned, but I hoped these would work," he said.

I licked my lips and curled my fingers into the scarves, needing them to anchor me because I felt like I might float away. "Work for what?"

"To make our home feel more like yours."

He pulled out a folded piece of paper from his back pocket and opened it, smoothing it out—so much like I'd done with my résumé the day I'd set us on this very path. "Starlight Cove doesn't have an elephant sanctuary or a mountain goat retreat. It's not Sedona or Marrakesh or Monaco. But we do have the ocean outside our back door and goat yoga and Mabel. And about five dozen other things that are just your brand of chaos."

I took the paper from him, my gaze skating over everything written in his neat, block lettering. He hadn't been lying—there were five dozen activities on the list, at least.

FIND THE BEST LOBSTER ROLL WITHIN FIFTY MILES
TEACH EMMA HOW TO ICE SKATE
SKINNY DIP IN THE OCEAN AT MIDNIGHT
DANCE IN THE RAIN
START A TRADITION THAT'S JUST OURS
GET SNOWED IN DURING A NOR'EASTER
CATCH FIREFLIES WITH EMMA
CLIFF DIVE (BUT ONLY IF I'M WITH YOU)
HAVE SEX SOMEWHERE WE ABSOLUTELY SHOULD NOT
GO KAYAKING AT SUNRISE

I scanned the rest, tears filling my eyes with each item I read, chosen and handwritten by Xander. And then I got to the last items on the list, and the tears I'd been holding back lost their will to cling to my lower lashes, and they rolled down my cheeks. Slow and steady and at complete odds with the racing beat of my heart.

RUN—BUT ONLY IF IT'S FOR ADVENTURE, AND ONLY IF WE'RE TOGETHER
FALL ASLEEP EVERY NIGHT AND WAKE UP EVERY MORNING NEXT TO SOMEONE WHO LOVES YOU

"Xander," I whispered, my heart so full it felt like it was going to burst straight out of my chest. "What are you saying? What does this mean?"

He stepped forward and cupped my face, brushing his thumbs along the curve of my jaw as if I were the most precious thing in the world. "I'm saying I want to add to that list for the rest of my life, Chloe. I want to give you adventures every day—whether we do that in Starlight Cove or we continue your yearly trip to Sedona or we swing by the elephant sanctuary in Thailand. It means I want you to go on the greatest adventures of your life. But I want you to experience them with me and Emma."

I closed my eyes as he pressed his forehead against mine, his breath ghosting over my lips.

"I'm in love with you, chaos." He kissed me then. Slow and sweet. Full of intent and devotion and the love he just confessed. "And I'm asking you to stay."

"What if I get restless?" I whispered, my bottom lip quivering as I admitted what I was really scared of.

Scared I couldn't do this.

Scared I was going to fuck it all up.

But he shrugged like it was no big deal. Just another adventure. "Then we buy a ticket to the first place that sounds good. We hop on a plane or a boat or a train or we jump in the car, and we go wherever that wanderlust heart of yours wants to go. But then we come back. Because this—you and me and Emma? *This* is home."

I swallowed hard, the lump in my throat continuing to grow with every passing second. "I've never had a home."

"Baby..." he murmured before tugging me to him. He gathered me in his arms and dropped his face into my neck, inhaling deeply like just the scent of me was everything he'd ever need. "You do now. Your home is with me. With us."

I'd never known what home felt like. Not a *real* home. Sure, I'd had a house with four walls and a roof over my head. I'd had food and clothing and all the necessities, but I'd never had this. Promises whispered against my skin and arms that didn't let go and a list of ridiculous little adventures written in block letters just for me.

I'd spent my whole life running—toward or away from something, I wasn't sure. But maybe I'd finally found what I'd always been searching for. Not found in a place or an escape plan but in the steady heartbeat of a man who saw all my broken pieces and called them beautiful. A man who knew every chaotic, unpredictable piece of me and loved me, not in spite of them, but because of them.

Maybe, finally, I was home.

CHAPTER FORTY-ONE

CHLOE

BY THE TIME Xander and I walked through our front door after the party, I already knew what was going to happen. I didn't wonder, didn't hope.

I *knew*.

He was going to do exactly what he'd told me he would because that was what Xander Steele did. He didn't break his promises, and he didn't go back on his word. When he went all in, he went *all in*.

Which meant he was going to fuck me. In our home. In our room. In our bed.

And it didn't feel scary or temporary. I wasn't spiraling or desperate to flee. I didn't need to escape. Not from this house and not from him.

Not ever again.

Not when this was the life I'd *chosen*. The one I'd handcrafted out of strangers who welcomed me, a little girl who chose me, and a man who'd never let me go.

Xander followed me upstairs, his hands firm on my hips

as I led us straight toward the bedroom, no words needed between us.

Holly had taken Emma back to her place when the little gremlin had conked out from too much dancing and the sugar crash of the century. Without the possibility of a surprise four-year-old audience, I could've pushed Xander down on the couch and ridden him right there in the living room. Could've pulled him into the shower and gone down on him until the water ran cold. Could've had him in a dozen different ways anywhere in this house, but I wanted him right where he said he'd take me.

Right where I belonged.

I stood at the foot of our bed, so attuned to him that I could *feel* him behind me, even though he wasn't yet touching me. My body hummed at his nearness, that ever-present urge to be closer buzzing beneath my skin.

"Still feel like running?" he asked, his voice low, his breath warm against my ear.

I shook my head—no hesitation. No uncertainty.

"The words, chaos," he said. "I need the words."

"No," I breathed. "I'm done running."

"You can still run, baby." He slid his hands beneath my—*his*—sweatshirt, pulling it up and off me before tossing it to the side. Then he stepped close, reaching around to cup my breasts as he brushed his lips against my ear. "You're just done running *without me*."

I arched against him, moaning when he pinched my nipples into stiff peaks. His hands were everywhere—tugging off the rest of my clothes while he caressed each inch of me he uncovered as if he couldn't get enough.

Before I could return the favor, he tossed me onto the bed, that dark glint in his eyes telling me exactly what he planned to do. In the next second, he dragged me to the edge of the mattress, dropped to his knees by the side of the bed, and settled his broad shoulders between my thighs.

And then he *devoured* me.

There was no teasing. No warm-up. He just dove straight into my pussy like a starved man. He groaned at the first swipe of his tongue through my slit—deep and filthy and *mine*—gripped my thighs hard enough to bruise, and ate me out like he had something to prove.

I cried out, arching against him as I grabbed for the sheets, the headboard, his hair—anything to keep me anchored here in this moment while he worked me over, sending me straight for the edge of a cliff.

"Fuck, Xander." I moaned, long and low, my eyes rolling back as he slipped two fingers inside me and focused his tongue on my clit. "*God*, don't stop."

"I'll never stop." He pulled back just enough to whisper the words, his beard brushing against my swollen clit with each one. "Gonna lick up every drop of what's mine."

As soon as he affixed his mouth back on my pussy and focused every ounce of his attention on my clit, I was done for. Game over. I came like I was breaking apart—back bowed, thighs quaking, shattered pleas falling from my lips.

And through it all, he kept going, never letting up. His tongue was relentless against me, those fingers, so thick and deep, sending me soaring again before I'd even found my footing from the last fall.

Xander groaned against my flesh like he couldn't get

enough. Like every ounce of pleasure he was coaxing from my body was his favorite flavor. Like I was his favorite fucking meal.

"Tell me," he growled against me before circling my clit with his tongue, thrusting his fingers inside me. "Tell me who this sweet cunt belongs to."

"Xander," I choked out, barely able to speak as every nerve ending in my body was strung tight.

"Uh-uh." He shook his head against me, the rough scrape of his beard making me squirm, hungry for more. "That's not good enough. I want to hear the words while you're just like this. Shaking and swollen and fucking dripping for me. Tell me this pussy's mine. And say it like you mean it."

Tears leaked out of the corners of my eyes as he focused his mouth on me again—his words, so gruff and possessive, along with the relentless stroke of his tongue taking me exactly where I needed to go.

"It's yours," I choked out, my fingers in his hair, tugging him closer as I arched against his mouth. Desperate now. "*I'm* yours."

"Damn fucking right you are. *All* mine. And I make sure my greedy little cunt's taken care of, don't I?"

This time, when he sucked my clit into his mouth, he didn't tease. Didn't work me up with slow licks. He just shoved me straight over the edge into pure bliss. I came so hard, I sobbed out his name as I rode his face and his fingers, pleasure I'd never found with anyone else tearing through my body.

I was still shaking when he finally pulled away, his lips shiny, beard wet, eyes hungry and focused on me. And then he stripped. Fast. Efficient. A man on a mission who knew exactly where he wanted to be. I couldn't even enjoy the show before he was there, flipping me over and settling in behind me.

"Hands and knees, chaos. I know how much you love it when I fuck you nice and deep, and I get the deepest like this, don't I, baby?"

God yes, he did. And I wanted it. Even wrung out like this, I still wanted it.

I scrambled to do as he'd asked, lifting my hips as I settled my cheek on the sheets. The cool air hit my pussy and the wetness coating the insides of my thighs, but I didn't hide what a mess he'd made of me. Why bother? He knew exactly what he'd done. And he fucking loved it.

"There's my dirty girl." He groaned low in his throat and knelt behind me, smoothing his palm up the length of my spine, the thick head of his cock nudging my entrance.

I tipped my hips back, seeking him out. Needing him to fill me in the way only he could.

"See?" He bent over me, his chest blanketing my back, hand wrapped around my throat as he pressed his lips against my ear. "That's *my* greedy pussy, isn't it? So fucking needy for me."

I nodded, clenching and unclenching my fists against the sheets, hips still arching...still searching. And then he was there, sinking in slowly. Like we had all the time in the world.

Because we finally did.

"Fuck me. And this is your cock, isn't it?" He gripped my hip with his other hand, his fingers digging into my flesh as he sank into me, inch by delicious inch. "You feel that stretch?

How you suck me in deeper? That's what happens when your pussy knows exactly who it belongs to. What happens when my cock slides home."

"*Yes*," I moaned, one hand fisted in the sheet, the other reaching back for him, my fingernails digging into his skin. Needing to leave my mark on him just like he was doing to me. "Please, Xander, don't stop. Don't stop. I need—"

"I know exactly what you need." He slammed into me then, his thrusts deep and punishing. Unrelenting. Not just fucking me, but owning me. *Claiming* me.

And I was all too ready to surrender.

"You think anyone else could fuck you like this?" he asked, his hips slapping against my ass, his cock so deep inside me. "You think anyone else knows your body as well as I do? Think anyone else could ever get you this wet, this desperate, this fucking *needy*?"

"No." I shook my head, eyes squeezed shut as my pussy clenched around him, my body strung tight. "Only you."

"That's right, baby. Only me." He slid his hand down my body, his fingers thrumming my clit and making me jerk against his touch. "Come for me one more time. I want this greedy little cunt to show me how much she loves being mine."

He brought his fingers down against my clit in three sharp slaps, and I went flying. I screamed as I shook and shuddered, the orgasm ripping through my body and splintering me into a thousand pieces.

Claimed. Consumed. Completely and utterly his.

Sinking as deep as he could, Xander came on a groan, his

lips against my ear, hand wrapped around my throat, body covering mine as he poured every bit of himself into me.

Our bodies were slick with sweat as we collapsed onto the bed, Xander still inside me, his face buried in the crook of my neck like he could breathe a little easier with me this close.

"I love you," he murmured before pressing a kiss to my shoulder. Soft and achingly sweet. "So fucking much."

I reached back, tangled my fingers in his hair, and turned my face toward him. I captured his lips in a kiss, then rested my forehead against his, eyes still closed, and breathed deep. "I love you too."

"I hope you know I'm never letting you go," he said, his arms tightening around me.

"I know." And I did.

That knowledge didn't scare me. Didn't fill me with the urge to flee. Instead, I snuggled closer, allowed myself to be wrapped up tight in his arms, content with the fact that I was finally home.

And I was never leaving again.

THE SUN WAS SINKING in the June sky, casting everything in that golden haze Chloe referred to as the magic hour. And hell if she wasn't right. Because across the yard, barefoot in the grass, hair a little windblown and skin a little sun-kissed, my girl was dancing with Emma like she'd been born to do just that.

The tutu-wearing birthday girl with frosting smeared across her cheeks, hands sticky and hair wild, was shrieking with laughter every time Chloe spun her around. The two of them giggled and sang and danced amid streamers hung from the swing set, bringing the heart and soul to our little family get-together.

And all I could think was, *this* was what home felt like.

Atlas stood in the yard, the weed whacker upside down in front of him, my toolbox open, tools spread out as he "fixed" something that hadn't been broken in the first place. Declan sat in a lawn chair, nursing a beer and marker-stained biceps, offering his arm like a sacrifice every time Emma dashed by on a coloring mission. And Lincoln grinned from the hammock, listening as Emma told the joke he'd taught her about a cantaloupe and a turkey on a loop like it was the funniest thing in the world.

Sutton, Laurel, and my mom were seated at the picnic table, the adults nursing glasses of wine and discussing their current read for book club while Laurel heckled everyone for sport.

It was too loud and too messy and absolutely fucking perfect.

Eventually, the dancing slowed as the sugar crash came. Conversations softened and everything mellowed into the kind of magic I wanted to experience every Saturday night.

Emma was perched on a chair next to Declan, carefully drawing another heart on his already decorated forearm. She reached for a different color—purple this time—but stopped suddenly, her brows tugged down in that way that said she was thinking. "LoLee?"

Chloe glanced over from where she was bent over the cooler. "Yeah, doodlebug?"

"When I'm six, can we make a unicorn birthday cake?"

"Absolutely, we can."

"How about when I'm ten? Can I have a unicorn cake then too?"

Chloe strode over and crouched beside her, wiping a smudge of frosting from Emma's cheek with her thumb. "If you want one, sure. You might like something else when you're ten, though."

Emma studied her for long moments, something heavy in

her gaze. "But whatever it is, you'll be here to get it for me, right?"

Chloe didn't even pause. No hesitation, just a bright, beaming smile aimed at our girl. "Of course I will."

Emma set down her marker and held out her pinkie, her expression deadly serious. "Pinkie promise?"

Chloe linked her finger through Emma's, a soft smile on her face. "Pinkie promise."

Then she wrapped Emma in a bone-crushing hug, pressed a kiss to the side of her head, and I felt something settle deep in my chest as I watched the two girls I loved more than anything plan a future together as if it were the most natural thing in the world.

AFTER THE SUN had gone down and the string lights lit the backyard, I was pretending to give a shit about a debate with my brothers over who had the best free throw in the family. Declan was building his case while Atlas shut down every point he attempted to make, and Lincoln... Well, Lincoln wasn't doing much of anything besides glancing toward the driveway like he was waiting for something.

Or someone.

After his fifth glance in that direction, I finally asked, "You got somewhere to be, Linc?"

He snapped his gaze to me. "No, why?"

"'Cause you've been staring at the driveway for half an hour like it's been giving you a striptease."

Declan leaned back in his chair, crossing his legs at the

ankles, and smirked at Lincoln. "Chloe mentioned Willa's bringing over something for Emma's camp this week."

"So?" Atlas said.

Declan shrugged. "So, Linc's probably waiting for his daily verbal beatdown courtesy of Hot Farmer Girl."

Lincoln tossed a bottle cap at Declan's head, nailing him right in the forehead and proving *he* had the best free throw in the family. "Shut the fuck up, Dec."

"I'm just saying—"

The gate slammed open, and in marched Willa carrying a wooden crate overflowing with mason jars and more wildflowers than any single person had any business hauling.

Lincoln was out of his chair and across the yard before Declan could even open his mouth.

"You hauled this by yourself?" he asked, already lifting it from her arms.

"You see anyone else with me?" She rolled her eyes and brushed a hand down her dirt-smeared overalls. "Yes, I hauled it myself, jackass. I'm not made of glass, you know."

"No, you're made of stubborn," he grumbled. "And you're going to hurt your back again if you keep trying to do this shit on your own."

Chloe settled onto the chair between my legs, leaning back against me, and I wrapped my arms around her. "They always this entertaining?" she asked, tipping her head toward the bickering duo.

"You have no idea," I murmured against her ear, pressing a kiss to her temple as I continued watching the show.

"Been doing a lot of shit on my own for a lot of years, Lincoln," Willa said, arms crossed, as she stared down my brother. "Besides, fucking up my back wouldn't be the worst way to get out of mowing the lawn."

Lincoln scowled, his mouth pressed into a thin line. "Real funny, wife."

I narrowed my eyes, sure I hadn't heard him right because what the hell?

Willa darted her gaze around to see who was paying attention before pinching Lincoln in the side. "It's not even real," she hissed, keeping her voice low, but that only made me listen harder.

"Don't care." He set the crate down on the picnic table and turned around to face Willa, his jaw tight, arms crossed over his chest. "My *wife*—real or not—isn't going to haul this shit by herself while I sit on my ass and watch."

Chloe shifted in front of me, turning around until her wide-eyed stare met mine. Then she whispered, "Did he just say *wife*?"

I stared at Lincoln and Willa as they stormed off, bickering like they hadn't just dropped a grenade in the middle of the backyard and walked away.

"Yeah," I murmured, lips twitching, because this? *This* was going to be something. "He absolutely did."

Thank you for reading The Live-In Temptation! Want to see what adventures Chloe and Xander check off from the list? To receive their spicy and swoony bonus chapters spanning five years—and multiple adventures—delivered straight to your inbox, scan the QR code below!

ACKNOWLEDGMENTS

I'm going to be honest—I was going to skip acknowledgments this time. After this long and this many books, it's sort of just a whole lot of the same over and over again. But then I did some calculations and realized this is my 25th book as Brighton (!!!), and that's a milestone worthy of a little extra note. I've been in this business for twelve years, and while the people in my corner have ebbed and flowed, the one constant is that there have *always* been beautiful souls helping me along the way.

My eternal thanks to the Emerald Elite for brainstorming this with me back in Galveston and then all the small pivots I had to make after the fact. Our virtual office is the best virtual office in existence, and no one can tell me otherwise.

Thank you to my amazing, phenomenal, miraculous, creative, hard-working assistant, Erin. Who, let's be real, is more like a magician than an assistant. I am beyond grateful for all you do to help keep me sane and my business running smoothly. Please, never, ever retire.

Thanks to Lisa for eeking out another tight one because I pushed this one right up to (*past*, if we're being honest) the deadline. Because I am who I am. Thank you for putting up with me.

Thank you to the bookstores—Blue House Books, Novel

Grounds, The Last Chapter, and Pages of Passion—who've partnered with me to bring the Steele Brothers of Starlight Cove series to more readers. Indie bookstores are simply the best.

Thanks to every colleague I've learned from, been inspired by, leaned against, accomplished along side, or been cheered on by over the past dozen years. Romancelandia is like a family—we might fight within the ranks, but we stand together when shit goes down, and I've loved being a part of this community for so long.

Thank you to my readers—the ones who've been with me through all 25 books and the ones who are only just finding me now. I quite literally would not be able to do this without your support and excitement over the worlds and characters I create.

Finally, to the guys in my life who've been on this wild ride with me every step of the way. Thank you for cheering me on, supporting me, and believing in me even when I didn't always believe in myself. Oldest, thank you for spilling the beans about my pen name at your third grade field trip because you were so proud your mom was a published author. Youngest, thank you for allowing me to inspire you to write your own fantasy novel. Hubs, thank you for being my sounding board and my biggest, unwavering cheerleader. Thank you all for thinking that what I do is a big deal when it oftentimes feels like just another day at the office to me. Thank you for reminding me that I create magic in this job I'm lucky enough to call mine. And thank you for making me lucky enough to call *you* mine.

OTHER TITLES BY BRIGHTON WALSH

STEELE BROTHERS OF STARLIGHT COVE SERIES

The Grump Next Door

The Live-In Temptation

STARLIGHT COVE SERIES

Defiant Heart

Protective Heart

Fearless Heart

Reckless Heart

Possessive Heart

Rebel Heart

HOLIDAYS IN HAVENBROOK SERIES

Main Street Dealmaker

HAVENBROOK SERIES

Charmer

Troublemaker

Heartbreaker

Faker

ABOUT THE AUTHOR

Award-winning *USA Today* and *Wall Street Journal* bestselling author Brighton Walsh spent a decade as a professional photographer before taking her storytelling in a different direction and reconnecting with her first love—writing. She likes her books how she likes her tea—steamy and satisfying—and adores strong-willed heroines and the protective heroes who fall head over heels for them. Brighton lives along the shores of Lake Michigan with her real life hero of a husband, her two kids—both taller than her—and her dog who thinks she's a queen. Her boy-filled house is the setting for dirty socks galore, frequent dance parties (okay, so it's mostly her, by herself, while her children look on in horror), and more laughter than she thought possible. Connect with her online at <u>brightonwalsh.com/quicklinks</u>.